LAST LOOKS

LAST
LOOKS

A Novel

Howard Michael Gould

DUTTON

DUTTON
An imprint of Penguin Random House LLC
375 Hudson Street
New York, New York 10014

Copyright © 2018 by Howard Michael Gould
Penguin supports copyright. Copyright fuels creativity, encourages diverse voices, promotes free speech, and creates a vibrant culture. Thank you for buying an authorized edition of this book and for complying with copyright laws by not reproducing, scanning, or distributing any part of it in any form without permission. You are supporting writers and allowing Penguin to continue to publish books for every reader.

DUTTON and the D colophon are registered trademarks of
Penguin Random House LLC.

LIBRARY OF CONGRESS CATALOGING-IN-PUBLICATION DATA
Names: Gould, Howard Michael, author.
Title: Last looks : a novel / Howard Michael Gould.
Description: First edition. | New York, New York : Dutton, [2018] |
Identifiers: LCCN 2017034561 (print) | LCCN 2017042630 (ebook) |
ISBN 9781524742515 (ebook) | ISBN 9781524742492 (hardcover) |
Classification: LCC PS3607.O8847 (ebook) | LCC PS3607.O8847 L37 2018 (print)
| DDC 813/.6—dc23
LC record available at https://lccn.loc.gov/2017034561

Printed in the United States of America
1   3   5   7   9   10   8   6   4   2

Set in Bell MT Std
Designed by Cassandra Garruzzo

This book is a work of fiction. Names, characters, places, and incidents either are the product of the author's imagination or are used fictitiously, and any resemblance to actual persons, living or dead, business establishments, events, or locales is entirely coincidental.

For my dad,
who'd have said he was whelmed

LAST LOOKS

ONE

As he scrubbed one sock in the day's supply of well water, noting that his stitches had not held and the hole in the toe had reopened, he considered once again the problem of the One Hundred Things, as he had every day, every hour of every day, for the past three years.

The wash bucket was a Thing, as was the work shirt he'd just scrubbed, as were the boxers. He knew some minimalists counted all of their clothing as one Thing, but not the serious ones. So the shirt and jeans and boxers he was wearing right now were three more Things, and the windbreaker slung over the post behind him was a fourth. Those were simple. Socks, though— socks were more complicated, drawing him into the tricky land of plurals and singulars and naming, where the line between reason and rationalization was the disputed border in nothing less than a war for his soul.

That battle had raged ever since he resolved to pare his possessions down to the One Hundred. His books, he had decided then, were not One Library, they were dozens and dozens of Things, so he donated them all to a home for indigent seniors and bought a Kindle. But the pins and needles and tiny spools of polyester and the needle threader—they were fairly elements of One Sewing Kit. Those choices were the stuff of certainty and easy conscience, true to the organizing principle of his life and the purpose of his days, the slim reed he'd grasped during the worst of times, the redemptive positive he'd built on a simple catechism of negatives:

Don't want, don't acquire, don't require.

Don't affect.

Don't hurt.

Ah, but socks. Back when he was whittling down his final list, struggling to find eight more Things he could live without, he decided, not without guilt, that his four industrial-strength boot socks were Two Things, not Four, that a pair of socks was *a* pair of socks, rather than a *pair* of socks, just as a pair of boxers was not in fact a pair. That decision helped him get down to the One Hundred, but it still gnawed at him some days.

Today was one of those days, what with one sock almost beyond repair yet its mate still good and sturdy. He could take out his iPhone, that indispensable Thing, and order another pair, but that would leave him with two untenable choices: either worsen the planet's landfill problem by throwing a perfectly good sock into the black trash bin (not one of the Hundred Things, since it belonged to Riverside County) and dragging it down the dirt road, or hang on to the good sock to couple with one of his others when *its* mate wore out—which in the meantime would leave him stuck with a hundred and first Thing, so that was no choice at all.

Maybe if he biked into Idyllwild, he could buy a pair there and find a Goodwill center and donate the good sock. But in his heart he knew that would be phony solace, that someone else would just throw the widow sock in the garbage. The very thought reminded him that when the socks originally arrived he had read on the label that they were ten percent something called polypropylene.

Such were the problems on Charlie Waldo's mind when he heard the tires in the distance, turning off the asphalt and onto the dirt road that serviced his twelve acres of wooded mountainside.

Nobody but Rico the mail carrier had been on Waldo's property in the years since he'd moved here, and then only when a package wouldn't fit in the roadside box. He tried to remember whether the last time had been just over or just under a year ago, when Waldo had ordered a sack of feed for his chickens. He realized that was the last time he had spoken to anyone aloud, and he wondered whether he'd have to talk to Rico now, or whether a polite thank-you nod would be enough.

Then he worried what the mailman might be carrying, because the last thing Waldo needed was a Thing.

A cloud of dust blew into the clearing ahead of the mail truck, obscuring for a moment that it wasn't a mail truck at all but a sleek Porsche 911, metallic blue. Waldo absently dropped the holey sock into the wash bucket and stood to watch the coupe approach, squinting into the sun. The Porsche pulled to a stop thirty feet away, but he had to shield his eyes from the blowing dirt and the gleam, so he recognized her first by her voice.

"Jesus, Waldo."

When he did see her face, he realized that he hadn't thought about his own appearance in a very long time—a mirror was one of the last Things he'd shucked to get down to One Hundred—so he could only imagine what three years without a haircut or shave must have done to him.

And here was head-turning Lorena, who had to be thirty now, standing in front of him in the swirling dust in a leather jacket and ankle boots and designer jeans, thick black hair still past her shoulders, taking off her oversize designer sunglasses and shaking her head slowly with a cool smirk, as if none of it had ever happened, as if Waldo had never felt compelled to break his own heart by breaking hers.

She said it again: "Jesus, Waldo." Only now she was walking past him, past his pond, to his miniature cabin. It was just sixteen feet by eight, like some playhouse imitation of a folk Victorian, seated at the edge of a forest, straight out of a fairy tale but for the solar panels and satellite dish. "You live in this? Seriously?"

"The average American h—" His voice broke, unfamiliar to itself. He tried again. "The average American home puts out eighteen tons of greenhouse gases per year. A hundred twenty-eight square feet is enough for anyone."

"You got plumbing?"

"I harvest rainwater."

"In California?"

"And there's a spring if I need it."

"Damn." She looked the house up and down. "Well, if anyone's hard-ass enough to put himself through this shit . . ." She let the thought hang there and started inside uninvited.

"Hey!" He trotted after her.

Waldo had to wait in the doorway while she inspected the tiny space, a normal home ingeniously compacted to the size of a freshman dorm room, the wood unfinished, the shelves shallow, the walls crammed with cookware and cutlery and any other of the Hundred Things that could be hung. The kitchen was a two-burner stove set atop a waist-high closet with a small fridge and toaster oven, all squeezed next to a tiny sink fed by a ceramic water jug.

"My new place, I got a walk-in closet bigger than this. What's up here?" Lorena started up a ladder to a tiny loft.

"That's where I sleep." Waldo knew she'd note the folded blanket; even though he never had company, only neatness and precision made life in this space tolerable, and he was as unforgiving about housekeeping as about all other aspects of his life.

Still on the ladder, Lorena twisted and took in the whole tiny room. "Where's all your stuff?"

"I've divested. Got myself down to a hundred things. You'd be amazed what you can live without."

"Like a badge?" Waldo took the poke without response. She pressed. "You got a gun, at least?" He shook his head. "Jesus, Waldo." She climbed down and continued her inspection. "I see you still got a MacBook. Guess you could've answered an email." Before he could find an answer, she asked, "How much land this mansion sitting on?"

"Almost twelve acres."

"Show it to me."

She followed him outside and into the trees. Waldo, pulling on his windbreaker, tromped through the woods he knew so well he could manage in the dark, so shaken in the presence of another, even her, maybe especially her, that he pulled way ahead, incognizant of her struggle through the underbrush in three-inch heels. "The agency's grown," she said, having to raise her voice. "I've got three ops full-time, three more freelance. You surprised?"

"Not even a little." It was a compliment, but it rang as something else, as a conversation ender, all the more so when Waldo picked up his pace, extending his lead in silence. He didn't want to make conversation, didn't know how anymore. It felt wrong; it felt cheap. Anyway, he was allowed to be a bad host. He hadn't invited her. He hadn't invited anyone. That was the point.

When she spoke next he wasn't sure he heard her correctly— she was far behind now, and it seemed too random. It sounded like she said, "Alastair Pinch." He knew the name, of course, which he'd been seeing every day online in the headlines of the *L.A. Times*. But Waldo stayed away from those kinds of stories.

"Alastair Pinch?" she repeated, a little louder, and added, "The actor?"

"Who killed his wife."

"I guess you *use* that MacBook." She continued. "Maybe he killed her, maybe he didn't. Even he doesn't know—he's a black-out drunk."

She's on a case, Waldo thought, and wants help. But why would she need it? She's talented, she's got ops, she sure as hell can't be looking for his connections at the LAPD anymore. Unless she's not really looking for help, unless the help was an excuse to come. Either way, he wasn't interested. He walked even faster.

"Could you slow down?" she called. He stopped and turned. She resumed her pitch as she closed the gap. "His network's got a lot riding on him. They hired a lawyer: Fontella Davis."

"Fontella Davis. So he did kill her."

"It means the money's serious. And they're looking to hire a

PI. This gig would jump me to the majors. Problem is, nobody's giving *me* that shot: woman, my age, midsize agency. *But . . .* if I could deliver the famous Charlie Waldo to work it *with* me . . ." She smiled at him. "You know these Hollywood types: always want to put a big name in it."

So that was it: she was here to make a business proposition, with the added benefit of showing Waldo that she'd survived and then some, that she was a success, and so completely over him that she could even handle working side by side. He realized he was glad for her on both counts. But he didn't want her getting the idea he wanted her here, so all he said was "I'm retired."

"From the force. Lot of ex-cops go PI. You'd be investigating a murder. What's the difference who signs the check?"

Waldo started walking again, this time dragging a little so she could keep up. "Difference is, cop's job is get the bad guy. PI's job is get the bad guy *off.*"

"Unless he isn't the bad guy. You don't even have to put in for a license; you can work under mine." A sharp light, a reflection, cut through the trees. "What is that?"

She walked straight toward the light, ahead of Waldo now, into a clearing, where she found the elephant, a modernist sculpture of sheet metal, anomalously placed in the middle of nowhere. Lorena circled it, studying, then turned to Waldo for an explanation.

"They say an artist owned this land in the seventies." He laid a hand on the elephant's gleaming flank. "It's why I bought the property, actually. It spoke to me."

Lorena looked him straight in the eye, her lip curling into that sly, lopsided grin of hers, the one that said she knew everything about him and that started him thinking about some other things he'd gone without. She said, "Oh, I know why it spoke to you." She ran the fingers of one hand suggestively along the elephant's upturned trunk, never breaking eye contact. Waldo, nonplussed, wondered if her flirting was obtuse or if he was simply way out of practice. As if she could tell he needed the help, she explained. "One of those times we were supposedly 'broken up,' I was coming out of the art museum on Wilshire with a date and ran into you?" Waldo shook his head like he couldn't recall what she was talking about, even though he did. Lorena had ditched the guy on the spot and she and Waldo had all but run to the back seat of his truck in the parking garage. "Yeah," she said now, taunting, "try and play like you don't remember."

"What does that have to do with this?"

"The parking garage was right next to the La Brea Tar Pits. By the mammoths."

She started back into the woods, pleased with herself.

She'd ruffled him, the way only Lorena could. It had been a long time since he'd felt that, and he didn't like it. "Wait, wait, wait." Now he was the one scrambling to keep up with her. "First of all, this isn't a mammoth; it's an elephant. Second, are you saying I bought this property because I had some subconscious sexual memory prompted by this sculpture—"

"—which you walked me straight to, the minute I came to visit you—"

"—*uninvited.*"

"Wasn't Detective Waldo's first rule 'There are no accidents'?" She kept walking.

He stopped, flummoxed, then started after her, insisting, "It's not a mammoth."

As they walked in silence back toward Waldo's cabin, side by side now, he didn't have to look at her to know she held on to that self-satisfied look the whole way. It was rattling and it was comfortable, which was worse. He wanted her to leave.

When they reached the clearing, she stopped walking and finally spoke. "So, this case: we'll go eighty-twenty, yours."

He knew he wouldn't take the deal but couldn't resist asking, "Why would you do that?"

"Because this is the biggest thing since O.J. It'll totally blow me up. And I've got too much marital. I want to branch out."

Waldo shook his head. "What would I even do with the money?"

"Buy a nicer hundred things."

"Pass."

She stood close to him, and Waldo wondered if she expected him to kiss her. He hoped not. He broke the moment and walked toward her car.

"You got any friends up here?" she asked. "You go into town? Anything?" Waldo shifted his weight, wondering what else he could do to hurry her into her car and back down the mountain. But she kept talking. "Lydell was a long time ago, Waldo. You don't have to keep punishing yourself. You don't have to live like this."

It pushed a button and his anger flashed, seeing her with her Porsche, everything he hated about the world, everything he'd rejected, and the words were out of his mouth before he had a chance to think about them. "*You* don't have to live like *that.*"

It was as if he'd slapped her. "Fuck, you expect me to *apologize?*" she said. "I grew up *poor*—for *real* poor, not with goddamn solar panels. So now I'm on Rodeo, I see a pair of suede D&Gs and I can drop a five-spot without even blinking? That is a moment of religious affirmation. That is God saying, 'Lorena Nascimento, *it is all good.*'"

He softened, even felt himself smiling for the first time since he'd moved up here. She smiled back. "Come on, Waldo. Let me pull you back into the real world. Just for a couple weeks. We'll have some laughs. And, hey—could be my guy *didn't* do it. You crack this one and keep him out of prison—maybe that'll even things out a little."

She'd meant well, but it was another misstep, bringing back for him everything that had gone so wrong. His smile disappeared.

"Hey," she said, trying to bring him back, "it was worth a try, right? Give me a hug at least," and she was in his arms before he could say no.

It took Waldo a moment to surrender to the embrace. But they fit, like they always had, and it was just like it used to be except it wasn't.

She said, "You ghosted me, Waldo."

He said, "I ghosted everybody."

"I know."

"It was a bad time."

She squeezed him tighter. After a moment she said, "You're skinny. But you smell better than you look."

"You're lucky—it was shower day."

She chuckled. So did he. She turned her face up to his. There was no doubt now: she did want him to kiss her. Seeing that, he was overwhelmed by a desire powerful and familiar, the desire to be left alone. So he said, "I *do* have to live like this."

She let go of him, stepped back and sighed, she registering the rejection and he registering what this visit had taught him:

that whatever each of them might still be, together they would never again be young.

"You got a bathroom, at least, before I drive back to L.A.?"

Waldo, knowing she wouldn't like it, told her, "It's kind of in the shower." She frowned but started for the cabin anyway, so he got more specific. "It's a composting toilet—after you go, you take some sawdust and spread it on top . . ."

She stopped. "There's a gas station in Idyllwild." She got into her Porsche, made a broken U, pulled up beside him and rolled down her window. "You can't stay up here forever, Waldo."

"No?" he said. "Why not?"

"Same reason you and I kept hooking back up," she said. "Unfinished business is a bitch."

With that, she finally left him alone. Waldo watched Lorena disappear behind the trees and the dust, realizing how much he wished she had stayed.

TWO

Junk television was Waldo's weakness, and he allowed himself an hour a day through his MacBook while preparing and eating his dinner and cleaning up. He was especially drawn to shows about lifestyles opposite to his—any of the *Real Housewives* or *Rich Kids of Beverly Hills* or, best of all, the old MTV *Cribs*. There was something irresistible and strangely soothing about watching Floyd Mayweather flaunting a twelve-person shower with, needless to say, no toilet built into the floor. Tonight, still roiled by Lorena's visit the day before, he was grateful to stumble onto a rerun of one of his favorites, Adam Richman's *Man v. Food*, and a particularly rewarding episode at that, the one where Adam conquers a twelve-patty cheeseburger.

Waldo finished his stir-fried vegetables and went outside to the compost heap to scrape the leavings, and when he came back inside, a junk commercial was playing. He even liked those, though not so much this ubiquitous fitness guru, this aggressive Savannah Moon with her fierce abs and fingerless gloves, always shouting at him through the screen like she was now: *"Face it, you feel like crap. You* look *like crap. I wouldn't want to be you—why would you want to be you?"*

Waldo shook his head and muttered, *"Believe* me," then washed his bowl with the last of the day's water.

As Waldo did every night to tire himself into easy sleep, he played four games of online chess against a computer opponent, choosing a setting too good for him to beat, believing that one didn't get better by winning, only by losing less badly, that the only thing you got out of winning was gratification and gratification was fool's gold. He lost twice as white and twice as black, countering a Ruy Lopez in the final game with a Berlin Defence and giving the AI a tougher go than usual before losing a bishop to a fork he should have seen coming. Per his own rules, Waldo played the game to the bitter end. Resigning was for cowards; it was almost like cheating not to pay for the loss in full by taking it all the way to the bittersweet taste of checkmate.

This time of year Waldo could awaken with the sunrise, dress and get straight to the business of the day. He fed the chickens, collected their eggs and put them in the refrigerator, mended the fence around his garden, and gathered some arugula, potatoes, snap peas and turnips for the two meals he'd eat today. He carried a basket down to the grove and picked eight navel oranges, snacks for four days, eating the first right off the tree. He drew his daily water and scrubbed yesterday's clothes clean, again pondering the problematic sock, currently on his left foot. The work complete, he took his daily hike through the woods, beyond his property line and on a loop through the undeveloped acreage beyond, six miles in all. It was the first day warm enough to go without his jacket.

Then it was time for lunch, a perusal of the news online and, this being a Sunday, a review of his finances. Three years ago he'd taken the equity in his San Fernando Valley home, a bank-owned fixer he'd shrewdly bought during the worst of the crash and on which in only four years he'd turned a mid-six-figure profit, bought the Idyllwild acreage and the prefab cabin for cash, and had plenty left over to invest in an income-oriented vehicle within a family of socially responsible mutual funds. He kept his expenses to a minimum—mostly things like property taxes, internet fees, content for his Kindle and, literally, chicken feed—and well within what that fund threw off. Waldo checked the numbers weekly, made transfers to his local checking account when cash was needed, and on the first Sunday of each month, if his account sat above ten thousand dollars, made a contribution of the excess, to the penny, to one of several environmentally oriented nonprofits. Today that meant sending thirteen dollars and forty-seven cents to the Natural Resources Defense Council, with the usual "In Memory Of."

The work of the day complete, Waldo stepped outside, shed his flannel shirt and tee, tested the sunshine and decided to pull the floating lounge chair from behind the cabin and drag it toward the pond. Waldo thought of the chair as his one extravagance, the one Thing he could most easily live without. The day Rico delivered it, Waldo renounced his comb.

He took his scrub brush and with pond water scrubbed off an entire winter's grime from the chair, thinking this would be so much easier if he could cover the chair with a tarp, though he couldn't imagine a Thing to part with that would justify that. Then he stripped to his boxers, settled into the floating chair with his Kindle, and pushed himself out into the middle of the pond to drift and read in the sunshine, the closest thing to luxury he knew anymore.

Waldo read mostly history and biographies, each by its conclusion confirming his theory of the world, that even the greatest triumphs came with unintended consequences, usually tragic. Washington and Jefferson begat Gettysburg and the Wilderness. Curie and Einstein and Bohr begat Hiroshima and Nagasaki. Gandhi begat half a million slaughtered in Hindu-Muslim riots. Now Waldo was halfway through David Halberstam's *The Best and the Brightest*, about how JFK attracted to Washington the finest minds in academia and industry, the candlepower that led us straight into Vietnam. In this way reading history made Waldo feel less alone.

For the second time in three days he was startled to hear tires turning off the asphalt and onto the dirt hill, but this visitor burned up the road faster than Lorena did, noisier, too. Waldo foot-paddled to the pond's edge, tossed his Kindle onto the grass and clambered to his feet.

A vintage Corvette roared around the bend, kicking dust and wheezing black smoke. It halted by the pond and a brawny man with thinning blond hair climbed out wearing a rumpled suit and holding a half-eaten sandwich. He looked Waldo up and down, making Waldo think again about his own appearance, unshaven and dripping, underweight and almost naked.

Cuppy shook his head, said, "Jesus, Waldo," just like Lorena did, and stuffed the last of the sandwich into his maw. Then he crumpled the foil and paper and tossed them into the pond.

"Shouldn't do that."

"No? Call a cop." Cuppy, who was still plainclothes LAPD, thought this was pretty funny. Then he pulled down his zipper and fished around for his dick.

"What are you doing, Cuppy . . . ?"

Cuppy pulled it out and began to pee into Waldo's pond. "Dub Gerhardt says hello."

Dub Gerhardt had been Cuppy's partner. Post-Waldo, there had been an independent panel that wound up spending a lot of its energy on Gerhardt: nine of his busts had been overturned and, according to the *L.A. Times*, Gerhardt avoided prosecution himself only by agreeing to resign from the department without pension. Waldo marveled at how rarely Cuppy's name surfaced in those articles; he'd always found Cuppy a bigger asshole than his partner and assumed he was dirtier, too. But here was Cuppy, still standing, and pissing in Waldo's pond.

"Tell me about Lorena Nascimento," Cuppy said. "She was up here a couple days ago."

"I'll have to check my visitor's log."

"What she say about Don Q?"

Lorena hadn't said anything that sounded remotely like "Don Q," but Waldo wasn't going to share even that much. "That a person?"

"I guess, if you're not too particular about what you consider a *person*. He's a captain of industry—pharmaceutical industry. Lorena works for him now."

"Bullshit."

"No bullshit. We got this guy wired so good, his balls itch, my cell phone rings. Notice baby girl's ride? Where you think she gets that kind of cheese?"

"Where does a cop with four kids get the cheese for a 'Vette?" Waldo pretended to remember. "Oh right." Waldo thought back to the first time he saw the legendary Big Jim Cuppy, shooting craps in the woods at Griffith Park at the L.A. Police Protective League picnic, Cuppy and Gerhardt and a half dozen other detectives holding stacks of twenties an inch thick, talking shit and rolling dice for dirty money while their wives ate macaroni salad and their kids ran sack races. Cuppy had the biggest wad and the biggest mouth.

Cuppy finished his whiz and zipped himself back up. "Your

girlfriend took something that belongs to Don Q—not exactly recommended by the *New England Journal of Medicine*. What *I* think is, she came up here to leave the thing with you. And if you're smart, you're gonna give it to me."

"You know I always love to help you, Cuppy, but I haven't seen her."

"Oh, she was here. Last thing she did on her computer was Google Map this asspile, and the last ping from her cell came through Idyllwild."

Waldo didn't like the sound of that. "What do you mean, 'last thing'? What, there a missing persons open?"

"No; that would require someone gives a shit. What are you lookin' at me? Even *you* didn't give a shit. She came up here for help and you probably stood there like Grizzly Adams in your panties and told her to fuck off, am I right?" Cuppy opened his car door. "Anyways, this one guy, pissed off Don Q? He got cut in half." He demonstrated with a hand, sawing the air in front of his waist. "Short way, like the Black Dahlia. Then Q mailed both halves to the guy's parents, UPS. They were divorced, so it kinda worked out."

"Lorena can handle herself. Better than you or me." Waldo wasn't kidding. One time Lorena had gotten video of a client's husband, a former NFL defensive end, taking two women into a motel room. After the lineman lost everything in the divorce, he was so angry he waited for Lorena in the garage of her apartment building with a few advantages on her, namely two hundred pounds, eleven inches and a hunting knife. He was the one who ended up in intensive care. When Waldo commented on the odds against a stun from her Taser giving the guy a coronary, Lorena said out of the side of her mouth, "Well, yeah—*a* stun."

Cuppy got into the Corvette and talked to Waldo through the open window. "Uh-huh. Could be she just blew out of town. And left her car in front of her house, and stopped using her phone." He turned the ignition, and the black smoke billowed again. "Let me know if you get any packages." He leaned out to spit near Waldo's feet and drove off.

Waldo found a fallen branch and lifted Cuppy's sandwich wrapper from the pond. Then he went inside for his iPhone and dialed the last number he had for Lorena. It went straight to voicemail.

It wasn't until after he'd finished his veggie omelet that Waldo realized he'd been too distracted to even think about finding junk to watch over dinner. He did play his usual games of chess, losing badly and losing worse. It was early still so he lost two extra times before stripping to his shorts and tee and climbing up to bed.

When he had moved into the miniature cabin, the sleeping loft was one of its most daunting features—an equilateral triangle at each end, three feet to a side, leaving him enough room to turn over but not much more. He slept with his head by the ladder the first night but found it cumbersome working his way in and treacherous climbing out, so the second night he started sleeping head-in, staving off claustrophobia by cracking the tiny window at the far end as much as the night would permit and, more important, by falling asleep quickly. There was a trick to that, too, he found: be physically active during the day, don't ever nap, and tap out what's left of your waking energy with chess. Most nights four games would leave him sleepy enough to drift off right away, wrapped in his cozy Cabela's Mountain Trapper sleeping bag, one of his most treasured Things.

Tonight, though, none of that worked. Cuppy's hints and warnings besieged him. The loft seemed smaller, the triangle more oppressive. Lorena hadn't asked him for help except on the Pinch case. Or was that code, was she trying to tell him something else he was too dense or too rusty to decipher? Was she inspecting him, testing him, trying to figure out whether he even had enough juice anymore to help her, and did he fail her test? Had she wanted to leave the thing Cuppy was looking for but decided Waldo couldn't handle it?

Or maybe Cuppy was just taking shots in the dark. And wanting to get to Waldo, that's why all the hard talk, to put pictures in his head, pictures of Lorena as the Black Dahlia, sliced in half and naked, naked, naked Lorena, and something done to her, naked Lorena, incredible naked Lorena, dark everywhere, and then Waldo had all the other thoughts to torture him, the old ones that most nights he could outrun by falling asleep quickly, the ones that usually didn't come until sleep began to wear off in the morning, at which point he could chase them by getting on with the day.

The triangle was small and getting smaller. Waldo went to his last, best trick, the one he used on the other occasional nights when sleep didn't come: chess, with its own minimalism, its white and black and sixty-four squares, infinity so economically packed into its own tight box. He tried to recall, in notation, all the moves from tonight's game, to see if he could remember every single thing that happened before the bottom fell out.

e4 e5

Nf3 Nc6

Bb5 Nf6

Nc3 Bc5

O-O d5 . . .

It worked. Waldo lost himself in the middle game and slid at last into a sound and untroubled sleep, dreaming of nothing but pawns and diabolically pinned knights until he felt the sleeping bag starting to move underneath him and himself being yanked with it and then the body blow the cabin floor put on him after a seven-foot drop.

THREE

Everything hurt so much he couldn't even tell what part of his body was injured. They found the light switch and he saw there were three of them. His instinct was to start marking details, but before he got a chance they grabbed the bottom of the sleeping bag, pulled it straight up and dumped him onto the floor, which at least clarified his left elbow as the locus of the pain. He reached for the ladder with his other arm, hoping to pull himself to his feet, but one of them stomped his hand with a work boot. "Get this bitch outside," another said. "They ain't room in this drum to kick his ass."

Waldo finally got a look: they were all in their late teens, twenty tops. One had dreadlocks dyed blond about halfway down, one was bare chested but inked all the way up his neck and even to one cheekbone, and the third had a grill and heavy gold ropes and a baseball cap on backward. All three were white.

Grill took Waldo by the back of his T-shirt and Tattoo grabbed one of his arms and they yanked him to his feet. Dreads held open the door and Grill, the biggest, kicked Waldo in the small of the back and out into the night. Waldo tumbled, rolled and scrambled far enough away to take a defensive crouch.

Grill sauntered over. "Ready to do the duggie, Grandpa?" He lowered his shoulder but Waldo came up faster with a surprise right that caught Grill in the throat. Grill sputtered, struggling for breath. Waldo couldn't resist a jab to the mouth, knowing the jewelry would mean a lot of blood.

Tattoo came at Waldo next, swinging high but missing, letting Waldo pop him with a right and follow it with a left hook that struck home but made Waldo's elbow howl. Waldo bulled him straight into the wheezing Grill and they stumbled over each other and both went down. These guys kind of blow, Waldo thought.

He barely had time to look around for the third when something caught him hard across the side of the head, setting him spinning and leaving white spots where the rest of the world should be. As he fell to his hands and knees he heard Tattoo call, "What you hit him wit', yo?"

Dreads grinned and brandished Waldo's cast-iron frying pan. "Rapunzeled him wit' dis skizzay."

Tattoo was getting up. "Fuck's a skizzay?" he asked.

"Skillet," Dreads said. "Skillet—skizzay."

"'At ain't a skillet, yo. 'At's a fryin' pan. An' nobody talk dat Snoop shit no mo'."

"I'm bringin' it back," said Dreads, adding thoughtfully, "Fryin' pan—frizzay?"

Waldo stayed down, dumbfounded by the chatter but tired of fighting. "Fuck do you numbnuts want?"

Dreads said, "We want you to keep yo' ass up on this muthafuckin' mountain, 'at's what we want. And stay away from 'at muthafuckin' Alastair Pinch."

"You don't, you gonna get mo' visits from the Palisades Posse," added Tattoo.

The Palisades Posse. For fuck's sake. He pictured these wannabes swagging around the toniest parts of L.A., walking badass and letting everybody at Whole Foods and Sam's by the Beach know whose turf it is, and maybe on Saturday night getting itchy and blasting 2Pac from the Priuses their daddies paid for while they cruised past Mandeville Canyon looking to mix it up with some Brentwood Boyz.

"You could've saved yourself the gas money," he said to Dreads, who seemed like the leader. "I got nothing to do with Alastair Pinch."

"Bullshit—you're workin' for the network! It's in the trades!" Dreads pulled something out of his back pocket and threw it on the ground in front of Waldo. He said to Tattoo, "Gimme 'at flizzay." Tattoo made a dismissive cluck but handed Dreads a flashlight and he shined it downward so Waldo could read. It was an issue of *Variety*, with the usual hype about box office and pilot orders, but near the bottom of the front page there was a picture of Waldo— younger, cleaner Waldo—and the headline:

EX-COP PINCH HITS FOR PINCH

"What the . . . ?" Waldo started to skim the article, about how some network president named Wilson Sikorsky was more confident than ever this would get straightened out quickly for Alastair and was pleased to be adding former LAPD detective Charlie Waldo to the team. Lorena must have told them he was in.

But he didn't get far into the article before Dreads said, "Just keep yo' mountain ass outta L.A., bitch," and Grill wiped the blood from his face, grabbed the frying pan and paid Waldo back for the bloody mouth with a wallop across the base of his skull. He dropped face-first on the paper.

Tattoo said "Let's slide, yo, 'fore he gets up," and they all made for the car. Waldo looked up, just lucid enough to see that, yeah, it was a Prius.

Waldo aroused the next morning with a stiff elbow and a thick knot at the base of his skull, cursing that he didn't own an ice pack because he hadn't let himself consider it part of his first aid kit instead of its own separate Thing.

He sat in his one chair and read the article in *Variety* twice. It referred to Waldo as "the controversial former LAPD detective" and overstated his promotion history, but at least there was no mention of Lydell Lipps. This Sikorsky character alluded to conversations they'd supposedly been having, as if Waldo had been on the case for a week. The issue was dated Friday, the same day Lorena came up the mountain.

Waldo looked up the network's Burbank headquarters on his iPhone and got through to Sikorsky's assistant. She said Sikorsky would return the call but Waldo had to stop her from hanging up before he could even give her his number.

The morning's chores still undone, Waldo went online and Googled himself and Alastair Pinch together and found to his chagrin that a score of other publications had picked up the story over the weekend. The *L.A. Times* went a lot further, with a full rehashing of the Lipps scandal and Waldo's meltdown, with a dozen hyperlinks to old articles. Waldo passed on these trips down memory lane but read up on the suspect.

Pinch, Waldo learned, was an English stage actor, legendary for his work at the Royal Shakespeare Company, who'd gone international with turns as a sadistic villain in a superhero movie and its sequel. For the last three seasons he'd been the center of a hit network procedural as a cantankerous southern judge with a complicated personal life, some show called *Johnny's Bench*, apparently a financial windfall like nothing he'd ever see playing Iago or Lear. One of the articles linked him to the tradition of storied British thespians like Burton and Harris and O'Toole, apparently hell-bent on matching them not only role for role but drink for drink and brawl for brawl. Judging by news accounts Waldo found on YouTube, when the police discovered him in his house at nine in the morning with a blood alcohol level of 0.103 and the doors locked and the burglar alarm set and his third wife bludgeoned to death on the living room floor and he claiming not to recall how it happened, friends and neighbors were surprised, but maybe not *too* surprised.

Before Waldo knew it he'd been surfing for an hour and realized that even if it weren't for half-assed Crip wannabes bashing his skull with cookware, he'd want to disassociate himself from this asshole as quickly as possible. He tried Sikorsky again, got the same assistant, and could hear her eyes roll through the phone.

He went outside and managed the chickens and the gardens and the wash, but without the serenity that had made the previous thousand days manageable. He could feel the stewing fury coming back, the pain in his elbow sharpening it, and he was ready to go at somebody, anybody, even before he heard yet another fucking car coming up the hill and before he could see it was a news van with CHANNEL 7 painted on the side.

A young and blandly attractive African-American woman stepped out of the van and into the line of fire. "Hi, I'm Tiffany Roper, Eyewitness—"

"This is private property, and I'm telling you to leave."

"You're Charlie Waldo, right?"

Waldo turned on the woman's partner, a fat guy with a backward baseball cap and a beard as wild as Waldo's who was already hoisting a camera onto his shoulder. "You're trespassing, and I've politely asked you to leave. Turn that thing on, I'll politely help you eat the lens."

Tiffany Roper gestured to the cameraman to put it down. "We weren't even expecting you to be in town; we were just hoping for some footage of where you live now. But as long as you're here, could we talk about Alastair Pinch, even off camera? Do you expect him to be indicted?"

"I have nothing to do with Alastair Pinch. Put *that* on television."

"We're probably leading with the story again tonight, and I have Wilson Sikorsky telling me you've been on the case since last week. Why are you saying you're not? Is it an advantage to your investigation if people don't know you're working on it?" She dropped the contentious approach and went for ingratiating. "This can be off the record."

Waldo looked off into the distance and silently counted a slow ten, then took the iPhone from his pocket. "I have nothing more to say. Leave now or I'm calling the Riverside County Sheriff's Department." He went silent and held the reporter's eye until she turned to her cameraman and nodded him into the van.

He watched them drive off, but this wasn't going to stop by itself, not if a network president was out there talking to the press about him. He needed to get Sikorsky to correct himself publicly, to put out a release saying Waldo had turned down the case. But he probably couldn't talk the man into that over the phone—if he could even *get* him on the phone.

Waldo didn't like it, didn't like it at all, but there wasn't a choice. Lorena had broken the peace and had brought on Cuppy and the punks and even the media, and the only way to restore the stillness that had made life bearable again was to go and reclaim it.

He'd have to leave his woods and go down the mountain.

FOUR

Idyllwild was only ninety miles from L.A., but it might as well have been a thousand, a rustic haven for society's peaceful misfits—artist colonies, Zen centers, Christian retreats, yoga retreats and motorcycle clubs drawn by Highway 243's steep, twisting jaunt. Waldo lived about three miles outside the tiny town center, but that might as well have been a thousand, too, so rarely had he visited.

He rode in on his Brompton folding bicycle, one of his more expensive Things, bought with an eye toward the possible need for a journey someday, having made the obvious commitment to permit himself only transportation that was public or self-propelled. He carried a bag for the compacted bike in his backpack, along with his other set of clothing, in case the trip spilled into a second day. Waldo could have bypassed Idyllwild altogether and headed straight to Banning to catch the Greyhound, but the trip to North Hollywood was three and a half hours including the change downtown and he could use something to eat on the way in addition to the two oranges he'd brought, taking advantage of the expedition to enjoy a little variation from his daily salad and eggs.

Though the town was happily free of chain stores and restaurants, he still hunted carefully for the grocery that looked most likely to offer truly natural food and chose the one with a hand-painted sign that read HARVEST MARKET in psychedelic Woodstock-era lettering and an aging, stringy-haired hippie type in a peasant dress behind the counter. Even with his rat's-nest mane, in this town Waldo didn't look threatening or out of place, and the hippie woman smiled warmly when he entered.

It was the first store he had been in since his transformation and he froze, unsure what he wanted or even how to begin deciding. She asked, "Help you find something?"

Waldo thought a moment. "What here's locally grown?"

"Everything. All local, all organic."

"Good"—he nodded—"good."

"Got sandwiches, too."

He hadn't considered a sandwich; it was like a world opening. "I haven't eaten a sandwich in forever."

She said, "I made a nice chicken salad this morning, if you like that. And we have some fresh twelve-grain bread."

"A chicken salad sandwich. God, that sounds better than you can imagine." She put on a pair of cellophane gloves and smiled at him again even though he wasn't anywhere near ready to reciprocate. The cellophane vexed him, but it didn't explicitly break a rule so he let it go.

Then something more problematic occurred to him. "Wait—how'd the chicken get up here? Truck?" The woman shrugged, *yeah, probably.* Waldo contemplated a second, said, "I guess you couldn't help that," and nodded for her to go ahead. She took out a couple of pieces of bread and started slicing a tomato. Then he remembered something else. "But it was wrapped too, I bet. Probably each chicken, individually?"

The woman stopped. "Of course." She wasn't smiling now. "Our food is fresh, if that's what you're worried about."

"No," he said, shaking his head and waving for her not to bother. "I don't eat anything that's had any kind of packaging." He had one more hopeful idea. "Did you make the bread yourself?" She shook her head. Waldo sighed, thwarted on all counts. The woman peeled off the gloves and gave him a peevish frown as he left the store, but Waldo couldn't let that bother him; some people just weren't as committed to preserving the planet as they thought themselves to be.

Then it was on to 243, the twenty-four miles downhill to Banning. He'd never taken it by bike before in either direction. As he approached, the prospect of the brutal return daunted him far more than the curvy glide down. Hitting the first loop, though, he saw that this direction would be hairy enough, the grade so steep that simply keeping the bike under control took every ounce of his attention and will, cars suddenly roaring out of nowhere, terrorizing him with whamming horns.

But he made it to the desert floor and the Greyhound station, flexed his fingers for a minute or two to get the blood flowing back into his knuckles and bought a ticket for North Hollywood. He folded and bagged his Brompton, conscious of a man studying him, all too interested in Waldo's process. He was of indeterminate heritage, Asian or maybe Native American, and flaunted his boxer's musculature under a tight white A-shirt. Waldo nodded at the man, who after all may just have been a cyclist himself, but the guy didn't nod back or even blink. For most of his adult life Waldo would have made a point to amble over to a dude flagging menace like that, a quick social call to let the fellow know there was a badge around, but now he just double-wrapped the handles of the bike bag through his fingers and confirmed his decision to carry it onto the coach instead of trusting the stowage underneath.

It was a straight shot west on I-10 to downtown L.A., then a change for the second leg up the 101 and then he was back in the city he'd never wanted to see again, the city that probably didn't want to see him either, and only a mile or so from the epicenter of the worst of it. He sat on a bench to unbag and restore his bike, then headed off in the opposite direction from the precinct house, down Lankershim and east to Burbank.

There were three cars ahead of him at the studio gate and Waldo took his spot behind the last one, a Lexus SUV. A guard with a russet mullet and Fu Manchu scoped him for a second but went back to his business, checking IDs and printing passes and raising the gate to let the cars through one by one. When the Lexus passed the drill, Waldo straddle-walked his bike to the gate, but the back of the mullet disappeared into the security kiosk, the door with its tinted window slid shut, and Waldo was left waiting in the sun by a five-hundred-dollar-a-week rent-a-cop who'd seen a shaggy bum on a bicycle and a chance to milk a power trip.

Waldo waited patiently until the guy finally came back out, running a comb through his hair with long, slow strokes. "Help you?"

"Tell Wilson Sikorsky, Charlie Waldo's here to see him."

"Beat it." Not even looking at him.

Waldo said, a little slower, "Tell Wilson Sikorsky, Charlie Waldo."

"You expect me to let you in to see Wilson Sikorsky, the president of the network." He kept combing.

"No, Rapunzel, Wilson Sikorsky, the makeup girl. But if she's busy, I'll take Wilson Sikorsky, the president of the network."

The guard sneered. "ID?"

"Don't have one."

"Pal," the guard said, seeming to enjoy his day better by the second, "you can leave on your wheels, or you can leave on your head."

"Look, I don't have an ID because I only have a hundred things and—" He saw in the guard's slack-jawed indifference that this wasn't going to get him anywhere, so he took his wallet from his back pocket and peeled a pair of twenties. "Make you a deal: call Sikorsky's office and have his assistant tell him I'm at the gate. If he won't see me, I got your next Supercut." The guard eyed the bills, then went back into his kiosk and dialed the phone.

While Waldo waited, a second guard sauntered toward him from a building on the lot, this one with mirrored sunglasses and flowing blond Thor locks. He passed the front wheel of Waldo's bike and bumped it accidentally on purpose. Waldo said, "Hey," and the guard took out his own comb and worked his own hair while he studied Waldo head to toe through the shades. Then the gate opened and Thor stopped combing and looked over at Mullet, questioning.

Mullet told his partner, "He's here to see Mr. Sikorsky," and handed Waldo a pass and a lot map. "Admin Building, turn that way at the water tower and it's three buildings to your right." As Waldo pedaled in, he heard Thor ask the other one, "Who *is* that?"

Waldo took the left at the water tower. A young woman with a headset and a clipboard flagged him down. Highly annoyed, she asked him, "Are you Wino Number Two? Why aren't you on New York Street?"

Waldo said, "I'm not Wino Number Two," and she looked even more ticked off. He pedaled on until he found the Admin Building, newer and shinier than the others around it, with an oversize network logo by the entrance. He spotted a rack, walked his bike over and was still kneeling to chain it when he heard someone shout, "Charlie Waldo!" He turned to see a fiftyish man in an Italian suit bounding toward him with a smile and an out-stretched hand. He had a strong Mediterranean face and dark curly hair and looked ready for his second shave of the day. "Wilson Sikorsky. Glad you made it." An African-American woman with straightened and gray-streaked hair and wearing an easy ten thousand dollars' worth of clothes and jewelry walked behind Sikorsky, frowning. Waldo knew her well from news channel appearances as the fire-eating lawyer Fontella Davis.

Waldo came right at Sikorsky, skipping the pleasantries. "Why are you telling the press I'm working with you?"

Sikorsky smoothly segued his rejected handshake into a two-hand *the answer's obvious* gesture and said, "When you land a star, you don't hide it under your ass, you tell the fucking world! You *were* the youngest captain in the history of the LAPD—did we get that right?"

"I wasn't a captain. I was the youngest Detective III—"

"Close enough. Ever meet Fontella Davis?" Waldo shook his head and pursed his lips; Fontella tipped her chin just enough to signal acknowledgment. The two weren't going out dancing anytime soon. "Let's walk," Sikorsky said, blowing past the friction and starting across the asphalt toward the soundstages, the others following. "Look, we want to start you right away, even though Lorena Nascimento's unavailable—"

"She's *missing*," Waldo corrected.

"And thus unavailable. But you were the one we wanted anyway; she just came with the deal." He handed Waldo a business card. "I've written my cell number here—don't bother with my office anymore; my new assistant's a fuckwit. Call me day or night—there is nothing more important to this network. I can get six mil an episode with what this dead wife thing's done for ratings. But only if I can get the fucker to a hundred, and we're at fifty-seven, so I need two more years of Alastair Pinch happy and healthy and off death row."

Fontella Davis finally spoke, telling Waldo, "You need to come on CNN with me tonight. I assume you know where to find a stylist, or at least a barbershop."

Waldo stopped walking. "I don't give a shit about Alastair Pinch. I never told Lorena I'd do this." The others stopped walking too. Waldo handed Sikorsky back his card.

Sikorsky's eyes flared, but he put on the *you'll pretend to love me because we both know I can kill you* charm, which gets you to the top of one of the biggest companies in Hollywood. "I tell you my nuts are in a vise, you give it an extra turn. Fine: you want to negotiate first, have your reps give me a call." He tried to hand Waldo the card again.

"I can't take that. I'd have to get rid of something else, and . . ." It wasn't worth it. "It's complicated."

Fontella Davis spoke to Sikorsky. "Let's go with one of the other PIs. I know I said we need to create distractions, but this—" She gestured at Waldo, running a hand up and down. "Come on."

"I'm a fan of your work too," Waldo said, and turned to Sikorsky. "I came here because I need you to put out a press release that says I'm not involved. That I turned it down and don't have anything to do with the case."

"Nobody would believe it. Not a job like this that everybody in town's been chasing."

"You got to make this right. Some punks showed up at my house last night to knock me around because of this. Called themselves the Palisades Posse. That mean anything to you?"

"No," Sikorsky said, "but 'Palisades Posse'—is that a title, or what? I wonder who has the rights." Then he said, "Look, sorry you had some trouble, but as long as you're on the lot, let me introduce you to Alastair." Davis tried to protest but Sikorsky was already walking again, headed for the door to the nearest soundstage.

Waldo said, "Not interested."

Sikorsky said, "Tell you what: I'll pay you for the day—whether you decide to stay with the case or not. What've you got to lose? Maybe at least you can straighten out that Posse business." He opened the door, holding it for the other two, but neither stepped toward it. Fontella Davis just shook her head, putting her disapproval on record one more time.

Waldo considered his options. He could work Pinch a little to see if he knew anything about the punks, maybe go shake them and put an end to that, at least. Plus if Lorena was really missing, there was a chance it had something to do with this and not the drug dealer story Cuppy was selling. The other choice was to go back up to his woods and hope everybody would forget about him, but that wasn't likely, and if he pedaled back up that mountain and it *wasn't* over, he'd have to pedal back down and take the bus, twice, and back up a second time—too big a pain in the ass to contemplate. So, fine, he'd talk to the asshole Brit.

Meanwhile, though, if this fancy suit was tossing around some network money, Waldo was going to take advantage. "What was your deal with Lorena?" he asked.

"A thousand a day, plus expenses." Sikorsky smiled satisfaction at closing the deal, but Waldo still wasn't moving.

"*Two* thousand." Sikorsky turned, and Waldo couldn't tell if he was pissed or impressed. Probably a little of both, which suited Waldo fine. "And not to me—to the Sierra Club. I'll give you the 'In Memory Of' information." Davis shook her head, that much more irritated. "That's the deal, or I'm out."

Sikorsky said, "Then that's the deal," and went into the sound-stage. The other two followed him in.

Waldo started to recalculate his day. He wasn't going to make it back to Idyllwild tonight, so he'd need a place to stay, and he considered the other parts of town he might still have to bike to before finding a motel. For two grand he should probably at least look at the murder scene. "Where's he live?" he asked Fontella Davis, dreading an uphill ride over one of the canyons to the Westside, where most of the stars' homes were, or possibly hours of bus rides and transfers. "Like Beverly Hills or something?"

Davis said, "Studio City," in a neutral way, saving the smirk for the extra screw, letting him know she understood the implications: "North Hollywood Division."

Fuck me, thought Waldo. I really am back.

FIVE

When they entered, Alastair was wearing a black robe and sitting in a director's chair behind a monitor, sipping from a teacup and holding court, a dozen people hanging on his anecdote. It was hard to mark his age: the creases on his face suggested he was pushing sixty, but his thick, still-chestnut hair suggested a much younger man. It added up to an arresting elegance. "So the two of us are at my country home in Cheshire, drinking absinthe, and several snifters in I decide: this is the night I'm going to teach Stevie Wonder how to drive." Everyone laughed. Alastair added, ". . . my Bentley," and they laughed harder. "And that it would be *most* entertaining to let him motor about the lawn with me *outside* the car, trying to dodge it!" They laughed harder still.

Waldo noted a couple of people at the edges of Alastair's audience surreptitiously checking their watches, probably producers responsible for keeping the show moving. Maybe this was some kind of official break, but more likely not: the camera guys looked like they were waiting by their cameras and the other actors seemed to be holding their places too.

A prop man carried a bottle of Stoli onto the set and Waldo wondered how vodka would fit into a courtroom scene. The prop man stepped onto the raised platform where the judge would sit and poured most of the Stoli into the judge's water pitcher, then left the set, taking the bottle with him. Oh, Waldo thought, that's how.

Alastair paused his story to drink a bit more from the teacup. One of the watch checkers gave a surreptitious but imploring head tip to a young production assistant in a miniskirt and leggings, who obeyed by approaching Alastair with a subservient smile. "Ready to shoot, Mr. Pinch."

Alastair handed her his cup and saucer, said, "Thanks, love," and sauntered onto the set. He stumbled on the steps to his bench and everyone pretended not to notice until he turned to a crew guy and said, "Fix that, would you?" and everybody laughed again. Alastair adjusted his robes, settled into his judge's chair, then poured himself a tall glass of "water" and downed it in two gulps.

Waldo noticed the girl in the miniskirt beside him and he took the teacup from her hand and sniffed it. Waldo asked Sikorsky, "Is he shit-faced?"

"Come on," Sikorsky said, "does he look shit-faced?" Waldo watched Alastair refill his glass from the same pitcher, hands steady, not spilling a drop, not looking shit-faced at all.

An assistant director bellowed, "Last looks!" apparently a signal for the hair and makeup people to rush over and fuss at the actor.

Sikorsky said to Waldo, "Watch the scene on the monitor; you can appreciate his work better. How much he does with so little.

It's a treat, being on this set. Greatest actor since fucking Brando—guy's got so many Shakespeare Awards he keeps them in a bedroom closet—and I've got him Wednesday nights after Jessica Alba."

Waldo took a spot where he could see the monitors, one for each of the two cameras, both trained on Alastair, one close and one wider. He stood behind and just to the left of a handsome and slightly familiar-looking man of about fifty, maybe a former character actor, weathered face and graying temples, who seemed like he might be battling some sort of compulsive disorder, twitching and picking at a cuticle. The man called out, "Are you ready, Alastair?" and, after Alastair nodded, said, "We'll go from Michael's objection, all right?" and Waldo figured that he must be the director. He called, "Action!" and the lawyer-actor at one table looked at Alastair and said, "Objection!" and the lawyer-actress at the other table said to Alastair, "Your Honor, the defense needs to be able to . . . ," but sort of let her line dissolve into the air when Alastair stretched with a monstrous yawn.

Alastair looked away from his fellow actors and over at the director. "Must I listen to this drivel?"

The director twitched and worked his cuticle and said, "Cut." He took a deep, slow breath and walked onto the set, to the spot in front of the bench where lawyers on TV stand when a judge gets irritated. Waldo edged closer to listen. The director looked up at Alastair and said, softly and carefully, "We do need your reactions to the other actors' lines."

Alastair spoke to him as to a child. "Yes, but I'm not on camera *with* them, am I, love. Simply tell me the reactions you want, and I'll give them to you."

The director twitched some more but decided not to fight it and nodded to his crew. "Let's go again," he said and went back

to his seat while Alastair downed what was in his glass and refilled it again.

The director called, "Action!" one more time and then said,
"Skepticism." Alastair tilted his head and looked skeptical. "Ir-
ritation," said the director. Alastair did irritated, basically the
same look he'd given the director moments before. "Infinite patience." Alastair gave him infinite patience.

Sikorsky leaned over to Waldo and whispered, "Brilliant, huh?"

The director called to Alastair, "We do have some lines—
would it be all right if Jodi called them out to you?"

Alastair gestured, *bring them on*, and the script supervisor
called out, "'No, I'll hear that.'"

Alastair took a moment, considering, in character, then said,
as if his own thought, "No, I'll heah-uh that," with a perfect Ala-
bama drawl.

The script supervisor called, "We need one 'Overruled' and
three 'Sustaineds.'"

Alastair said, "Overruled," then "Sustained," then a different
"Sustained," and finally a much more emphatic "Sustained!"

The script supervisor said, "Now we've got the big speech.
'Let me tell you—'"

"I know this one," Alastair snapped. Alastair closed his eyes
and kept them closed for so long that Waldo, watching on the
monitor, wondered if all the vodka had put him to sleep. But when
he opened them again he seemed to have found a new clarity. "Let
me tell you a story from when Ah was just a tyke in Tuscaloosa.
Mah granddaddy Raymond Forbishaw, he was a jurist himself.
Fam'ly couht." Waldo found himself leaning in to listen more
closely. "Granddaddy Raymond, he used to set me on his knee
and say, 'Johnny, foh ninety-nine days a judge's job is me'h'ely to

be that blahndfold on the statue of Lady Justice, to make ce'htain that neithuh prejudice noh predisposition interfe-uh with each sahd havin' its say. Foh ninety-nine days, do that, and justice in its own natural wisdom will fahnd its way. But, Johnny,' he'd say, 'on the one hundredth day, a *great* judge knows that he needs to *be* justice.'" Judge Johnny looked down with a tiny smile, recalling something special and private about his grandfather . . .

. . . or at least that was what Waldo *thought* Judge Johnny was recalling, until Waldo reminded himself that Judge Johnny wasn't a person at all but a make-believe character, and was struck that even he, Charlie Waldo, Detective III, who'd made a career of seeing through people, had been fooled for the briefest moment into believing that there actually was a Judge Johnny and that Judge Johnny had an actual grandfather and a lifetime of memories. Waldo didn't know anything about acting but he could tell Alastair was doing something intrinsically different from what he'd done with those artificial "overruleds" and "sustaineds."

"Now, Ah wouldn't be so bold as to call mahself a great judge," Alastair/Johnny continued and sipped from his glass—drained it, actually—"but Ah do know that as Ah sit here today Ah'm thinkin' 'bout mah granddaddy Raymond. And that's why Ah'm goin' to *direct* this vuhdict, and find this heah-uh defendant . . . *guilty.*"

A moment passed, and then the director leaped from his chair shouting, "Cut! Alastair, that was terrific! *Terrific!*"

Alastair snapped back to his British self. "Terrific? It was bloody genius! We're not going to top that one, are we. I'll see you all tomorrow, then." Having decided to dismiss himself for the day, he started to take off his robe.

But at the monitors, right in front of Waldo, Jodi the script supervisor leaned over to the director, ashen. "He's supposed to say, 'Not guilty.'" The director looked at her, not getting it at first. She made it clear: "He said, 'Guilty.'"

The director ran a hand through what was left of his hair and said, "Couldn't you just tell me I have ass cancer?"

"I'm sorry."

The actor had already handed his robe to a wardrobe assistant when the director reached him. "Um, Alastair, I hate to do this to you, but we need one more."

"Well, that's *your* problem, isn't it, love, because you're not getting it."

"We need it."

"Good God, why?"

"The last line is 'Not guilty.'"

"So?"

"So . . . you said, 'Guilty.'"

"The fuck I did."

"Please, Alastair. One more."

"I know what I said. It wouldn't make *sense* to say 'Guilty.' Why would I say that?"

"If you want, we could look at the playback—"

But Alastair wasn't listening anymore, distracted by someone across the stage who'd apparently been observing the exchange in a way Alastair didn't appreciate. "What are you smirking at?" he said, then brushed past the director and accosted a ruggedly handsome young camera assistant, a kid a quarter century Alastair's junior and at the opposite rung of the Hollywood food chain.

The kid, all innocence, said, "What? I didn't do anything."

But Alastair was having none of it, face reddening, nostrils flaring, a taunted bull. "You think it's easy to carry this bloody piece of shit on my shoulders week after week? You think I need a twat like you standing there hoping I'll cock it up? How long have you worked on this show?" Alastair was nose to nose with him now.

"It's my first week."

"Your first week," Alastair said, shaking his head. "Your first bloody week." He seemed about to turn away in disgust, but instead reared back and bushwhacked the assistant with a head butt. Blood from the kid's brow spattered the soundstage floor.

Waldo took a step toward them, but Sikorsky halted him with a gentle hand on his arm.

Before the assistant could process the shock, Alastair followed with a high roundhouse that caught him square. The kid, having had enough, shoved the actor backward, then came at him with a couple of body shots, but Alastair, clearly no stranger to fisticuffs, answered with an ambidextrous flurry and capped it with a haymaker that sent the kid tripping over a camera wire and careening into the props table, which he toppled before landing amid briefcases and fake legal briefs and the near-empty vodka bottle.

Alastair stood over him, ready to dish out some more if the kid dared to get up. But he didn't. He'd had enough.

The fight was over, and nobody had moved a muscle to stop it. Waldo, astounded by the crew's lack of response, tried to make eye contact with Sikorsky, the director, anyone. But everyone was clinging tight to neutral, disinterested looks, no one wanting to risk being the next to antagonize the star.

"All right," Alastair said, clapping his hands together and restoring order to the production day. "Let's do this." He stomped back to the set and let the wardrobe assistant help him into his robe.

The director turned to his assistant director and said, "Roll.

Just roll." The AD confirmed it for the camera and sound people with a hand gesture.

Alastair, settling into his judge's chair, said, "Do we need the whole speech, or can we do a pickup?"

The director quickly answered, "Pickup's fine."

"All right, then." Alastair called it himself: "Action!" Waldo didn't know an actor was allowed to do that. Alastair composed himself, then, matching perfectly his position and inflection from the end of the speech from the previous take, said, "Ah'm goin' to direct this vuhdict, and find this heah-uh defendant," and paused before bellowing the final words at full volume, *"not . . . guilty!"* Then he said, "Cut. Cheers, mates," and made tracks for the sound-stage exit, this time not bothering to remove his robe.

Sikorsky said to no one in particular, "Now, *that's badass,"* and to Waldo, "Come on, I'll introduce you," and started toward the same exit. Fontella told Waldo that she needed to get to the CNN building and made tracks in the other direction.

Waldo considered the scene outside the scene: his would-be client was a blackout drunk whose wife died from a blow to the head, who sucked down vodka on the job and punched out co-workers, and everybody let him.

The assistant director watched until Alastair had safely cleared the door, then hollered, "That's a wrap!" Waldo watched the crew go about the technical business of shutting down the set for the day. The director had already found a paper cup and was heading for the water pitcher on Judge Johnny's bench.

SIX

While Sikorsky knocked on the door to the double-wide just outside Alastair's soundstage, Waldo circled the trailer and found a sunning area on the far side with what looked like a covered Jacuzzi, the whole mini-estate surrounded by a privacy fence cozied by well-tended hyacinths and forsythia. Waldo estimated the dimensions and did a little math: Alastair's dressing room was eighteen times the square footage of his own home.

When he heard the door open and Alastair say to Sikorsky, "Ah, the lord of the manor, down to slum with the vassals," Waldo swung around to the screen door and followed the network boss inside. There was a full kitchen and a hallway to what looked like several bedrooms; the actor was already going into one of them and peeling off his wardrobe.

Sikorsky said, "Alastair, this is Charlie Waldo, the detective we told you about—the one who used to be King Shit at LAPD." Waldo liked him less by the minute.

"Ah yes, the fallen angel!" said Alastair, tossing some clothing into one of the bedrooms and crossing to Waldo bare chested to shake his hand. "Come in, come in." Alastair said to Sikorsky, "So you landed him after all."

Sikorsky said, "Didn't I promise I'd get him for you? You know I'd give you the shirt off my back."

"How about the watch off your wrist?" Alastair turned to Waldo. "Have you seen what this man wears? It costs more than the house I grew up in."

Sikorsky held out for Waldo his steampunkish Kudoke Skeleton, nifty indeed, open face, the workings visible. Waldo studied it, wondering why any wristwatch, let alone an expensive one, was a Thing anyone needed anymore. "Much as my wife loves you," Sikorsky said to Alastair, "I don't think she wants me giving away her anniversary present. Maybe I'll get you your own as a wrap gift."

"I'll hold you to that." To Waldo he said, "I'm done for the day, Detective. Do you have plans? Where do you live?"

"I'm a civilian now; you don't have to call me that. And I'm only in town for the night. I'll find a hotel." Alastair turned to Sikorsky, confused. Waldo added, "I haven't said I'd take the case."

As if fearing another Alastair outburst, Sikorsky amended that quickly. "Waldo's with us for the day as a consultant. But I'm hoping we can convince him to stick around."

Alastair said to Waldo, "You don't need a hotel, love. You'll stay at my house tonight. It'll make everything easier—scene of the crime and all that." He unbuttoned and unzipped and stepped out of his pants. "You don't mind sleeping amidst the yellow tape, do you?"

Waldo tried to imagine what this could mean, how the police could have let Alastair back into the house if they were still collecting physical evidence and how the man could be so casual about it all, when Sikorsky broke up laughing, recognizing the joke a second late but still before Waldo. "This fuckin' guy," said Sikorsky. Alastair grinned in his boxers, then disappeared into the bedroom and shut the door. Sikorsky said to Waldo, "Nobody like him," as if this were a wonderful thing, then said he had a sitcom run-through to get to and gave Waldo his business card again before leaving him alone in the trailer.

Waldo entered all Sikorsky's info onto his phone so that he wouldn't have to take his card, then inspected Alastair's refrigerator and kitchen cabinets, finding mostly liquids of varying proof. The actor emerged from the bedroom in jeans and polo and sport jacket, a *GQ* page, and Waldo's toe again fussed with the hole in his sock.

Alastair suggested Waldo follow him home in his own car. When Waldo said he had a bike, Alastair pursed his lips, considered him anew, then asked if he had an aversion to *riding* in a car. The question froze Waldo. On the one hand, Alastair's car would be neither public transportation nor self-propelled, so it was theoretically off-limits; on the other, if Alastair were going to be driving it anyway, then riding along wouldn't actually add to Waldo's carbon footprint, so why not. "I can go with you," he answered.

They crossed the lot to the Admin Building to fetch the bike, an eccentric pair drawing discreet double takes. Waldo unlocked the bike chain and stuffed it into his backpack and walked the bike alongside Alastair toward the parking lot nearest his trailer. Waldo knew this time with the suspect ought to be the moment to start his investigation but found himself stymied, unable to initiate even a simple conversation after the years of solitude. He wanted to ask about the night of the murder but figured that would be easier once they got to the spot where it happened. He thought about attempting light chatter about Alastair's work but couldn't imagine how to broach what he'd just witnessed on the soundstage without putting Alastair, his theoretical client, on the defensive. The very word "client" stopped Waldo's thoughts dead. The silence was becoming oppressive, and it was apparent that Alastair wasn't going to help. Waldo finally decided to open with the problem that had brought him here in the first place. "You know a bunch of white teenagers, try to act black?"

"That's all of them, isn't it?"

"These ones want me to stay away from your case. Any idea why?"

"Perhaps they don't care for my telly program. Can't say I blame them."

Waldo blanched when they arrived at Alastair's car: a big yellow Hummer, the original four-ton H1, unapologetically straddled across two spaces in the closest corner of the lot, A. PINCH stenciled on both concrete parking stops. Alastair slapped the side of the behemoth like the proud owner of a Belmont winner and said, "If I'm going to cost myself a knighthood playing a cracker magistrate on some American 'procedural'"—those last two words dripping with mocking disdain—"I owe myself a vehicle the size of Manchester, don't you think?"

Before Waldo could tell him that he'd rather ride behind after all, Alastair opened the rear for the bike and asked, "Do you mind driving?"

"I don't have a driver's license anymore."

"That's all right, neither do I."

Waldo considered the amount of vodka he'd seen Alastair

consume, extrapolated that across the rest of Alastair's working day, and accepted the keys. He lifted his bike into the Hummer's massive cabin and started for the lot exit at about eight miles per hour and, he was certain, fewer than that per gallon.

He followed Alastair's directions through Toluca Lake and Valley Village. He hadn't driven anything for a while, and never anything bigger than the Crown Victoria black-and-white that LAPD had put him in as a rookie, so the Hummer made him overcautious as well as self-conscious. It was wider than his lane and he had to keep choosing between road hogging or risking a sideswipe on the right, and the rush-hour slowdown on Moorpark made him feel even more piggish. At least the streets were familiar, even if the merchants weren't. "That was Henry's Tacos forever," he said to Alastair at one corner, distracted enough by driving to forget his conversational inhibitions. "I can't believe they let that change."

"Yes, you Angelenos and your profound cultural attachments. They demolished a Bob's Big Boy, one of the producers carried on like it was Westminster Abbey. It amused my wife no end."

It was an opening, at least. "Monica?"

"Monica."

"Tell me about your marriage."

"My marriage?" Alastair sighed. "When a woman is killed, the husband is always the first suspect. That tells you about everyone's marriage."

They turned left onto Laurel Canyon and Alastair said they'd be turning right on Fryman, a couple of miles up the hill, so Waldo edged into the right lane when he had a chance. At one of several long waits for the light at Ventura he had the feeling of being watched. There was a Smart car next to him, and indeed the woman in the passenger seat was looking up and staring. She rolled down her window, worked up a loud gob of spit and hocked a loogie that hit Waldo's window at eye level, leaving Waldo simultaneously pissed off, embarrassed, sympathetic and impressed. If Alastair saw what happened, he didn't let on.

That two-mile crawl took a good ten minutes. Waldo didn't know whether he was just unused to traffic, whether this was a particularly bad day or whether it had all gotten worse while he was gone. He remembered a conversation with an L.A. Department of Transportation exec he once had to arrest for bloodying a protester's nose with a clipboard when a community informational meeting about extending the Green Line devolved into a full-blown melee. "People bitch about rail construction disrupting their neighborhoods," the guy told Waldo as part of his statement, "but if they could see the studies *we* see, what L.A. traffic is going to look like in twenty years? People would be rioting in the streets."

After the turn onto Fryman they were rid of the other cars and it was just another few minutes up into the hills until they got to Alastair's Tudor, a two-story baronial spread. Alastair raised the garage door with a remote and Waldo docked the oversize Hummer into the normal-size bay with excruciating deliberation but eventual success, to the delight of his British host. "Well done, sir!" he said. "I strip off a bit of molding twice a week."

They entered the house through a mudroom into a grand kitchen with two full-size refrigerators, four ovens and a marble center island that could comfortably sit sixteen. "How big is this place?"

"A little over eight thousand square feet. Monica and I were going to add on. If the show makes it to syndication and if I'm still living here—as opposed to, say, San Quentin—I might still."

"How much more do you need?"

"Twice the size should do."

Waldo couldn't stop himself from running the numbers in his head or from sharing the results. "Eight thousand more feet. That would emit another four hundred thousand pounds of CO_2 a year."

"Would it."

He could tell Alastair didn't want to hear it, and why would he? Even people who'd recoil at the thought of driving a Hummer didn't want to reckon with the facts about how their comfy and seemingly harmless homes were quietly destroying the planet. Waldo's compulsion to talk about this was, he realized, one more reason he'd be better off sticking to his woods. Still, the malignancy here, the *shamelessness*, affronted him too mightily to keep it to himself. "That's what five hundred Kenyans produce in an entire year. Or eight Australians."

The notion seemed to amuse Alastair, who apparently hadn't much use for the latter. "Eight Australians, eh? I'll take the Kenyans." He headed toward another room. "Come, let me show you where I found my wife."

Waldo followed him through an oversize family room and through the vaulted foyer into an even larger and plusher living room. "It was in here." Alastair paused, taking in the space. "She did all our decorating herself. She was particularly proud of this room. It was in *Architectural Digest.*"

"Walk me through that morning."

"It was a Saturday. I woke up—'came to,' the uncharitable might say—in my study upstairs. It must have been around eight thirty. The first thing I noticed was that I had no recollection of the previous night." Alastair, as if reading Waldo's mind, or perhaps simply accustomed to the public's disbelief, said, "I've been a highly seasoned blackout drunk since my youth, as many can attest. So this incident has precedent in kind, if not in degree. Generally just the odd chipped tooth or paternity suit, that sort of thing."

The glibness was discordant, here in the room where the man's wife had lain dead on the floor, and though it might not confirm the actor's guilt, it wasn't endearing. Waldo kept the thought to himself and let Alastair find his own way back to his narrative.

"Anyway, I went to the kitchen"—he tilted his head to indicate the part of the house they'd come from—"made myself an espresso, came in here and found Monica." He gestured toward a spot on the floor near the middle of the room. "There was so much blood, and a shattered vase . . ." He trailed off, took a moment to collect himself. "She was obviously gone. So that's what I told the 911 woman, and they sent the police instead of an ambulance. The officers asked me some questions and had me sit out in the garden while they poked about for a few hours. Then the coroner came and took her."

"They let you stay in the house after that?"

Alastair shook his head and said, "They let me pack a few things and kept me out for four nights, I think it was, while the forensic boys had at it. It took another two days to clean up after them. Nasty stuff, fingerprint dust. But that was that, except for the indignant dudgeon on cable television, the impassioned talk of Bringing the Villain to Justice," pronouncing the words with capital letters.

"Who else had a key to the house?"

"Besides Monica and myself? To the best of my knowledge, only Rosario, our nanny—and she was in Venezuela, visiting her family."

"Nanny? There were kids in the house?" It was the first Waldo had heard of children.

"We have one child, Gaby, and she was sleeping at a friend's. She likely wasn't the killer, either—but she'll be back from kindergarten soon enough, if you think it's worth trying to wrest a confession."

Waldo finally had to say something. "You know, being that flip won't help you with the indignant dudgeon."

Alastair dropped the ironic curl and looked him straight in the eye. "The world is certain I murdered my wife, Mr. Waldo, and I can't even tell you the world is wrong. If you know a man who's handled similar with an élan of which you more approve, point me to him and I'll gladly emulate."

"Ever think about trying to stop drinking?"

"With every sip."

They heard footsteps outside and a key in the front door lock. A yellow-haired five-year-old pushed the door open, her pained visage a disquieting echo of her father's. The actor shouted, "Princess Ozma!" He lifted her and swung her in a circle, father and daughter not mere centers of each other's worlds but their totality. In seconds, miraculously, both were giggling. Waldo and the solidly built, fiftyish Venezuelan nanny, insignificant intruders both, exchanged wordless acknowledgment of each other's existence.

"Daddy, remember 'Brush Every Morning'? I said it in front of the class today!"

"Of course!"

Gaby recited: "Brush every morning, brush every night, I brush and I brush so my teeth will be white. Teeth can be shiny, teeth can be gold—"

Alastair joined her for the last line. "I hope I still have some when I'm very old!"

"Do you like that poem?"

"I certainly do. It's a most excellent bit of verse." Lowering her to the floor and turning her to face their guest, he said, "Gaby, meet our new friend Mr. Waldo."

"He looks scary," she said. "Like a lion."

"He *is* a lion," Alastair said, "but not a scary one. In fact, you can barely get him to growl." He grinned at Waldo.

Gaby frowned and studied every inch of him, shamelessly, as only a little girl can. Finally she turned to her dad and said, "Can I show Mr. Lion my school tomorrow?"

Waldo answered her himself. "I'd love to see it." Alastair looked at him, surprised. Waldo said, "You never know what you might learn at school."

"All right, then," Alastair said to him. "Rosario will show you to your room. Gaby and I are going to spend some Daddy time before bed." He lifted her again and tossed her over his shoulder. "Wait!" he said. "Do I see a slice of upside-down cake?"

"No!" she squealed and giggled.

"I *do* see a slice of upside-down cake! I'm going to have to eat it!" He held her by the feet and buried his face in her tummy, tickling her with his scratchy chin, and she squealed some more. Then he slung the little girl over his shoulder and turned back to Waldo. "You and I can drive Gaby to school together in the morning, Mr. Lion, and we can continue our conversation after that." Then, remembering, he said, "Oh right: you haven't yet agreed to take the case." The girl squirmed in his arms to look at Waldo. Alastair asked, "What say you, Detective? Will you retreat to your mountain and leave me to the fates? Or will you extend your stay in the City of the Angels long enough to see that the authorities get it right this time? Whatever right may be."

Get it right this time. It had been Lorena's angle, too, a prod at the old wound, only on the mountain it had been theoretical and here it was real, with this fascinating entertainer and now this daughter, whose life had already been darkened enough. Waldo said, "What time do we leave for school?"

Alastair, pleased, said, "Seven twenty-five sharp," and again tucked into his upside-down cake, carrying his daughter away in peals of innocent laughter, your typical loving dad with a six-million-dollar mansion who couldn't happen to recall whether he'd bludgeoned the life out of his little girl's mother.

SEVEN

I s all right?" asked Rosario, showing him the palatial guest suite, with silk bedding, sitting area, thirty-six-inch flat-screen and expansive marble bathroom with sunken tub.

Waldo said, "It'll do."

He put his backpack in the corner, wondering how long the case would keep him away from his chickens. He'd left them a completely full feeder and left both waterers in the shade, adding a couple of teaspoons of vinegar to keep them from going sour, so they'd probably be all right for a while, but this would be his first time away for more than a day.

There was a magazine on the coffee table, *Architectural Digest*. He thumbed it to see if it was the issue featuring this house, and there it was, six pages, the two largest photos showing off the room where Monica died, more or less as it still was. There was a smaller photo of Monica and Alastair in their garden, sharing love, laughter and a pot of tea amid white roses, looking like they'd last forever. The issue was dated the previous August.

It was still early but Waldo was spent. The news van's intrusion this morning already seemed like it had happened a week ago. He realized he'd eaten nothing all day except the two oranges but decided he'd rather hold out until breakfast than find his way back to the kitchen and poke around for whatever he'd feel least self-conscious helping himself to. Better to distract himself with a little junk TV and drift off to sleep, too tired even to access the chess website on his phone.

He had to search for the television remote, found it camouflaged by the tablecloth and half-hidden by a bouquet on a circular bed stand a little too large for its corner of the room. As he waited for the TV to come to life, he found himself annoyed by the way the round tabletop hung over the edge of the bed. He tried to slide the piece away, gently so as not to topple the floral arrangement, but it was flush with the far wall and wouldn't budge. Waldo was struck by how inefficient people could afford to be with their space when they lived in this kind of monstrosity.

There was a soccer game on. Unfamiliar with Alastair's cable system, Waldo had to scan channel by channel to find something more to his liking, ideally a program about some celebrity's house even bigger than what Alastair had in mind for this one. Instead he stumbled onto the program Fontella Davis had wanted him to go on with her.

"I'm hearing there could be an indictment as early as tomorrow," the aggressive CNN host was saying. He'd never seen the woman before, but she looked like she was angling to be the next Nancy Grace.

Fontella Davis said, *"We have not been told that."* Waldo wondered whether there was any reason to believe Fontella, on TV or otherwise.

"Well, have you been told that according to the LAPD, there were no unidentified fingerprints found anywhere in that living room?"

"No, that would be news to me."

"Well, it shouldn't be. It's what the L.A. Times *is reporting."*

"That doesn't mean it's true."

"No, but if it is," the host said, *"what would that suggest to you?"*

Fontella Davis said, *"It would suggest that the real killer knew what he was doing. We need to let the justice system do its work, and turn down the volume on the media circus—"*

Pricked by Davis's hypocrisy—Waldo was too—the CNN host lit into her. *"Oh, come on, Fontella—you* live *for the media circus. And if you want to turn down the volume, what are you doing putting out a press release about a million-dollar reward? And for God's sake, what are you doing bringing in Charlie Waldo, from Lydell Lipps? Charlie Waldo? Seriously? Where did you dig* him *up?"*

Charlie Waldo, from Lydell Lipps. He turned the channel.

Sixteen years earlier, while still a Police Officer III and prepping for his detective exam, Waldo had taken a call from dispatch about a robbery-homicide at a 7-Eleven on Oxnard. There were no cars out front; through the windows the store looked empty. His partner at the time, an unpleasant old-timer named Rusty Hollander with a comb-over and a candy-bar problem, clomped around to the back of the store and Waldo carefully edged open the front door. A decal on the glass read PREMISES PROTECTED BY SECURITY CAMERA, but the next morning he'd learn that it had been on the fritz for months; the owner, too cheap to fix it, was trying to protect the premises by decal.

Waldo followed the metallic smell of blood and found the first two bodies on the floor between shelves of snacks: Manuel Uribe, a lineman crew foreman who'd been visiting his ailing mother in Arizona, and his wife, Vitoria, a pediatric nurse who'd just picked him up at the Bob Hope Airport. They'd each been shot in the face, as was the twenty-three-year-old behind the counter, Damien Banks, who'd been working nights to put himself through an accounting program at Cal State Northridge. The till was empty.

Hollander spotted the fourth body before he did, but that's the one Waldo never forgot: Manuel and Vitoria's nine-year-old son, Lalo, slumped in the corner against a beer fridge, one eye blown out and the other wide open in what Waldo imagined was the terror that came with being shot last, a half-eaten, blood-soaked Hostess blueberry pie in his lap.

The San Fernando Valley saw fifty or sixty homicides a year, give or take, but most of those were gang related or domestic, so the randomness, the brutality, the child, the decent neighborhood and the absence of witnesses or leads made this the crime of the year in the North Hollywood precinct, not to mention the Valley section of the *Times*. A raft of detectives were assigned, but after several fruitless weeks they began drifting away to more promising cases.

Officer Charlie Waldo, though, couldn't forget the faces of the victims, especially the boy's. So he did all he could to keep the case alive, mentioning it to everyone on his beat, the junkies, the gangbangers, the guy who sold him tacos at lunchtime, asking over and over if anyone had heard anything at all about 7-Eleven. It was almost four months later, after he'd already aced his exam and passed the interview, that now-detective Charlie Waldo caught the break that made his career.

Driving solo through Valley Glen on his way to check a lead on a chop shop that would probably go nowhere, Waldo swung a couple of blocks out of his way to give Grant High a once-over and recognized a low-level dealer talking to a couple of kids, a raw-boned, gang-adjacent nineteen-year-old he'd arrested the previous year. The guy's name was Lonnie Lipps and Waldo guessed he wasn't hanging around Grant to go back and finish his math requirement.

Lonnie was scoping the passing traffic carefully, so when Waldo pulled over in his unmarked, the kid spotted him right away and broke off from the others, sprinting toward the school. Waldo jumped out and gave chase on foot, yelling, "Police!" as often as he could, conscious of his new plain clothes. Lonnie scampered over a chain-link fence more nimbly than Waldo, stretched his lead to a good thirty yards, and would have gotten away were it not for one Cleanthony Gaines, an assistant football coach whose boss had just given him so much shit over Friday night's defense against Verdugo Hills that he was in the perfect frame of mind to clothesline a punk running from a cop.

Waldo found four gram bags of marijuana and seven loose joints in Lonnie's jacket pocket. California hadn't yet relaxed its three strikes law, so bad news for Lonnie, who already had two convictions for possession with intent and was suddenly looking at a lot of years for not a lot of weed.

Which made Lonnie talkative. Sitting in an interrogation room, wrists shackled to the center of the metal table in front of him, he offered Waldo a handful of crumbs—which Crip just got his own crew, which tweaker robbed that liquor store on Saticoy—none of it, Waldo told Lonnie, worth enough to bother putting his suit jacket back on. Waldo felt in his gut that Lonnie was sitting on something better, that the kid wouldn't have even mentioned trading if these scraps were all he had, and that if Waldo could figure out how to lean hard enough, Lonnie, third-strike desperate, was bound to give it up.

Waldo's simple play was to put the kid in mini-solitary. He told Lonnie he'd give him a few minutes to think about what else he might have for Waldo and what was in front of him if he didn't. Then he left Lonnie there, alone and cuffed, for an hour, and another hour, and another, six hours in all, until Waldo, checking periodically through a one-way mirror, thought he could see Lonnie Lipps start to lose his mind. And then he gave him one more hour.

When Waldo finally came back into the interrogation room, all he needed to say was "Well?" Lonnie Lipps looked at the floor and said, "7-Eleven—but no more till I get me a lawyer." Waldo called the public defender's to send somebody over, then, while he waited, climbed up onto the roof of the precinct to smoke a rare cigarette, look at the night stars and feel pretty fucking good about himself.

Turns out Lonnie had been riding around with his wilder younger brother Lydell, who showed him a gun and said he wanted to rob the convenience store together. Lonnie resisted but finally agreed to wait behind the wheel while Lydell went in. The gunshots surprised him and pissed him off—in fact, he was *still* pissed, he told Waldo and the other detective taking the statement; he never would have gone along if he thought Lydell was going to do anything crazy-ass like that.

In exchange for getting his would-be third strike dropped, Lonnie Lipps was the star witness in the triple-murder trial of his own brother Lydell, with their mother sitting right behind one son and crying through the other's testimony. Lydell got twenty-five to life, on the light side because he had no priors and was just seventeen at the time of the murders, but got sent anyway to Pelican Bay, the worst of the worst.

As for Detective Charlie Waldo, the good times were about to start rolling. The *Times* did a profile, which caught the eye of Brad Pitt, who convinced Warner to option the rights to Waldo's story. The studio hired the flavor-of-the-month screenwriting team Pitt wanted, who, after cashing their checks, quietly pointed out to the studio exec that there was nothing intrinsically dramatic about waiting hours for a low-level drug dealer to rat someone out. But Pitt insisted he knew how to make it work and swore he'd make Waldo his next movie if they'd just move on to the next hot writer he needed. The process repeated itself for two years, burning through three-point-something-million studio dollars before Pitt lost interest and the option lapsed.

By then Waldo himself had blown his own tiny fraction of that wasted money on a vintage second-generation Camaro, pineapple yellow with teal racing stripes. Appropriate, because he was about to leave his fellow detectives in the dust.

He ascended the ranks quicker than anyone in memory, his clearance rate regularly the highest in the division. When a Valley crime got any kind of public attention, the precinct commander would usually pull Waldo off his regular rotation to help out, even loaned him out to commands elsewhere in the city when downtown asked. One high-profile clearance led to the next two high-profile opportunities, a virtuous cycle, and Waldo played it for all it was worth.

Not long after his inevitable transfer to the more intense and prestigious Robbery-Homicide Division downtown, Human Rights Watch began to make trouble about Lydell Lipps, pressing

the state of California to offer Lydell, who'd been a model prisoner, a resentencing hearing in consideration of his age at the time
of his crime and his spotless record before it, with the possibility
of parole to follow. Trends in prison reform were creating that
possibility for young offenders in California and across the country, in light of new notions of brain development and impulsive
behavior in teens and the capacity for change. But Waldo, remembering little Lalo Uribe's one terror eye and his parents and
Damien Banks and not seeing a whole lot of difference between a
seventeen-year-old shooting four people in the face and an eighteen-
year-old shooting four people in the face, jumped in with both feet
and found himself once again working with prosecutors to prepare
the state's case against Lydell Lipps, toward an upcoming hearing
in superior court that had no business happening.

The DA's office believed that a vivid narrative would be the
best counter to a plea for leniency, so Waldo and the lawyers
worked at reassembling every detail, with special focus on whatever they might get that wasn't already in the trial transcript.
That led Waldo to Chuckawalla Valley State Prison to talk to
his old friend Lonnie Lipps, who in the meantime, to no one's
surprise, had found a way to pick up his third strike without any
help from Waldo and was now going by the name Rahman
Hashim Abid.

Waldo asked him if there was anything about that night he'd
never told before, and Rahman/Lonnie, sinewy and tatted now,
gave him a slow grin, and not a friendly one. "Shit, yeah," he said,
"I didn't tell you that me and Lydell wasn't nowhere near there."

"What do you mean?"

"7-Eleven. I made that shit up. Whole thing."

The room spun. "Why? Why would . . . ?"

"Man, my girl Keesha was pregnant, and like two days before you busted me I found out it wasn't mine, it was Lydell's. I wanted to fuckin' kill that little muthafucker. Then you there bustin' my balls, lookin' at life for a couple reefer? And sittin' in that room all fuckin' night? And you always askin' everybody 'bout 7-Eleven—so I go what the fuck, two birds, know what I'm sayin'?" Rahman watched Waldo sweat, loving the shit out of the best moment he was ever going to have in here, maybe the best he'd ever have again. "I kept wantin' to hug you, man, 'specially durin' that trial, watchin' that piece a shit Lydell gettin' fucked like that, but I knew I couldn't say nothin'. Guess I can thank you now, right?"

Waldo vomited. Rahman Hashim Abid laughed at him.

Charlie Waldo's next surprise was how much harder it is to get an innocent man out of prison than to put a guilty man in. The district attorney and his people didn't want to believe the brother's new story, and why would they? A wrongful conviction would not only make them look incompetent but make them the latest poster boys for the growing racial narrative about prosecutorial injustice. Lydell got the backing of lawyers at the Innocence Project, but the DA took advantage of the claim of new evidence to get the original resentencing hearing postponed, and postponed again. Waldo and his superiors got pressure from Sacramento, too, where state officials worried about a lawsuit against the state for wrongful imprisonment and maybe an eight-figure payout.

But that was nothing like the pressure Waldo was feeling from the PD itself, not least from his former colleagues at North Hollywood Division, still his closest friends in the department.

Owning a mistake like that would be toxic to all of them, damage their credibility with the public, with the press, with the street, with their families, everybody. Besides, most of the North Hollywood cops didn't *believe* it was a mistake, there being no reason to believe this guy was any more truthful now that he was Rahman Hashim Abid than when he was called Lonnie Lipps.

Still, the pregnancy story had checked out, the girl corroborated everything, and besides, Waldo just knew. He knew how he'd scared a nineteen-year-old shitless, how he'd exploited sledgehammer-stupid laws to jam the kid so bad he'd say anything, how he'd been so hell-bent on solving 7-Eleven that he'd made himself the perfect buyer for the bullshit even a third-rate dealer knew to sell him.

Waldo, whose only contact with Lydell Lipps had been the arrest and the original trial, drove thirteen hours up to Pelican Bay, near the Oregon border, not even sure what he'd say when he got there. It didn't matter anyway; Lydell wouldn't see him. He did all he could to help Lydell's new lawyers and anything he could think of on his own, calls and letters to lobby the DA, the chief of police, the state and the city and even the US attorney general. He went on the record with the *L.A. Times*, which put it on the Sunday front page, above the fold. The chief himself called Waldo in after that one, warned him that if he didn't go through Media Relations from now on, he'd be placed on indefinite administrative leave.

But all the pressure worked: after a campaign of more than a year, the Innocence Project finally got a judge to grant Lydell a full retrial, with Waldo set to testify on his behalf.

Thirty-seven days before the trial date, while pulling into a cheap Peruvian seafood place he liked for a quick lunch, Waldo took a call on his cell from one of the lawyers. Lydell Lipps had changed Waldo's life once more, this time by sticking his stomach in front of a knife in the yard at Pelican Bay and bleeding to death.

Lydell Lipps was thirty-one years old and had been locked up for the last fourteen of those years.

Charlie Waldo quit the LAPD in a fury and talked to anyone with a microphone about those who needed to be held accountable. Some people burn bridges; Waldo burned the river. He set everything he could aflame—the DA's office, the government and especially the department, whose opposition to getting it right was the betrayal Waldo could never forgive, and who deserved the worst hell Waldo could figure out how to wreak. The press ate it up, not just the *Times* and local TV but the big papers back east and cable news and the national magazines. Waldo kept talking, talking, talking, to anybody who'd listen.

But, as happens, people got tired of listening.

And in the silence, Waldo started to think more and more about the one person who should be held *most* accountable but hadn't been. It was time to start wreaking hell on himself.

EIGHT

That same infomercial queen, in barely there workout clothes broadcasting her muscular perfection, pointed down at Waldo from a billboard over Ventura Boulevard:

YOU DON'T HAVE TO BE YOU!

He knew she was just a cynical huckster tapping into self-hatred and peddling superficial (if pricey) change; still, he contemplated this existential challenge she was posing and wished to God she were right.

Gaby rode in back, silent and pensive. Alastair, sober at this hour, steered onto Chandler and quickly into a near-hidden entrance to the Stoddard School. "Welcome," he announced to Waldo, "to Kindergartens of the Rich and Famous." A slow-moving line of cars safely offloaded elementary schoolers, but Alastair apparently had other plans: he cruised around the line and glided into a space with a sign marking it as RESERVED FOR THE PINCH FAMILY. Actually, the Hummer laid claim to a chunk of the adjacent handicapped space as well.

"What'd you do to deserve this?" asked Waldo.

"The school auctions off a space every year at their insufferable fund-raiser. I put in a bid to allay the boredom."

"What it set you back?"

"Thirty." Alastair shrugged. Waldo chose not to ask thirty what.

Gaby, freed from her car seat and distracted by the sight of her friends, jumped down and ran shouting into the playground, where she blended with a hundred other kids in identical white polos and navy shorts, wealthy and clean, protected from the bad world by oaks and fences, attentive faculty and sacrificing parents. Waldo watched Gaby and another girl with buckteeth and braided pigtails find each other like magnets and hug like sisters after a long separation. What did this little pal know about Gaby's mother? Gaby's father? And all these other kids—had *their* parents told them? Or was news, even scandalous news so close to home, one more thing they were protected from?

Every adult on the playground kept a careful eye on Waldo, a stranger and not a safe-looking one, strolling among their children alongside their presumptively lethal fellow parent. Only one approached, a reed-thin middle-aged man in rimless glasses, blazer and repp tie. Alastair introduced him as Dr. Sebastian Hexter, the headmaster, and left him to chat with Waldo while he collected Gaby and escorted her to her classroom.

"I'm happy to answer any questions you have," Hexter said, "but I don't expect that I or anyone at Stoddard would have much to offer that could help you."

"At this point I'm trying to get a picture of the Pinches as a couple. How well have you known them?"

"Not well. Gaby's in kindergarten, so this is their first year at the school, of course. My early impression has been that they'd be generous financially, if not particularly involved. We rarely see him at all, and she's more of a drop-off mom." He corrected himself. "*Was.*"

"Could I talk to Gaby's teacher?"

"I'd prefer you didn't." The bluntness was surprising. Hexter might look like an effete New England preppy transplanted under the California sun, but he was in command of his world and wanted to let Waldo know it. "This tragedy has rocked our campus, at least on the parent and faculty levels. There's not much a headmaster can do in a situation like this, but I've been able to shield our students from the chaos, and I plan to keep it that way." The children on the playground did indeed look untroubled playing tag and four square, but the headmaster's pride rankled Waldo.

"Gaby Pinch is one of your students. I'd say the chaos already found her."

Hexter's smugness dissipated. He said, "Her name's Jayne White. Room 2. I'll walk you over." They crossed the campus in a disagreeable silence. Hexter indicated the door without a good-bye and headed back toward the playground.

Waldo stepped into the classroom and saw a life-size plastic skeleton holding its own skull in an upraised palm. Alastair was standing behind the skeleton, his head atop the spine where the skull should be. Gaby and her bucktooth friend, sitting on the floor in front of the show, were already squealing with delight.

Alastair quieted them and began: "Alas, poor Yorick! I knew him, Horatio: a fellow of infinite jest, of most excellent fancy . . ." He worked the bones like a skilled puppeteer, the arms expressive and elegant, the legs punctuating with an occasional twitch or kick. The girls were riveted; they didn't need to understand the words, only that they hadn't seen anything like it. Neither had Waldo.

". . . he hath borne me on his back a thousand times; and now, how abhorred in my imagination it is! My gorge rises at it. Here hung those lips that I have kissed—" Alastair bussed the skull square on the mouth and turned to the little girls with an icked-out face. They screamed and giggled; the man knew his audience.

Alastair played the speech all the way to the end and the tiny crowd hung on every word. When he finished, all three applauded, and so did a fourth. Waldo looked over his shoulder and saw the teacher Jayne White, twenty-six maybe, simply and practically adorned for a day among five-year-olds, yet still so striking, hair so dark and eyes so pale, that Waldo took a second glance despite himself.

"Ms. White?"

"That's me."

Alastair affixed the skull to its rightful spot and said, "Come, girls—I'll push you on the swings until the bell rings. Mr. Waldo wants to ask your teacher whether Daddy plays nicely with the other children." They each grabbed a hand and he led them out, winking at Waldo and saying, "I'll meet you at the car so you can gather your bicycle."

When they were alone he said, "My name's Waldo. I'm a detective working for Alastair."

"Really." She gave him a once-over. "I'd have guessed you were his stylist."

The crack knocked him off-balance. But he recovered: "Give me some credit—not a lot of people could pull this off without looking scruffy."

She smiled, then sobered. "I'm sorry; we shouldn't be joking. My heart breaks for Gaby. This has to be all kinds of unreal for her. I can't even imagine how she's processing it. Mr. Pinch does a lot to keep her spirits up."

"What was *Mrs.* Pinch like as a parent?"

Jayne thought before answering. "We have the children memorize these poems? I like to ask the kids whose mom and dad can recite them, too. Half the time the parents can't, but the nanny can, in two languages."

"And the Pinches?"

"Mrs. Pinch never knew the poems. Mr. Pinch, always."

"Her death must have shocked the hell out of this place."

"Not me." That got his attention, but before he could follow up, a cluster of little boys broke the moment, tumbling into the room, screaming and knocking the carefully ordered desks askew. Jayne was gentle with them but firm. *"No running in the classroom,* you guys know that. And we use our *inside* voices, remember?" The boys settled down as Jayne took a marker and began writing on a sheet of construction paper.

Waldo said to her, "I want to hear more."

"Come tomorrow night and hear me sing," she said.

"You don't look like a singer."

She handed him the construction paper. It had an address on La Cienega, the other side of the hill, and below that she'd written, *8:30.*

"This is Hollywood, Waldo. Who is who they are?"

NINE

Like many Angelenos, he had never actually ridden the subway, but his thighs cried for mercy after yesterday's hours on the bike, so he looked up the Metro on his phone. He calculated that the Red Line, which ran all the way to Union Station, could clip fifteen blessed miles off the ride downtown.

Rush hour hadn't thinned yet at the North Hollywood station, so he had to jostle his bike through the crush and onto the long escalator down from the plaza. At the bottom he took a spot behind two other passengers waiting to pay for the ride. When his turn came, it took him a moment to decode the vending machine's payment system, and when he finally did his heart sank: the Metro apparently required him to load the dollar seventy-five fare, or multiple fares if he preferred, onto a reusable card, which itself had to be purchased separately for a dollar. No way around it, the reusability made the card itself a Thing, which would have to live alongside his cash and single credit card (two Things) in his threadbare wallet (a third Thing). "Shit," he muttered.

He looked at the wallet, which he'd owned for a decade and rarely used, and considered shedding that in favor of the Metro card. But aside from the mild undesirability of keeping his cash and credit card loose, he wasn't expecting to spend much time in Los Angeles or come back often; a rarely used fare card was precisely the kind of Thing he'd learned to strip from his life.

Someone behind him cleared her throat and shuffled impatiently, and he realized that there were already three people waiting for him to finish, the first in line—probably the throat clearer—a young Latina in what looked like a nurse's uniform.

If he used the card just once and disposed of it immediately, he could consider it currency—and part of *that* Thing—as he would, say, if the subway ran on old-fashioned tokens. Of course, if he rode the Metro more than once, as was likely, that would raise each fare by more than fifty percent, to two seventy-five, steep for a subway ride, but maybe the best available choice. That is, if it didn't mean throwing away a piece of plastic every time he rode a subway, a nonstarter. "Shit, shit, shit," he muttered.

"Need some help?" said the nurse, not gently.

Waldo didn't answer, put his credit card in the machine and figured out how to purchase a card with one fare loaded.

At the turnstile he watched other passengers tap their cards on the sensor to continue to the trains and he imitated them with one hand while lifting his bike with the other. There was still another short escalator to ride down to the platform, and he was relieved to see a security guard standing beside it, eyeballing him. Waldo approached him, holding out his Metro card. "Can I give you this?"

"What for?"

"I can't keep it. Can you take it, give it back to the . . . whoever?"

"You keep it. For next time you ride."

"I don't want to keep it."

"Keep it."

"Please."

"Look, man," said the guard, "you wanna chuck it, chuck it. I can't do nothin' with that." He held up his hands, not wanting to touch something that Waldo had been holding, and Waldo realized that, given his appearance, it was understandable. He decided he'd look for the vending machines at Union Station and see if he could give the card away to a passenger about to buy one, and if not, leave it on the ground nearby in hope that someone would pick it up.

Waldo descended the short escalator with his bike just as a train was pulling into the station. The car was empty, North Hollywood being the first stop on the line, and Waldo took a seat that allowed him to rest his bike against the wall of the car beside him. In the quiet of the ride his mind drifted not to Alastair and Monica Pinch, but to Lorena and to Cuppy's ominous claims. It was possible, even likely, that Cuppy was just trying to push his buttons. But Lorena must have seen the media attention that Waldo was getting in the past twenty-four hours; you'd think she'd know he was working on Pinch and reach out. Then again, when she came to see him, he'd rejected a lot more than a case. Maybe she was humiliated, maybe even angry at him all over again.

Besides, mystery had always been her default. In fact, she counted on his acceptance of that; it had been an essential element of their equilibrium. Even in their early days, when he was still with the department and had means legal or otherwise to check the dirt behind anybody's ears, he had never asked around about her, never even ran a simple online search. He'd allowed her to be as much or as little a cryptogram as she wanted to be, a choice that sometimes served as a love drug and at other times magnified his torment, but which, he could tell from the beginning, was the only way to be with a woman like Lorena Nascimento and keep himself sane.

The reverse had never been true, he was sure.

They'd originally met at a double-homicide scene in Echo Park. Hours before, Lorena—an op in those days for an eastside schmo named Tejano—had played her client recordings of the woman's husband and au pair cavorting in the couple's own bed while she was out at her book group talking about *The Help*. The wife, a devotee of cooking shows, decided to consult the Food Network website rather than a divorce attorney, then put her own twist on one of Rachael Ray's favorites and served both husband and au pair a zucchini linguine with curried arsenic pesto.

As Detective Charlie Waldo, called to the scene, guided the murderous wife into the back of his car, he thought he noticed the woman's alluring PI looking him over with a curiosity dissonant to the occasion. The second time he met Lorena, at her boss's office to take her statement, the look she gave him while she lingeringly palmed him her business card told him she'd moved well beyond curiosity—in fact, it made him feel like he'd already been fully vetted. And during their first date, dinner in a reconstructed speakeasy she suggested downtown, it was like she was three steps ahead, like she'd somehow combed through his bank accounts and quizzed a handful of former lovers. She was almost smirking while she let him tell stories she already knew, even finishing one or two for him. Whom she'd talked to, what she'd actually seen—that was part of the enigma that Waldo intuitively knew to let stand.

So by the time the train pulled into the next stop, Universal

City, and the car started to fill, he had convinced himself not to worry about Lorena. There were all sorts of reasons he might not hear from her.

But then he started to think about the darker ones and reached for his phone, only to learn there was no connectivity this far belowground. He felt suddenly helpless, penned into a close space as he hadn't been for ages, with no idea how long the rest of the ride downtown would take or even how many stops before they got there, and fifty people, easy, between him and the map that could tell him. He closed his eyes, drew as deep a breath as he could, and promised himself he'd be back in Idyll-wild before long.

At Vermont/Sunset a disfigured woman limped aboard, four and a half feet tall and no more than eighty pounds, skin a mottle of angry blotches, a disconcertingly long tongue hanging straight down to her chin, possibly without bottom teeth to hold it in, a ratty wool cap covering whatever the top of her head might look like. Waldo couldn't begin to guess her age. The kinder teenagers by the door shied away; the cruel ones giggled. Whatever her afflictions, it had to be an unimaginable existence. Dragging a green plastic bag full of something, she hobbled over to Waldo and squeezed past him into the vacant window seat.

She settled in and from her rancid cloth coat pulled out a smartphone with a shattered screen and half a pair of earbuds and began tapping it with maculated hands. Soon she was laughing, full guffaws ringing through the otherwise quiet car. Waldo couldn't resist peeking down. Through the cracks in her screen he made out a fat man in what looked like a Nazi helmet and recognized it as an episode of the old prison camp sitcom *Hogan's Heroes*. The commandant with the monocle smacked his bald head in chagrin and the misshapen creature chortled, stomped her foot and drooled a little. Why, of all the things she could have downloaded for subterranean playback, had she chosen this? The anomaly so vexed Waldo that he almost tapped her leg and asked, but the last thing he wanted to do was disrupt her delight and jar her back into wretchedness. Then again, maybe it wasn't that complicated, and no different from his connection to MTV *Cribs*—these goofy Nazis played the right chords, the ones that somehow worked for her, distracted her and gave her respite. Same reason anyone watched anything, maybe. Same reason so many people watched *Johnny's Bench*.

Which brought him back to the case. Why hadn't Alastair been arrested yet? Did the police have doubts? Or was it just particular caution because of the high-profile suspect, wanting to have the case fully locked down before they pulled the trigger? One of his first pieces of business would be to find out whether they were looking at anybody else. He also needed to learn whether those buffoons from the Palisades were even on their radar. Why were they so intent on scaring Waldo off the case? They weren't just a piece that didn't fit; they seemed to be completely misboxed, from another puzzle entirely.

Waldo locked his bike to a stand outside the pretty brick building on Mission Road that used to be the old Los Angeles County General Hospital and now housed the coroner's office. He went up to the second floor and past the sign for Skeletons in the Closet, the eccentric little gift shop, discreetly set off from the rest of the building's grim business, which sold chalk-outline towels and boxer shorts along with crime scene tape and toe tags. There was a time when its morbid irony tickled him, but now he knew it to be, like all its brethren, an apotheosis of the world's problem, silently poisoning the planet one playful bit of kitsch at a time.

He asked the receptionist to see Freddie Dellamora and gave his own name, which didn't seem to mean anything to her, a good sign, and took a molded plastic seat in the waiting area. Waldo didn't know how many friendly pockets he'd be able to find after everything that had happened, but this was a safe place to start. Though Freddie was seven years older, they'd hit it off on a drive-by killing during Waldo's rookie year and quickly became after-work buddies. Beyond their friendship, Freddie owed Waldo more favors than either of them could count: he'd introduced Freddie to his wife, a public defender with a lot of business at North Hollywood; later on, when Freddie grew tired of the marriage, Waldo had reluctantly let him invent a fiction about splitting a pair of Dodgers season tickets, to cover Freddie's once again robust dating life.

Now Freddie emerged from behind a heavy door, a little thicker under his scrubs, eyes droopier, gray hair peeking out from under his cap. Time hadn't been kind to him, but this was the first friend Waldo had seen since he'd gotten to town, and he felt himself smiling.

Freddie wasn't smiling back. He gave Waldo a once-over and said, "Jesus, Waldo." It was something he was hearing a lot. Freddie tipped his head toward the heavy door and Waldo followed him through. Freddie moved fast, making no effort to let Waldo keep up, and once in his cramped office shut the door quickly behind them. Stacks of file folders covered the floor and every inch parallel to it except for Freddie's desk chair, onto which he dropped, frowning. "Outside this room, you don't know me anymore. Understand?" Waldo held out his hands for an explanation. "You're poison."

"Even at the coroner's?"

"Coroner's, sheriff's, LAPD, DMV, PTA. Poison. Fuck were you expecting?"

Waldo frowned. "Can I sit?"

Freddie waved permission for Waldo to move the files from the chair. "What kind of welcome they give you at division?"

"I came to you first."

"Thanks for that. Ticker tape, you'll get over there. Rose petals."

"Yeah, I know. Probably twenty guys in that building who'd like to knock my teeth in."

"Twenty? A *hundred*. Twenty who'd like to knock 'em in with a bullet."

Waldo got right to it. "I want the autopsy protocol on Monica Pinch. All the slides, all the photos—"

Freddie scoffed. "Good luck with that."

Waldo said, "The defense has the right to everything—"

"*Defense*. He hasn't been arrested yet."

"Is he going to be?"

"Fuck *you* think."

"So, what—I'm asking you for it a couple days early." Freddie shook his head. Waldo tried another tack. "Or you can wait and deal with Fontella Davis instead. Who's every bit the delight she looks like on TV, by the way." Waldo saw that wasn't enough. "And who never went in with you on Dodger seats."

Freddie looked out his window. "Barb left me. Right before Christmas."

"There's a surprise."

"Charlie fucking Waldo." He plucked a file from one of the

stacks on his desk. "Wait here while I make copies. *Door closed.*" He started out of the room.

Waldo stopped him with a question. "Straight up: how do you make this?"

Freddie stopped and exhaled to signal a serious and thoughtful response. "Severe blow to the right temple, cerebral hemorrhage, secondary contusion back of the head, probably where she fell." Waldo nodded, following. "Subject locked in a house with a drunk who likes to beat people up. Front door's got a dead bolt locks only from the inside. I'm guessing . . . suicide?" He screwed up his mouth, wiseass. Waldo shifted in his seat. Freddie went on. "And the alarm—you heard about that, right?"

Waldo shook his head. "I just came on."

"Burglar alarm was set when the cops got there; they saw him turn it off. Alarm company says it was armed straight through since the previous night."

"Before or after time of death?"

"Too close to call." Freddie leaned on the edge of his desk, pushing a stack backward with his butt. "Fucking guy's got two assault convictions in England, did you know that?" Waldo shook his head. "He's a drunk and a hitter and a liar and he clobbered his wife with a vase. Nothing complicated about this one: he did her. I hear the DA's dotting every *i* twice before they bring him in because he's going to shoot for life."

Waldo absorbed it. Maybe he'd be back in Idyllwild sooner than he thought.

Freddie said, "Seriously—three years off the grid, and you come back for *this* piece of shit?" Waldo looked up at his old friend, whose annoyance had liquefied a bit, a glimmer of empathy peeking through. "You ran out of money, right?"

TEN

Waldo spent two hours diving deep into Freddie Dellamora's files, sitting undisturbed in the spare modernist courtyard of the Los Angeles Cathedral, an old favorite retreat where he used to grab a quiet moment on either side of a downtown court appearance. He scrutinized every page, then stuffed the files into his backpack and rode the Metro back to the Valley, nettled by a couple of dissonant points but mostly discouraged for his client and wondering how he'd gotten sucked into giving a shit about what a likely killer was facing.

That was, after all, exactly the aspect of PI work that had made him sneer at Lorena's original offer, the inherent corruption of the investigation, which ran counter to his constitution. He was built and trained to attack a case without prejudice, to rely on his intuition to inform but never to guide, let alone determine; the very notion of a "client" was anathema to all that. Still, there was no quitting before he was sure Alastair was guilty: if there was one thing he'd learned hard, it was to play it to the end and make sure the answers weren't just quick but righteous.

Back in the Valley after wasting a dollar on a second Metro card, he got on his bike and, for lack of a plan, started west on Chandler while he moved on from private eye work's moral compromises to its practical ones. As a police detective, he'd start by examining the murder scene in its raw state; needless to say, the uncorrupted location wasn't available to him anymore, nor was whatever the police might have gleaned before turning it back over to Alastair. As a police detective, he'd comb the neighborhood for potential witnesses; he could still do his own canvass, though it wasn't likely to be very fruitful in a neighborhood built for privacy, gates and hedges dividing one big lot from the next. As a police detective, he could work from forensic reports much wider ranging than the coroner's; he'd never see any of that, though, as nobody else would be as helpful as Freddie, at least not until it moved toward trial and the DA was obliged to share with Alastair's lawyers during discovery, long past the point Waldo hoped to be gone from the case. In all, working as a PI would mean working without any of the normal investigative assets he was used to.

Coming at it from another direction: what would he be doing next, if he were still LAPD, and if those investigative assets had already been properly mined by the police and if they had indeed pointed to Alastair's certain guilt, as they seemed to? He'd focus on Alastair, on breaking him down and looking for the hole in his story, to prove not only that he'd killed his wife but that he remembered full well doing it, toward helping the DA prove intent and secure a tougher sentence.

Of course, that objective would be contrary to his actual intuition; Waldo's read, admittedly without factual backup, was that even if Alastair had killed his wife, he truly had no memory of it.

So in that sense his current obligation to his client squared—
more than his old job would have—with his instinct for what
would actually constitute justice. The recognition gave him his
first glimmer of peace since the encounter with Freddie. Could
he find an approach to the case, a way in, that could build on that
comfortable moral ground?

No doubt the first impressions on the PD—the locked house;
the truculent alcoholic; that the husband is, as Alastair said, always the first suspect—were powerful. Also powerful would be
the temptation to arrest and convict a killer as shiny as Alastair
Pinch, all the more given the perverse irony of his representing
justice itself to America every Wednesday night. Might those
powerful forces have influenced the police investigators, even
subconsciously?

Maybe that was the way he could serve both his client and the
truth and be square with the work: he could question whether the
police had gone about their business with the requisite level of
dispassion. How did the investigation begin? What were the first
minutes like? Who was on the scene? How much information had
they gathered before they made up their minds that Alastair was
the doer?

Basically, did anybody fuck up?

Of course, there was only one place to begin asking those
questions, and it was the last place he thought he'd ever visit
again: North Hollywood Division. Not only would he have to
return to that river he'd burned, but they'd see him coming with
a can of gasoline and a book of matches, ready for another go.

Tires screeched and a black Toyota SUV bore down on him.
He swerved into a hedge, then popped to his feet, bracing for an
attack—the Posse in a new ride?—only to see a mom behind the

wheel, holding a cell phone and mouthing apology. Waldo gave her a baleful glare, though he knew he himself hadn't been paying full attention either and might have drifted too far toward the middle of the road.

In fact, he realized as the woman drove on, in his distraction he'd absently cruised along old routes into his former Valley Village neighborhood, where he'd lived for his last five years in L.A. Trying to convince himself he wasn't just forestalling the trip to division, he rode the two blocks to his old house on Cantaloupe to take a look.

It was a two-bedroom stucco bungalow on a dead end, with purple trim that had been white when Waldo sold it. He got off his bike and leaned it against an overflowing blue recycling bin on the street awaiting pickup. There was a basketball hoop attached to the garage now, a tricycle in the driveway and a couple of yellow Adirondack chairs. Like the Camaro, this house had meant so much to him once: first an emblem to himself of early accomplishment and great future, and later of pride and corrosive ambition. It was the place where he and Lorena had spent so many indelible nights together, including that mendacious final one, when he knew what he was about to do but couldn't bring himself to tell her. In the end, it was the agent of liberation, the canny investment that gave him the freedom to quit the world cold. Now it was just a structure, essentially interchangeable with hundreds of others near it, a structure where a family of strangers kept their many, many Things. Waldo, who'd once spread his solitary life over two whole bedrooms *and* a living room *and* a dining room *and* a full kitchen *and* one and a half bathrooms *and* a garage, was almost physically ill, mortified and disgusted by his decades of consumption and waste.

"Get out of here or I'll call the cops!" someone shouted from across the street, and Waldo turned to see his retired neighbor, Marty Schraub, standing outside his front door. "And stay out of *my* recycling!"

Before Waldo could identify himself, Marty's wife, Gerta, called from inside the house, "Who's out there?"

Marty turned toward their screen door and said, "Some bum, stealing the Faustos' recycling."

Waldo took a step in his direction, into the street. "Marty . . ."

"Get away from me! I'm calling the police!" He turned and fumbled open the screen door, but Gerta had appeared in the doorway, blocking him, and was peering around him toward Waldo, wearing her bathrobe even though it was almost lunchtime. "Get inside!" Marty barked at her.

Gerta said, "That's Waldo, you dummy. Charlie Waldo, from across the street." She waved. "Hi, Waldo!"

"Hey, Gerta."

"Waldo?" Marty said, as if it couldn't be true. He turned and looked at him.

Waldo nodded.

Marty walked out into the middle of Cantaloupe Street, squinting, studying him and finally screwing up his face. "Jesus, Waldo."

Across the street from the North Hollywood Division driveway, Waldo straddled his bike and took inventory of the relationships he'd enjoyed over his LAPD career, trying to decide which of his closest friends was most likely not to despise him. Freddie Dellamora's wariness troubled him even more than Big Jim Cuppy pissing in his pond. The truth was, if Waldo's mission was to focus on the police work itself, to investigate the investigation, even the guys who were totally *his guys* back in the day—Conady, Dinkley, Segura—wouldn't be his guys anymore.

A cruiser pulled out and passed him. Neither of the uniforms looked in his direction, nor did either look familiar. He tried to recall how fast the division turned over and wondered how many people in the building would even know him.

He stared at the entrance. He was here, he needed to go inside, but he didn't have the play yet.

His phone dinged with a text from a number he didn't recognize. It read:

I know who killed Monica Pinch.

It had been years since he'd even received a text. He wrote back, *Who is this?*

The answer came back quickly. *Meet @ yr cabin.*

In LA—let's meet here.

This time the person at the other end made Waldo wait for a long, long minute. Finally:

Cabin. And then, *Tonite.*

There was the possibility that this was some kind of ambush, of course, but he didn't see any option other than the long trek back to Idyllwild. There'd be time for North Hollywood later.

ELEVEN

The pedal up 243 was even worse than he'd anticipated, the lactic acid setting his legs on fire, his heart hammering so hard he could hear it. He tried to remember the tips he'd read online on the bus back to Banning, to keep his breath steady, to bend forward and keep a low center of gravity, to slide back in the saddle to leverage more force from his glutes. But if any of it helped, his thighs weren't getting the message.

His canteen was empty before he hit the top of the mountain and he considered stopping in town to refill it with tap water, but the sun had almost disappeared and, as it was, he'd probably be managing the last stretch to his house in the dark, so he rode on, parched and spent. He'd tested his mystery informant with four more messages over the course of the day, proposing they establish a specific time to meet and keeping him—Waldo was thinking of him as a male, based on the curtness of the initial texts—apprised of his progress toward Idyllwild, but the informant never responded. Now he worried that after all this, the guy wouldn't show.

He indeed had only the light of the gibbous moon to guide him when he turned onto the dirt road to his property. Approaching, he heard voices from his cabin. So there was more than one. He hoped they wouldn't be the dipshits from the Palisades again. He pedaled faster, the pain in his legs returning as he gained speed, but then his front wheel rammed something and he wiped out, landing on his elbow, still swollen and aching from the last night he was here.

He rolled over, hoping to leverage his good arm to raise himself up, and found himself inches from what looked like the back of a man's head, or what was left of it. He got to his feet and poked the body with his toe to roll the corpse onto his back for a better look. He still didn't look familiar.

Waldo pushed his bike out of the dirt path and made his way toward the cabin, from which the noise had not abated, treading as silently as he could. There was an SUV parked outside, a black Escalade, which he hadn't been able to see at a distance.

He found two men waiting for him inside his cabin and his possessions trashed and scattered. He recognized one as the bodybuilder who'd been eyeing him at the bus station, wearing the same kind of muscle shirt. The other was a head shorter, a wiry, thirtyish Hispanic in a print guayabera, with one small hoop earring, wisps of a chin beard and carefully landscaped sideburns. He was holding Waldo's Kindle. "How you like this thing? I'm tryin' to decide between this and a Nook."

"You can get a Nook cheaper, but Kindle's better for content."

The short man considered the device carefully and said, "Uh-huh. How's their tech support?"

Waldo said, "Excellent."

"Good." He picked up Waldo's hammer and smashed the

screen. He tossed it aside, turned to Waldo and twirled the hammer ominously. "I'm Don Q. You hearda me?"

Waldo nodded and took stock of the situation. Body on the lawn notwithstanding, if they were here to kill him, they probably would have gotten right to it without the dialogue. Then again, if they were here to make some kind of point, he was pretty sure it wasn't going to stop with his Kindle. They were in close quarters, three in the tiny room. He flashed a peek at Don Q's gorilla on his right, wondering if he might be too muscle-bound to block a coldcock left to the Adam's apple and whether Waldo's own healing elbow had enough left in it to make it worth the trouble.

As if reading his thoughts, Don Q introduced his associate. "This is Nini. You do not want to fuck with this man: he was the number one ranked Inuit light heavyweight, and that was *before* he started goin' all apeshit on the Bowflex."

Waldo turned to Nini. "Inuit? That the same as Eskimo?"

Don Q answered for him. "Not exactly. All Inuits are Eskimos, but not all Eskimos are Inuits."

Waldo, still looking at Nini, said, "Then you *are* an Eskimo."

Don Q said, "Well, see, Nini's from Canada. You can say 'Eskimo' in Alaska, but in Canada, they ain't down with that. They want to be called 'Inuit.' To them, Eskimo is pejorative." In case Waldo didn't comprehend, he added, "That means it's insultin'."

Waldo nodded to indicate he'd be sensitive to the ethnic nuances.

Nini sucker punched him in the jaw.

"*Fuck!*" said Waldo, realizing that Inuit, Eskimo or Australian aborigine, he didn't stand a chance against him.

"Thing is, Waldo, as you may have already surmised, all this chitchat 'bout heritage ain't the reason we visitin' your castle. So. Where is it?"

"Where is what?"

Don Q nodded at Nini, who telegraphed it this time but still drove a lead fist into Waldo's stomach. Waldo doubled over, gulping for wind, which came even harder now than it did on the hellish slog up the mountain.

Don Q twirled the hammer some more while he waited for Waldo to stop heaving. "The item Lorena left with you."

Waldo, hands still on his knees, looked up and wheezed, "I'm starting . . . to think . . . you're not here to tell me . . . who killed Monica Pinch."

"Waldo, Waldo, Waldo. You just give me the muthafucker, we'll go on our way and you'd hardly know we was here."

"Except for . . . the lawn ornament . . . you left me . . ."

"Oh, you met that gentleman."

"Who was he?"

"Business associate of mine. Former."

"Why's he here?"

"Why's he here? Shit, Waldo, he's here to tell you somethin'."

"What's that?"

"What's that? That I'm one fuckin' serious individual, that's what's that." Don Q looked around the cabin. "Thing is, there ain't even much here to look through. This the only property you got? Where you keep all your possessions? Mementos, knickknacks, what have you."

"This is everything."

"Come on, man. You know that ain't true."

"I'm a minimalist."

"*Minimalist?* Fuck's that? Like those artists, with that white on white and shit?"

Waldo squinted at him. Apparently traffickers had gotten more erudite since he'd left the force. "It's a lifestyle. I've divested. I'm only allowed to have one hundred Things."

"Allowed? By who? You in one of those funky-ass churches be hidin' up here?"

"Not a religion. Lifestyle. Self-imposed."

"*Self-imposed?*" He looked around the cabin again. "A hundred things. That's fucked up, Waldo. Especially if one of 'em is mine." He said to Nini, "Backpack," and the Inuit yanked it from Waldo's shoulders. "Pockets," he said, and Nini went through Waldo's pants while Don Q dumped the contents of Waldo's bag onto the floor and rifled through its compartments. "So what you tellin' me— this, like, all your clothes?"

Waldo nodded.

"Paira socks," Don Q said. "That one thing or two?"

"One."

Don Q raised an eyebrow. "Kinda cheatin', ain't it, Waldo?" Before Waldo could decide where to begin, Don Q said, "I'm becomin' convinced that you ain't storin' my item on the premises after all. What I'm thinkin' now is, you stashed it someplace in L.A. May even be you got into this Pinch bullshit as a cover."

Waldo shook his head, though he knew it wouldn't make an impression.

"Here's the deal, Waldo: you got twenty-four hours, and then I want my Mem. The alternative, you end up like your friend Lorena."

"Where is she? And what's a Mem?"

Don Q gestured toward Nini and said, "You telephone my

man here when you got it in hand. Easy to remember his number: 818-ME-NANOOK."

Waldo looked at Nini and said, "Me Nanook? *Really?*"

One more Inuit uppercut and Waldo's endless day was finally
over.

TWELVE

Consciousness took a halting approach shortly before daylight, dragging along a trio of regrets. The first was having refused Lorena. The second was—again—not having an ice pack. The third was not making room in the Hundred for a gun. Lorena had seen the danger of living in isolation without one; it had been her first question when he told her about divesting. Well, he'd need one now. He'd figure that out in L.A., where he'd also need to start looking for her. And he still had to figure out how to handle division.

But he was facedown on a floor and his first job was to figure out what floor. It was his own, it turned out, in what was passing for good news this week. His ruined Kindle was right in front of him. He would order a new one, so there would be a net-zero impact on his Things, but one also had to consider environmental costs incurred in producing each Kindle. The breakeven on those costs, relative to traditional paper books, came with the download of 22.5 e-books, but Waldo had been hoping to get several more years' use out of this one and read easily a hundred books a year, and if you called it three hundred books that meant about a thousand pounds of CO_2 he'd still been hoping to save. Looking at it in a more forgiving way, the manufacture of a new device would be adding "only" about seventy-five pounds' worth. But of course that didn't account for the abhorrent practices behind the gathering of the columbite-tantalite required to manufacture the Kindle's capacitors, two-thirds of the world's reserves of which resided in war-torn Congo, rendering virtually every electronic device on the planet complicit from birth in financing African military conflict at least and, at worst, human rights abuses up to and including slave labor.

It was paralyzing to contemplate.

But he needed to focus on imperatives closer to home. The priorities today were Lorena, a gun, and Alastair. Then he remembered one bit of priority housekeeping that couldn't wait: he'd have to do something about the dead man in his driveway.

He sat up and phoned the Riverside County Sheriff's, then spent an hour freshening his chickens' provisions and putting his cabin back in order while he waited for a cruiser to make its way up the mountain from Hemet. They sent two men, Oquendo and Foy, a fortyish buzz-cut sergeant and a young African American with the skittery eyes of a trainee. The dispatcher apparently hadn't passed on the word that Waldo was former law enforcement, and they were far enough from L.A. and the old scandals that his name must not have triggered anything for them.

In fact, Oquendo, who did all of the talking, seemed pretty sure that this long-haired freak living alone in the woods had shot a man on his property and was trying to cover with some babble about LAPD and drug dealers and Eskimo prizefighters and a body being left to intimidate him. Waldo didn't have a lot to back up his story: his three-year beard covered the evidentiary bruises and swelling on his jaw. When Oquendo asked him again if he was certain he didn't recognize the dead man, Waldo suggested he take a picture of the corpse and shoot it to a detective named Jim Cuppy at North Hollywood Division, because he'd been up here days ago asking about the drug dealer who was here last night and maybe he could provide an ID. The specificity of an LAPD contact gave Oquendo pause, so he told his partner to stand with Waldo by the body while he got back in the car and made the call. In the awkward silence Waldo asked Foy if he was a rookie and the kid decided it was safe to say yes. Then they both watched Oquendo through the windshield. He hung up and got out of the car and told them that Cuppy wasn't reachable but that dispatch would get a message to him.

The sergeant stared dumbly at the corpse, frozen, overmatched by the situation. In the vacuum, Waldo declared that he needed to leave soon to catch a bus back to L.A. That roused Oquendo. "I don't think you should leave town."

"You arresting me?"

"Not sure yet."

"Get sure, or I'm going."

"What's the hurry?"

"I've got business." He moved for his bike, which was still near the body.

"What kind of business?" said Oquendo, easing his hand toward his belt.

Waldo couldn't believe what he was seeing. "Are you going for your piece?"

"Sir, I need you to keep calm."

"Tell you what, put your right hand on your gun, put your left hand down your pants and while you're being an *actual* jerk-off, have your trainee here Google 'Charlie Waldo, Alastair Pinch.'" He had worked in L.A. long enough to know when to drop a name.

Foy looked to Oquendo. Oquendo took his hand from his gun. "Judge Johnny?" Waldo nodded. "What do you got to do with Alastair Pinch?"

"I'm working for him, as a PI. Go ahead, look it up."

Doubtful: "*You* are." But he nodded to Foy, who quickly found the *Variety* story. He showed his phone to Oquendo. "I'll be damned," said Oquendo.

Foy said to Waldo, "So what are you, like, famous?" Waldo picked up his bike and inspected it for damage from last night's collision with the dead man. Foy, reading his phone over Oquendo's shoulder, said, "He really *was* LAPD."

Covering, Oquendo said, "I could tell," as if he had been in Waldo's corner all along. Waldo let it slide. Oquendo said to no one in particular, "Fucking Idyllwild, man. Every time I have to come up here it's something screwy. But this wins the goddamn prize." Then added to Waldo, "No offense."

"None taken."

While Waldo finished checking out the bike, Oquendo got up his nerve. "Ask you something? How much they pay you on a case like that?"

Waldo was enjoying the upper hand too much not to share. "Two thousand a day."

Foy blurted, "No shit?"

"But I'm making them give it all to the Sierra Club."

Oquendo headed toward the cruiser shaking his head. "Fucking Idyllwild."

It was another harrowing ride down the mountain. A motorcycle club passed and one biker buzzed so close Waldo could smell the weed on the guy, then saluted him with a middle finger as the crew roared off around a bend. But he made it to the Banning station, sweat-soaked more from nerves than from exertion. The Greyhound was over-air-conditioned and chilled him in his wet clothes, but it had Wi-Fi and as it merged onto the 10 he searched Lorena and found her agency, which was called Very Private Eyes. *Shit*, he wanted to tell her, *with a name like that*, of course *you get too much marital.*

The website had a phone number—not familiar, not Lorena's cell—and a PO box for an address. She had claimed to have some full-time ops—was that just a fiction to impress him? Was the agency really doing business? That Porsche she was driving wasn't cheap. Then again, Cuppy said she was in the drug trade now, or at least drug-trade adjacent, working for Don Q. Waldo hadn't wanted to believe it . . . but so far Cuppy was proving right about the rest. He sighed. Lorena Nascimento. Three years could do a lot to someone. Look in a mirror.

He tried the number on the website, got a machine with Lorena's voice. No receptionist. He said, "Waldo. Call me," and hung up. He buzzed around the net some more, found Very Private Eyes on all the social media platforms, but it was studiously anonymous, no pictures of Lorena, no names of other staff. Yelp seemed to swear by her, at least the few semi-anonymous but possibly actual people who shared their stories. Giving up on finding a toehold online, he turned off his phone to save the battery. He shifted his thoughts to the challenge of securing a gun without a license, not something he'd ever had to worry about before, and let the Greyhound rock him to sleep.

A sudden slowdown for freeway traffic jolted him awake with the answer handy. He restarted his phone, searched "gun shop sunset blvd," but didn't find what he was looking for until he remembered that the store might be just beyond the line where Sunset turns into Cesar Chavez and tried again. There it was: Alberto Suarez was still in business.

Alberto was a two-decade fixture at the police academy armory, everybody's favorite, an equal-opportunity ballbuster who remembered every cop who came through and left you laughing whenever you did. Then his only daughter, Marisol, went to her first high school party in Panorama City and never came home, found two days later raped and strangled and left in a Dumpster just over the Tujunga Wash, the boundary between North Hollywood and Mission Division. For the first and only time in his career Waldo forced himself onto another division's case, spent a week pulling every string he had downtown until they initiated a loan-out. Mission had been working one suspect: the football player who'd gotten Marisol Suarez drinking Southern Comfort and Dr Pepper and brought her home to an empty house, his parents off at his mother's college reunion in North Carolina. They didn't believe the kid's story about falling asleep together on the sofa and waking up to find her gone, but the case jammed when the kid's DNA didn't match the swabs.

A month later the investigation was running dry and Waldo was starting to get pressure to go back to his division when he played a hunch and ran a check on the kid's relatives, even the out-of-town ones, and found an uncle in New Mexico with a rape jacket, then found the same uncle had rented a car in Las Cruces the day before the murder and reported it stolen the day after. Turned out a surprise visit to his sister's family had gone in a different direction, and now, thanks to Waldo, Marisol's killer was at Mule Creek, on a cellblock with one of the Menendez brothers. But Alberto Suarez was never the same, stopped busting balls, finally pensioned out and spent a couple of years watching the Dodgers before he decided Kershaw every fifth day wasn't enough of a distraction from the hell and opened a gun shop of his own.

When Waldo entered the empty store, Alberto recognized him even through the beard and almost smiled but not quite. Business was good, Alberto told him, plenty of cops coming his way, the years of goodwill paying off. Most of his stock, in fact, was LAPD-approved weaponry, familiar stuff. Waldo searched the glass case for an eight-round semiautomatic Beretta 8045F, the weapon he'd carried on duty and off for most of his career, and found one. Alberto unlocked the case and handed it to Waldo. He couldn't say it felt good in his hand, but it felt like his.

Waldo tested the safety, then tested Alberto. "One thing. I don't have a license."

"Anybody asks, I thought you were still a cop."

Waldo raised an eyebrow, doubting the play. "You don't watch TV?"

Alberto was confident. "Don't even have one no more."

Waldo nodded gratitude, laid the Beretta on top of the case and said, "This'll work." He took out his wallet and gave Alberto his one credit card, which reminded him of the other issue, that the gun would be the Hundred and First Thing.

"Problem?" Alberto said.

Waldo didn't want to explain it all again. He reconsidered the wallet, which he would rather not give up, then emptied his pockets onto the counter in hope of finding an alternative. A Swiss Army knife—eight Things in one and thus indispensable—plus the keys to his cabin and bike lock; that was it. The wallet had to go. He plucked from it his cash and credit card and showed the ratty wallet to Alberto. "You know anything about Goodwill? Think they'd want this?"

Alberto's brow furrowed at the odd question but gave the wallet a once-over. "Probably not."

"Throw it away for me?"

"Why'n't you get a new one first?" Waldo waved off the question. Alberto tossed it in the garbage can behind the counter. Then he said, "Let's get you some bullets."

Waldo froze. "Bullets. Shit." He thought for a moment, then kicked off his shoes and started pulling off his socks. One had a hole in the toe anyway.

THIRTEEN

The PO address on Lorena's website was a dingy little mailbox store on Hollywood Boulevard. Waldo wheeled his bike inside and leaned it against a wall. The place was empty save the young woman behind the counter, and she didn't glance up from her phone when he came in. Waldo found 173 on the wall of rental boxes and peered in the tiny glass window: empty. Lorena had been missing for the better part of a week; not even junk in there, which meant somebody was picking up her mail.

He took another look at the girl on duty: sleeve tattoos, a dozen piercings, pigtails ironically high on her crown, thumbing her phone a little too fast. "Hey," he said, and she still didn't look up. A little louder—"*Hey*"—and she did. "You got a name?"

She frowned for a good five seconds, less like she wasn't sure what to answer than like she didn't remember what a question was. Finally she said, "Theola." One eye twitched a little.

"Tell me about 173, Theola," Waldo said, coming over to her. "Who owns it?"

Her hands trembled too. After another odd hesitation she said, "My boss doesn't want me to, like—" Before she could finish, Waldo stormed around the counter and snagged the studded leather handbag from the chair next to her.

"Hey!" She lunged but he turned away, blocked her with his body and dumped the contents onto the counter. Along with the usual wallet and keys, sunglasses and lighter, loose change and mints, he found what he expected, an amber prescription bottle from Rite Aid. "Your boss doesn't want you to, like, take dexies on the job, is that what you were going to say?"

"Gimme that!" She grabbed at the bottle but he held it out of reach.

"Not your day, Theola. I'm a cop." It wasn't just a lie, it was a felony, but in his experience, tweakers didn't tend to file formal complaints.

She stopped trying to wrestle for the bottle and went with a shaky indignation instead. "I'm ADHD," she said. "I have a prescription."

"I'm sure you got several." Then he repeated, "Box 173."

She scowled, cornered and resentful, then went to the desk computer and struggled to work the mouse with a jittery hand. "You don't look like a cop," she grumbled as she brought up the info.

Waldo looked over her shoulder and read out loud, "Willem Vander Janssen, 511 North St. Andrews Place." He looked down at her. "You know him?" She shook her head. When she held his eye he decided she was probably telling the truth. "Thank you, Theola," he said, friendly, and went for his bike.

"Hey, do I get my pills back?"

"Nah. I'm keeping 'em."

"If you're a cop, I wanna see some ID."

Half out the door, he turned back. "Feel free to call my captain and tell him what a prick I am. North Hollywood Division. My name's Cuppy."

"Come on. Please?" She looked frightened.

What would he do with them anyway? Dump the bottle in a sewer, feed Dexedrine into the ecosystem? Save it until he went to division and toss it in the drop box there? That visit was going to be complicated enough. He could hold on to it without a short-term plan . . . but, well, then it's a Thing. He tossed her the bottle and was surprised when she caught it clean.

She looked up at him, grateful like a child, and said, "Thanks, Cuppy."

A stakeout without an automobile was another first, exposed and conspicuous on a street of one-story houses and little traffic. To cover, he leaned the bike against a mailbox and dropped down to fuss with the gears and pretend a repair. In case anyone was watching from inside one of these houses, every hour or so he moved the bike to a different spot on the block, keeping 511 North St. Andrews in sight.

As the afternoon of squatting and kneeling ground away and he wondered whether it was time to move to yet another vantage, his fourth, his conscience began to trouble him almost as much as his knees. It had been well over twenty-four hours since he'd done anything on the case he'd been hired to handle, given that the trip to and from Idyllwild ended up having nothing to do with Alastair Pinch. Waldo rationalized that more of Alastair's neighbors would be around to talk to him in the evening anyway, his intended next step. Of course, by the same token it was likely that he was right now staking out an empty house, that Waldo would waste the rest of the day here waiting for Willem Vander Janssen, whoever that was, to get home from work, and even after that it would take him a good couple of hours to get over the hill to Studio City. Being honest with himself, he knew that if he stayed here until, say, eight o'clock, he'd end up giving his clients nothing for today's two thousand dollars.

He'd just decided to give St. Andrews Place one more hour, when a shirtless blond man emerged, locked the front door behind him and trotted into the street in Waldo's direction. He was more fashion-ad handsome than TV-star handsome, tall and muscled like a swimmer, his perfect three days' beard nothing like Waldo's raggedy three years'. Even the skimpiness of his running shorts suggested a life of being looked at. And why not? Waldo thought. He was the flavor of beautiful you find in maybe a dozen American zip codes. The two men nodded strangers' acknowledgment as the jogger passed; then Waldo stood and called to his back, "Willem Vander Janssen?" The man stopped running and turned, corporeal confidence giving way to corporeal fear.

Waldo said, "I'm looking for Lorena."

The man took a couple of steps backward, like he was thinking about making a run for it. "Who are you?"

"My name's Charlie Waldo."

"Oh," Vander Janssen said, visibly deflating with relief. "Oh. Waldo. Thank God. Hi." He came to Waldo and pumped his hand gratefully.

Waldo said, "You know who I am."

"Lorena's talked about you. Plenty."

"You know where she is?"

"I haven't seen her since last Thursday. She borrowed my car. She said she was scared to drive her own."

Waldo said, "Lorena used that word? 'Scared'?" It was hard to imagine this woman, who had once left a pro athlete three times her weight in critical condition, being afraid of anything.

Vander Janssen said, "You're probably wondering why I'm going for a run, with her missing and all. But, *you* know." He gestured vaguely to his body, as if its perfection were explanation enough. He bounced nervously on the balls of his feet, took a glance in each direction down the street. "Truth is, I'm pretty freaked out. Are you helping her? She said you'd help her."

"When did she say that? Before or after she came to see me?"

Vander Janssen said, "I didn't even know she saw you. She only told me she was going to reach out."

"She came up to where I live, in Idyllwild." The guy shrugged: news to him. Waldo said, "Your car she borrowed—was it the Porsche?"

"The 911? Uh-huh."

"Why's she doing business out of your PO box? Who are you?"

"Oh. I'm her husband."

It was a gut punch.

Then again, what should he have expected? He was the one who disappeared, and stayed that way—of course there would be somebody, probably a whole series of somebodies; still, with the reality standing in front of him, this pretty boy with his shorty-shorts body off a Sunset Boulevard billboard, the world tilted off its axis. His own erotic memories, his thoughts in the night, everything he had so tenaciously chased away, were all of her, still, but here was a living demonstration that her erotic life had moved on. And yet—and how did this square with the fact of a *husband*—Lorena wanted Waldo back, didn't she? The visit to the mountain, the way she held him, looked at him—wasn't that what she'd been telling him? Evidently not. How had he misread that so badly?

The time away had made him wholly incompetent to live in the world.

"You want to go inside and talk?" the man said. *Lorena's husband* said. Waldo nodded dumbly and followed him back inside the house.

Her house. With these oversize arty photographs of birds on the wall (was this her taste now? since when?) and framed photos of older people (the darker-complected ones familiar, the blond ones not) on the end table of the living room set, this living room set they probably shopped for together, Mr. and Mrs. Willem Vander Janssen, out on a Saturday afternoon with a joint Master-card, looking to fill up their home together with shared Things. Because none of this would have been Lorena Nascimento's alone. Her downtown apartment had been cluttered with secondhand gems discovered at swap meets and yard sales, eclectic but all comfortable and interesting and *hers*, not these anodyne prefabs straight out of some anodyne chain at some anodyne mall, clean and well matched but aggressively *not* interesting. Had she subordinated her taste to this guy's, to everything she wasn't? Did she love him that much?

And then he found himself furious for wondering about any of that, for letting his mind, his weakness, distract him from the only question about Lorena that mattered: *Was she even alive?*

Vander Janssen himself was asking him a different question, though: "Would you like a kombucha?" Waldo didn't know what that was but knew he didn't need one and shook his head. "Is it okay if I get one?"

"Your house."

Vander Janssen went into the kitchen. Waldo followed to see what that was like. More Lorena, the new-model disinfected Lorena: white marble countertops, even the small appliances well coordinated, everything placed perfectly as if staged for a real estate showing. The notion that she lived like this was as foreign to Waldo as his cabin must have been to her.

Vander Janssen took a bottled tea-looking drink from the fridge and leaned against the counter. Waldo asked, "Did she tell you who she was scared of?"

"No. She never talked about her work." That, too, was strange: she'd always been candid with Waldo, their respective investigations part of the daily fabric of their lives together. Early on they'd established a sort of inviolate confidentiality agreement with regard to their business-related conversations, and each trusted that the other would never misuse anything shared. It was part of their intimacy, and it held even when they were in one of their off-again stretches. A Lorena who walled off her work from her life partner would be a different Lorena. Then again, he was a different Waldo. Three years.

More important, it meant that her husband might not be much help. "Can you tell me *anything* about her business? Like, does she have an office? The website only has the PO box."

"No office. She goes to the client, and if they want to meet her somewhere else, she uses this thing LiquidSpace." That plus kombucha, two words in less than a minute that Waldo didn't know, and when Vander Janssen explained by saying, "It's like Airbnb, for offices," that made three. Waldo decided he'd be better off nodding false comprehension, but when Vander Janssen added, "Saves her on overhead," he interpolated some sort of short-term rental service.

"What about the ops? She said she had full-time employees."

"She does. Three. It's all online or phone."

"Know their names?"

"Sure."

"It'd be good if you could write them down for me." Lorena's husband opened a drawer and took out a pad, then stopped, overcome by some thought. "What?" Waldo said.

Vander Janssen said, "Do you think anything happened to her?"

The things they had in common made Waldo queasy. He got back to it. "If Lorena was hiding, where would she go?"

Lorena's husband didn't have any idea. It was stunning how little the man seemed to know about his wife. The realization that the relationship must have been primarily physical made him queasier. Vander Janssen said, "You can look at her room if you want. She might have some files up there."

"Her home office?"

Vander Janssen shifted his weight. "It's really like her, you know, *room*. Like where she lives." Waldo didn't get it. "We're kinda, like, separated. Even though we're both living here." He added, apologetically, "That's why I don't know very much." The ground kept shifting under Waldo. He couldn't even tell what he was feeling—relieved or angry or jealous or just pissed off at the guy's uselessness.

They passed the husband's bedroom, as flawless and flavorless as the front rooms, but when they reached Lorena's he recognized the woman again. "Sorry about the mess," said Vander Janssen. But it wasn't a mess; it was a revolt: there was a queen bed with discrepant sheets and pillowcases and a heavy afghan Waldo recalled her bringing home from the Rose Bowl Flea Market. He'd slept under it many times.

There was an overstuffed closet and shoes that overflowed across the carpet, but no desk and no file boxes. She had a laptop but, unsurprisingly, Vander Janssen didn't know the password. He did know the names of her three employees—all men, Willie Williams and Lucian Reddix and Dave Goldberg—and even had a phone number for one of them, but Waldo doubted they'd be very useful either.

The two men who'd shared Lorena's bed, probably the bed they were standing next to, talked for a while about how she and Vander Janssen met, and how quickly they got married and bought the house, and why it made financial sense to keep sharing it platonically while they figured out how to untangle their lives. The talk satisfied some of Waldo's curiosity but shed no light on whether Don Q had harmed her or where she might be hiding if he hadn't.

His phone rang. "Waldo."

"It's Fontella. Got anything yet?"

He felt guilty again for ignoring the case for a day and a half. Half turning from Vander Janssen, he said, "I've got the coroner's report."

"Jeez, *I* can get *that.*"

He'd almost forgotten how much he hated having a boss. He flashed on his pond and his Kindle. He said, "I'm going to hit Alastair's neighbors this evening, when people are home from work," feeling the need to justify himself, then immediately hating himself for doing it. Davis didn't respond. He could feel her disdain through the static. He said, "I could use access to phone records from that night."

Davis sighed annoyance. "Nothing there. Monica had two calls on her cell: one outgoing early in the evening to order Indian food—delivery man saw Monica, didn't see Alastair; one incoming later, a friend confirming a tennis date the next day. Nothing on Alastair's cell. One call to Sikorsky from the landline."

"What was Sikorsky about?"

"Chocolate."

"Chocolate?"

"Alastair called to tell him American Milky Ways aren't as good as they make in England and he needed his trailer stocked with the British kind. Mars bars."

"Alastair called the president of the network for that?"

"Doesn't remember doing it, either. Sikorsky says he was completely tanked already. Let me know if I can do anything else for you." She didn't need tone to sell the sarcasm.

Waldo said, "I could use the times of all those calls," but she'd already hung up.

FOURTEEN

He was back in Studio City by five, leaving him plenty of time to talk to Alastair's neighbors. Or, as it happened, plenty of time to realize how few neighbors Alastair had. The house sat on an acre-and-a-half lot, big for L.A., and backed onto a hillside that abutted public land, separated from Fryman Canyon Park by cyclone fencing topped with razor wire, ugly but practical and tucked deep enough into a hillside eucalyptus grove to be unnoticeable from the Pinch yard. The only neighbors with a chance of seeing or hearing anything the night of the murder would have been those in the houses on either side, or possibly the one across the street on what looked like an even larger property, though that home was hidden by forbidding ivy walls and a solid gate. Waldo tried it first.

The entrance, directly across from Alastair's driveway, had a doorbell and keypad for gate entry. While he waited for a response to his ring he noticed a security camera pointed at him. *"Yes?"* a woman said through an intercom. He looked straight into the camera and said he was an investigator and that he'd like to talk to her about Monica Pinch. She told him she'd already said everything to the police. When he started to ask how well she knew the Pinches, she said, "Please go away," and he heard a click.

The house to the Pinches' left looked more promising. No wall, just a friendly red picket fence behind which a fresh-faced young woman with copper hair watched two little kids on training-wheeled bikes pedaling loops around a driveway the size of a small playground. She wouldn't come outside the fence or let Waldo inside, but she chatted over it for a few minutes while she kept an eye on her charges. Her name was Shelagh and she was spending two years in America as an au pair for this family, the Goodwins. She was homesick for Edinburgh and said she loved the kids but she didn't seem to care for their parents, who'd gone out for the evening, as they did almost every night. She'd never personally seen Alastair but knew from the Sparkletts man that he lived in the house next door. She said she'd heard shouting from over there once but couldn't make it out, and also that their nanny, Rosario, seemed nice though her English wasn't good enough for them to really be friends. Waldo thought she gave him this much time mostly because she was lonely.

The only actual homeowners he got to meet were the ones on the other side. Waldo had seen Chase and Martha Shinn before, on a local news segment on the murder that he'd found on YouTube that first morning he'd researched the case, after he'd been linked to it in *Variety*. They were both executives at what they called content providers, neither of which Waldo had heard of but whose names they seemed to think would impress him. The couple was happy, even eager, to talk some more about the Pinches, whom they clearly couldn't stand. Waldo got the sense that they both disliked Monica even more than Alastair, especially the wife, but he could see them trying to focus their scorn tactfully on the spouse who hadn't just been murdered.

They took Waldo out to the street to show him the torn-up lawn in front of their house and the stump of an orange tree, which they claimed Alastair had cracked so badly with his Hummer one drunken night that they'd had to cut the whole thing down. Then they showed him a toolshed that the Pinches had built a foot and a half over their property line, and also described at length the ugliest point of contention, a birthday party invitation that the Shinns' daughter had extended to Gaby but which went unreciprocated, a slight that escalated to tears on the day of Gaby's birthday when little Alexa Shinn saw that the Pinches had brought in a pony *and* a moon bounce for the day. As for the murder, Alastair's guilt was self-evident to them, though they hadn't actually seen or heard anything the night Monica died.

The third time the conversation circled around to the contretemps over the moon bounce, Waldo found a way to extricate himself and walked back to Alastair's house. Rosario let him in and told him that Gaby was upstairs in her room and that Alastair wasn't home from work yet. Waldo decided to take advantage of the unsupervised time to give the house a closer inspection and see if he might glean something the cops had missed.

He checked out the security system, which supposedly had been armed through the night, until right after the police saw Alastair turn it off. It was from a well-known alarm company and pretty standard issue for this kind of house, everything in order and working right and all the accessible windows fitted with alarm screens.

He studied the front door, which had two locks: a typical single cylinder, opened by key from the outside and a twist knob from the inside, plus a one-sided dead bolt with a twist knob on the inside but no access at all from the outside. With that one locked, nobody could enter through the door, and nobody could secure it from the outside, either. This was the lock Freddie had mentioned and the immutable fact that most incriminated Alastair.

Waldo retrieved the *Architectural Digest* from his guest room and surveyed the living room from the camera's vantage in each of the two large photos in the magazine. The issue was a year old, but little in the space had changed: there were different flowers, naturally, some art and a new Oriental rug. A side table had been swapped for another, and a small sculpture and a floor vase were gone. Other than that, the magazine shoot could have been this afternoon.

"What say you, Detective? Ought I hire a decorator and refurnish completely?" Alastair had entered behind him and he hadn't noticed.

Waldo tapped one of the magazine photos. "Where's this vase?"

"Ah, the amphora she was killed with. Gone, gone. Smashed to bits."

"What was it, ceramic?"

"Earthenware. We bought it in Istanbul." He sighed. "Beautiful piece. I miss it."

Waldo wondered how a jury would take to him. Could be a catastrophe, but then again, with all that star power and that disarming twinkle even when tossing out a casually outrageous remark like that, twelve star-struck citizens might eat this guy right up. Waldo indicated the magazine again. "How about this table?"

Alastair considered it a bit but didn't have an answer. "That photo's a year and a half old, you realize. Monica was a tinkerer; no room was ever finished. That painting's changed, too."

"I saw. And the rug."

"Well, that's because of the blood," he said softly. Waldo nodded gravely. Alastair added, "With the stains, it didn't match the sofa." Waldo doubled back: catastrophe for sure.

He said, "And this sculpture?"

"That's not a sculpture—it's an Olivier Award, for my Richard the Third."

"Where is it now?"

"I couldn't tell you. I've never been much for Acting Trophies," Alastair said, making plain what he thought of them. As always, Waldo couldn't tell where the genuine insouciance ended and the posing began. "Monica liked to keep that one on display for sentimental reasons—that was the production on which we met. Truly, I haven't thought about it in years; I've no idea where she moved it. For all I know, the police may have stolen it." Waldo frowned, his patience thinning, but Alastair kept the act going. "There were a number of things missing when they were through. Some photographs, petty cash from the cookie jar."

"Really."

"They haven't exactly been gentle with the process." He flopped onto a sofa. "Or perhaps it went into the trash with my other Oliviers and my People's Choice Award." He pronounced the last with extra-big capital letters. "For that one I had to beat out two crusty doctors and a vampire."

"What do they give Oliviers for? Plays?"

"British theater. The equivalent of your Tonys."

"And you've got so many you throw them away?"

"Honestly, I don't know where any of them are. Anyhow, it's not the number; it's the notion. They're fakery. Fakery to celebrate fakery."

"You don't seem to think much of your work."

Alastair gazed out the window at his California-style English garden, jasmine and succulents instead of tulips and lavender. "The perfect performance would be King Lear, done in a sealed black box with no audience. Every deviation from that is compromise. The more you're *willing* to compromise, the more the forces of commerce stand ready to palliate the damage to your soul with statuettes and luxury, until the palliative becomes the thing itself, and then, my dear friend, you are lost." He thought about that for a moment, and added, "Of course, as your presence attests, lost I may already be."

"Or maybe," Waldo said, "somebody just wanted to say they like your acting."

Alastair exploded with a guffaw. "Yes! Yes, Detective! It could be that!"

Gaby bounded into the room with a picture book she wanted her dad to help her read, and Alastair excused himself for the night. Waldo had plans anyway: he was going to hear Jayne White sing.

He considered taking a shower, though he'd just had one the morning before. Living in Idyllwild, he did that only every third day to conserve his well water. Even then his careful bucket shower used but a small fraction of what a few minutes under the spray in a normally plumbed house would use, so two traditional running-water showers a mere thirty-six hours apart felt dissolute, considering the water crisis threatening the globe. But since yesterday morning he'd had the grueling, sweat-soaked bike up the mountain, the scuffle with Don Q and Nini, and then today's long wait in the sun outside Lorena's house, and the level of hygiene adequate for solitary life in the woods probably wouldn't do in Los Angeles, especially not at whatever kind of club in West

Hollywood Jayne had invited him to. So shower he did, mitigating the extravagance by running the water only briefly to wet himself, then turning it off to soap, shampoo and lather, then on again to rinse as quickly as he could.

After he dried himself he flipped the channels until he found something promising, two morbidly obese women on the ground clawing at each other in front of Maury Povich, apparently over the results of a paternity test. Waldo put on his clean underwear and, when the security guys began to pry the women apart, moved to the bathroom to listen to the *Maury* denouement while he hand washed his other set of clothes in the sink. The job was quicker today without socks. In fact, he thought, if the skin on his feet could get accustomed—no sure thing, as nasty irritations were already in bloom behind both heels—he might eventually go sockless full-time, opening two permanent slots to spend however he wanted. The thought made him feel like a rich man. For now, though, he was glad to still have one pair and that this would be a socked night.

Maury went to break and another truculent Savannah Moon commercial. *"Have you taken off all your clothes and looked in the mirror?"* Waldo, in his boxers, appraised his own body, something he hadn't done in a long time. Lorena was right: he *was* skinny.

"Seriously, how fat are you going to get before you do something?"
How *skinny*?
"Well, guess what, Shamu—I'm your something."
Waldo finished dressing while he pondered his options for the trip to West Hollywood. His legs were shot, so riding over the hill and back was an intimidating proposition. The 218 bus went north-south over Laurel but would stop running before

he'd need it to come home. Then there was the danger of the curvy canyon roads in the dark. He decided to coast downhill to Ventura, catch the bus and double back up and over to the other side, and choose later whether to brave the tough ride back or figure out something involving multiple transfers.

Waldo got off the 218 at Sunset and biked to La Cienega, then carefully down its first steep blocks. Beyond Santa Monica most of the stores were dark, shut down for the night, but in the distant blocks ahead he could see pockets of light and people in the street. The first club he approached had a crowd milling out front and he figured that was Jayne's until he got closer and realized that there were no women among them and the music inside was pulsing EDM. He checked Jayne's construction paper and saw he was probably still a block away.

The address she'd written had to be a mistake, because it matched a Lutheran church called Saint Luke's. There were a couple of places open on the other side a block down and he tried those. One was a sports bar and the other a hipster joint with a jukebox loaded with sixties songs; neither was set up for live music.

Waldo went back to the church and this time as he neared he heard a choir from within: "I Know That My Redeemer Lives." Waldo locked his bike to a rack near the heavy wooden door and took a look inside.

It was a rehearsal, not a service, the choir in its stalls but in street clothes. Sure enough, there was Jayne among the altos, in a simple white blouse, hair pulled back in a blue ribbon. *Come hear me sing.* The setting was even more unsexual than the kindergarten, but still she had something ineludible. Waldo slipped into the rear pew to watch and listen. Near the end of the hymn

Jayne noticed him and smiled; she might have winked, too, but he wasn't sure. Between the classroom and the church, he'd been around her less than five minutes, but she'd already knocked him off his pins a dozen times. He listened to "Lift High the Cross" and "Go, My Children, with My Blessing" before the rehearsal broke and Jayne said her good-byes and walked down the aisle to Waldo's pew. "You came," she said.

"I like music."

She told him she knew a place they could get a soda or something and he followed her out. They made small talk on La Cienega, Waldo asking how long she'd been in the choir, Jayne answering that she'd just joined, Jayne asking if he went to church and Waldo saying not lately. She led him into the hipster bar, where the jukebox was playing Jan and Dean. They slid into a wooden booth with high backs.

When a waitress came over, Waldo waited for Jayne to order, but she said to him, "You first." He looked at her demure ribbon and thought about her singing about Jesus and his cross and asked the waitress for a cranberry juice. Jayne said to the waitress, "Double Maker's, rocks."

The waitress said, "Right up," and started away.

Waldo said, "Check that," and changed his order to match Jayne's, then said to her, "Who is who they are?"

Jayne smiled at the playback and said, "Could be I'm exactly who I am—a kindergarten teacher choirgirl who happens to like whiskey."

Waldo shifted in his seat. This was feeling more social than he'd expected and he wanted to get back to work. "So why weren't you shocked that Monica Pinch was murdered?"

Her smile didn't fade, but she said, "Let's hold that till our drinks come." She made him feel ham-fisted, like he wasn't up to the job, like he didn't know how to do any of this anymore, not how to chip away at a case, not how to order in a bar, not how to have a simple conversation with a woman he was attracted to. Jayne was watching him and waiting for his next line and all he could think of was that he didn't have one.

Finally she said, "So—you dressed up for me."

He looked around the bar at the rest of the clientele. There were hipsters wearing jeans and work shirts that seemed similar to his, but if she was saying this now he must be conspicuously untrendy, the stuff he bought for its durability wrong in some way obvious to everybody but him. "Sorry," he said. "Where I live . . . I don't have to think much about fashion."

She untied the ribbon and shook her hair loose, holding his gaze as she did it.

Without thinking about it he said, "There goes the kindergarten teacher choirgirl," but wondered right away if he'd gotten it wrong again.

She said, "Just wait till I have a couple whiskeys in me," and he thought maybe he was okay. Then she said, "Don't get the wrong idea. I'm *totally* a kindergarten teacher choirgirl. Who happens to like whiskey and has good hair."

The waitress came back with the drinks and they both thanked her. Jayne raised her Maker's to Waldo in a silent toast and they both sipped. He hadn't had a drink in his years on the mountain, not out of principle but because he didn't see its place among the new habits he was creating.

He asked again, "Why weren't you shocked?"

But Jayne was distracted by something over his shoulder. Waldo turned: the TV behind the bar, running silently while the oldies played—Buffalo Springfield now—was showing an update on the Monica Pinch murder, footage of Fontella Davis, footage of Alastair, helicopter shots of his house. Jayne said, "I have a confession to make: I've been watching CNN ever since the arrest. I knew who you were the minute you walked into my classroom, even with the new look." Waldo wanted to ask again what she had to say about the Pinches, but before he could she said, "Who was Lydell Lipps? They keep talking about Lydell Lipps."

It was inconceivable that she didn't know, that any Angeleno who even thought to turn on any cable news talk show, anyone who recognized Waldo at first sight even with all his hair, wouldn't know all about him and Lydell Lipps. And given the way she'd been misleading him, teasing, taunting, flirting, toying, she had to be messing with him some more. Or at least trying in a playfully obvious way to get him to tell the story in his own words. But there was no guile in her look as she awaited the answer, no hint at double meaning. He said, "You really don't know?"

She shook her head.

"Were you living in L.A. three years ago?"

She nodded and said with apology, "I was busy, I guess."

"Usually I can tell when someone's screwing with me. But you . . . something jams my radar."

"Maybe your radar's just rusty."

He weighed it, wasn't convinced.

"Honest," she said, "I never, ever heard of Lydell Lipps until I heard about you getting hired to help Mr. Pinch."

Waldo took a drink and a good long look at her before he decided to tell her the story, the central story of his life, the story he'd never told aloud. He started haltingly, but something about the fully present way she listened—in sympathy, concern, horror, hanging on every word and never looking like she was waiting for her turn to talk—made him keep going. The alcohol, which hit quickly, made it easier. He told her about all of it, even the aftermath. About how, when he was still living in town after he'd quit the PD, he couldn't look at the yellow Camaro without remembering that if it weren't for what he'd done to Lydell Lipps, he wouldn't have that car. Or his house, for that matter. Or even that girlfriend he'd been with off and on since the high-flying days. "I didn't know how to be with anybody anymore," he told Jayne now. "If somebody said something funny and I laughed . . . I'd start thinking, *Lydell Lipps* can't laugh at jokes any more, what right do I have—" He stopped midsentence.

Why was he doing this? He'd come here tonight to ask *her* things, to find out what she had to say about Monica and Alastair Pinch, but the evening had gone completely off course. "Sorry," he said, "I never really talked about it."

"It's okay. I'm glad you're talking to me." She reached across the table with both her hands and took his, comforting him. "Did you get any help? Therapy?"

"Someone made me an appointment, but when I got to the guy's door, it was, *Lydell Lipps* can't go to therapy . . . and I turned around and went home. I got to where I couldn't get through the day, you know? Couldn't live in the world."

"So what did you do?"

"I stopped."

He finished his drink. She said, "What do you mean, you stopped?"

So he told her about how he sold the Camaro and renounced materialism, about Idyllwild and the Hundred Things and the three years alone. He didn't tell her about Lorena's visit or any of what followed, only that somebody approached him about helping out with Alastair Pinch's case and that he decided to come down the mountain and do it.

After that they sat together quietly for a long time. When the waitress came over, Waldo motioned for the check. Jayne reached for her purse but he said, "I've got it," and paid in cash.

Talked out, he walked her back to the church, still unspeaking. She was silent too. He didn't feel awkward with her anymore, just drained.

"This is my car," she said, stopping at a white Civic hybrid, a sensible kindergarten teacher ride.

He remembered that he still hadn't taken care of the business he'd intended and felt incompetent again. "Why weren't you shocked about Monica Pinch?"

"God, of course I was shocked! How could I not be shocked?" He was completely baffled now, about the entire night. She looked at him like he was a fool and said, "Don't you know when a girl just wants to have a drink with you?" and when he still didn't know what to do she kissed him. Not a flirty kiss, either, an all-in kiss, her tongue darting between his teeth, then her own teeth tugging at his bottom lip, the fingers of one hand on the back of his neck and the other tangled in his mane, and soon his own hands were moving all over her. Like everything else, more than everything else, it had been so long. He slipped a hand under her blouse and she drew a breath.

"Kindergarten teacher choirgirl," he muttered into her mouth.

"When I like it, I like it," she said and sucked on his tongue, leaning against him and pressing his back against her passenger door.

He eased his fingers under her bra and found hard pebbles

and squeezed and she gasped. "Jesus," she breathed, kissing him harder . . . then suddenly broke from him and pulled away. "I said, a *drink*." She spun out of his arms and continued around to the driver's side. She staggered a little; Waldo himself was reeling. She opened her car door, looked back at him and said, "Three years in the woods—you haven't been with anybody all that time?"

He shook his head.

Her mussed hair hung in front of her face, wanton, and she said, thickly, "That's kinda hot, Waldo," then slipped into her car and closed the door. Waldo stepped back from the curb and watched her pull away and disappear down La Cienega and into the night.

He was bewildered and alone again and he still had to get back to the Valley. He decided to risk the traffic in the dark, straight over the canyon. Do it the hard way.

FIFTEEN

H is sleep wasn't deep, even though it was only the second time in four nights that he hadn't been tucked in with a blow to the cranium. Jayne's teeth and tongue and hands kept coming back to him in dreams and in half-awake moments; he'd spent the whole night trying to sort out which was which. In the early morning light he heard footsteps and he remembered where he was and why and grabbed hold of wakefulness and pulled himself out of sleep though he was still exhausted.

He padded to the bathroom and washed his face and hands, scrubbed yesterday's clothes in the tub and, swapping them with those that had been drying over the glass shower wall, got dressed and followed voices out to the kitchen.

Rosario and Waldo traded good mornings and Gaby said, "Mr. Lion! I forgot you were here! Rosario, can I make breakfast for Mr. Lion?"

Waldo asked Rosario where Alastair was. The housekeeper froze, caught between betraying her boss and being rude to his guest. Waldo, to help her out, asked if he was in the house. She nodded. "Still asleep?" She nodded again. "Does this happen sometimes—he has trouble getting up in the morning?" She nodded a third time. "Who takes Gaby to school on those days?"

She hesitated but said, "If Mr. Alastair is not up by seven thirty I drive."

Gaby walked up to Rosario and said, "Can you go away and let me make breakfast for Mr. Lion?" Rosario told her not to bother Mr. Waldo but Waldo said that she wasn't a bother, that he could even keep an eye on her in the kitchen if Rosario needed a few minutes to get ready.

When Rosario left, Waldo smiled at Gaby and said, "May I please have an orange for breakfast?"

"No."

"But there are oranges right there."

"You're gonna have *cereal* for breakfast." She dragged a chair across the kitchen and climbed up onto the counter, opened a cabinet and stood on tiptoe to reach the boxes on a top shelf.

He crossed the kitchen to spot for her. "Are you allowed to do that?"

"Uh-huh."

"I'd rather have an orange."

"You're gonna have Frosties and Lucky Charms and Froot Loops." She put each of the boxes on the counter by her feet, squatted and sat on the counter, swung her legs down and dropped to the floor.

Waldo said, "I can't eat any of those."

"Are you allergic?"

"Can't I please just have an orange?"

"*Are—you—allergic?*"

"No. It's something different." She made a face she must have learned from television and waited for an explanation. He said, "It's because cereal comes in boxes."

"You're allergic to *boxes*?" Not buying it, she opened a lower cabinet and took out two bowls.

"Seriously—don't pour any of that for me; it'll just go into a landfill."

Ignoring Waldo's protests, Gaby started carrying the cereal boxes and bowls one by one to the table. "What's a landfill?"

"It's a place in the ground where they put all the millions and millions of tons of garbage. It ruins the whole planet we live on." He had to raise his voice a little; a helicopter was hovering close overhead. Even in a six-million-dollar house, you couldn't avoid the sound of chopper blades—one more fact of L.A. life he hadn't missed.

As she put the box on the table she said, "My mommy's in heaven." He didn't answer, hoping she'd just change the subject again. She didn't. "Do you know my mommy?"

"No, I never met her."

"She died and went to heaven."

"Yes, I heard about that."

"Daddy says everybody goes to heaven someday and when I'm very old I'm going to go there too and see her again and everybody's allowed to have a dog."

"That sounds about right."

"These cereals are really good all mixed together. It's my secret recipe. If you're not allergic you're gonna really like it."

"How about I just watch you eat it?"

Gaby poured way too many Frosties into the first bowl and said, "Is your mommy alive?"

"No, my mommy's in heaven too."

"Maybe your mommy and my mommy are friends."

"I bet they are."

"Do you have a dog?"

"No, but I have chickens."

"*Chickens?*"

Gaby poured from the second box and Waldo was trying to figure out how to get out of tasting her secret recipe, when he realized he was hearing a second helicopter. He went to the window and looked out but could see only one of them. Then he saw two more approaching from a distance and realized what was happening. "Shit," he said.

Gaby gasped dramatically and said, "You're not supposed to say that word. Don't worry, Mr. Lion—I won't tell."

But Waldo was already heading out of the room. He said to Gaby, "Show me where your daddy's bedroom is."

She said, "I'm not supposed to wake him up unless it's a 'mergency," but followed Waldo up the stairs. At the top he let her lead him to a closed double door at the end of a hallway. Waldo knocked, got no answer, knocked louder. "He's sleeping, but it's okay. Rosario'll take me to school."

Waldo cracked Alastair's door and looked inside. The bedroom itself was oversize, opulent, with a chandelier and a sitting area complete with divan and coffee table and a pair of its own hallways leading presumably to walk-in closets and a bathroom or two. In the center of the bedroom stood a luxurious bed with luxurious linens, on top of which Alastair lay snoring with his bare ass pointed toward the luxurious canopy.

Waldo looked back at Gaby in the hallway. "Go tell Rosario I said not to open the front door until I come downstairs. Tell her it's important." Gaby ran to the stairs and back down.

Waldo went into Alastair's room, slammed the door behind him and said, loud, *"Hey."* Alastair didn't stir. Waldo grabbed one of the canopy posts and gave the bed a hard shake. Alastair groaned annoyance. Waldo yanked at the comforter underneath him.

Alastair groaned louder. "Go away."

"Wake up. The cops are coming."

That got a response. "What?" He rolled onto his back.

"Put some clothes on. How hungover are you?"

"I am not hungover."

"Uh-huh."

"For your information, Detective, I am still drunk."

"Where's your closet?" Alastair pointed to one of the hallways. Waldo followed it and came to an enormous walk-in closet. He picked an Oxford and a pair of khakis and rifled through a highboy until he found where Alastair kept his underwear and socks, and not just *some* socks, either—dozens and dozens of pairs, probably a hundred Things in the sock drawers alone, even counting the lenient way.

Waldo came out of the closet to see Alastair padding toward him nude from the bedroom proper; the actor took the pile of clothes from Waldo without comment as he passed and continued into his bathroom and shut the door. "Don't lock it," Waldo said. "There are helicopters all over—news. LAPD is putting on a show. You need coffee. You keep any instant?"

From behind the door, Alastair said, "Does my home resemble a Holiday Inn Express?"

Chimes rang downstairs. Waldo said, "Is that your doorbell?"

"Detective Waldo," the actor bit off from behind the door, "would you please allow a living legend to move his bowels in peace?"

Waldo had had his day's fill of Alastair and the day hadn't started yet. "Come downstairs when you're dressed."

He could hear the pounding and shouting before he got to the staircase. In the foyer he found Rosario standing looking scared and wondered if she might have INS worries too. "Policemans," she said.

A cop pummeled the front door incessantly, adding an "LAPD, open up!" every few thumps. Waldo opened the door wide, recognized the lead officer and grinned at him. "Pete!"

Lieutenant Pete Conady, shoulders like an ox and a face like a manhole cover, the residue of unfortunate childhood acne, scowled at Waldo. As academy recruits they had been close, and when Waldo became a star and began rising through the ranks, he had done all he could to pull Conady up behind him. Their longtime affinity apparently left Conady all the angrier when Waldo launched his post-Lipps nuclear assault on the department without warning his friend it was coming, and angrier still when Waldo didn't return his phone calls; at least, that's what Waldo had heard from a reporter from the *Times*, who also told him that it was Conady, of all people, who'd torn apart Waldo's old desk in a rage after his notorious *60 Minutes* interview. When Waldo learned that, he had almost called Pete to try to mend fences, but it was right about the time he decided to disappear and he knew that if he wasn't calling Lorena, he wasn't calling anybody.

Seeing Conady now, almost shaking with long-held resentment, a grim passel of uniforms behind him, Waldo knew the chance for mending fences was long past. Conady looked him in the eye and said, "We're here for Pinch."

Waldo stalled to buy Alastair a little more time. "That's all you have to say to me?"

"Go fuck yourself. How's that?"

"It's a start."

Conady kept his voice low but didn't muffle his bitterness. "Ten thousand good men and women and you knew it, but you couldn't live with your own fuckup, so you had to take it out on everybody else, make the rest of us look like the fucking Klan." One of the patrolmen put a hand on Conady's arm but he shook it off; if anything, that made him angrier. "You were too much of a pussy even to tell your own lieutenants you were turning in your badge."

Waldo felt his own blood rising. "What would be different if I told you? What would you have done?"

Conady took a step toward him. "I'd've made you eat the fucking thing."

"Yeah? How about we go around to the backyard and you take off *your* badge, see which one of us is pissing through tin tomorrow?"

"Gentlemen, gentlemen, no fisticuffs, please." Alastair strode into the foyer, somehow looking like he'd had a full night's sleep, a shower, and maybe a massage. He gestured to the skies beyond Conady. "Not with the good people of the fourth estate hovering."

Conady stepped into the house, brushing past Waldo, and said, "Alastair Pinch, you're under arrest for the murder of Monica Pinch."

Waldo calmed and said quietly, "Come on, Pete. Let him come in and surrender himself."

Conady ignored him and reached for his belt. "Hands behind your back."

Waldo said, "*Cuffs?* You don't need to—"

"Step back, Waldo, or I'll bring you in, too, for interfering with an officer." He turned Alastair around. "You have the right to remain silent and to refuse to answer questions. Anything you say may be used against you in a court of law."

Waldo said, "Why are you doing this to him?"

Conady looked him in the eye and said, "He runs with scum, he gets treated like scum."

It took a second to get his meaning. "This is about *me*?"

Conady turned back to Alastair. "You have the right to consult an attorney before speaking to the police and to have an attorney present during questioning."

Waldo said, "Pete—"

Alastair, voice full of mock wonder, said, "This is just like on television!"

"If you cannot afford an attorney, one will be appointed for you before any questioning if you wish."

Alastair said, "I can probably afford one, but may I call my broker first to make certain?"

Waldo turned from Conady. "Stop talking. Don't say anything else, no matter how fucking cute you think it is."

Alastair said to Waldo, "Oh, Detective—are you helping me? I couldn't tell."

Their relationship was growing knottier by the second. Waldo said, calmly, "Don't talk. I'm serious."

Conady, finishing up with the handcuffs, said, "If you decide to answer any questions now without an attorney present, you will still have the right to stop answering at any time until you talk to an attorney."

Waldo said to Alastair, "I'll call Fontella Davis."

Conady said, "You can tell her the DA's going for no bail."

Alastair held his tongue, but the withering look he gave Waldo needed no words.

Conady pointed Alastair to the door. "Say good-bye to your pretty house. Last time you'll ever see it."

"Daddy?" They all turned and saw Gaby, in the foyer now, watching with Rosario. Everyone froze.

Then Conady said, "Let's go," and steered Alastair to the door.

Waldo asked Rosario, "You can get her to school?" Rosario nodded. He said to Gaby, "Your dad's going to be okay." Gaby watched her last parent being led out of her house. Waldo knelt in front of her and said, "I promise," and hoped she couldn't tell he was lying. Then he headed out after Alastair and Conady.

There were four black-and-whites in the driveway. Conady shepherded Alastair into the one nearest the house, putting his hand on Alastair's head and pushing it down to keep it from banging on the roof. Waldo counted seven news helicopters, the local stations no doubt cutting into morning programming and the cable news channels breaking away from deconstruction of the new president's latest tweet to broadcast the spectacle. Waldo approached the cruiser. Conady said, "Where do you think you're going?" and Waldo realized he didn't have an answer.

As the cherry tops came to life and the black-and-whites started backing out of the driveway one by one, Waldo phoned Fontella Davis and told her what was happening. She asked a couple of gruff questions and hung up on him. He knew she'd take over from here but he felt partially responsible for the morning's drama and thought it was important to be there for Alastair at his arraignment, so he ran inside for his backpack and an orange from the counter, then got on his bike.

It was easy enough to stay close to the police caravan as it made its careful way down the residential hills, but as soon as they reached Laurel, the cops hit the sirens to clear traffic and avoid stoplights and Waldo realized he'd have no chance of keeping up. Still, it would take a while for them to process Alastair and get him in front of a judge, so he had time.

Taking the less-trafficked Moorpark to bypass the morning rush on Ventura, he pedaled hard, pissed. The last thing he wanted was to become the story himself, especially in this new role, an ally and employee of a guilty man. It would trivialize what had happened to Lydell Lipps, could even tarnish Lydell with Alastair's brush. Maybe that was exactly what Conady wanted. But Conady didn't have to do what he just did to that little girl, make her see her father handcuffed and scare her after all she'd been through already, all she still had coming. Waldo reproached himself for his own role in bringing that on her. The world was full of collateral damage, collateral damage he couldn't stop causing.

Thus preoccupied, Waldo didn't notice the absence of cars in front of him until he heard a honk. He glanced over his shoulder and saw a long line crawling behind him at bike speed, led by a blue Cadillac coupe. There was no need for it, though; Waldo was well to the sidewalk edge of the broad single lane, leaving more than enough room to pass, but for some reason the Caddy was being overly cautious. The penned-in rush-hour drivers were all joining in a full serenade now to let the Caddy driver know how they felt about being made late for work. More collateral damage. Waldo turned up Fulton to get away from the noise.

When he got to the courthouse complex he found a bike rack and dialed Fontella Davis to ask her the time and courtroom of the arraignment, but she didn't answer. News vans were lined up and Courthouse West seemed to have more than the usual bustle, so he headed that way.

Among a pack of waiting reporters, Waldo saw the overweight

cameraman from Channel 7 who'd been on his mountain last week. Waldo asked him, "Are you here for Alastair Pinch?"

"Fuck off."

"Do you know where the arraignment is?"

"Fuck off."

"Come on, I've got to be in there."

"Too late. They just finished."

"Already? Did he get bail?"

The Channel 7 reporter, Tiffany something, worked her way over to where they were standing and heard Waldo's question.

"Twenty million," she said. "Will you go on air?"

"Twenty. Holy— Are they still in there? What floor?"

"They're coming down to talk to the press out here."

Waldo thought about running inside to intercept them but suddenly remembered the gun in his backpack and realized he'd have a problem with security. He should have thought about that before he left the house—one more reminder that he wasn't ready for this.

Fontella Davis and Wilson Sikorsky came out and reporters bombarded them with questions. Davis said that despite the arrest they were as certain as ever of Alastair's innocence and Sikorsky said they had no plans to shut down production of *Johnny's Bench.*

Waldo couldn't tell if they noticed him, but as soon as Davis said they had nothing further at this time, she pushed through the pack to where he was standing, put an iron grip on his bruised elbow and pulled him back toward the building, Sikorsky on their heels. Just inside the door Waldo said, "Where are we going?"

"We're getting a conference room."

"I can't go through security."

"Why not?" He looked at her and she got it; it only ticked her off more.

Waldo said, "How did the arraignment happen so fast?"

Davis steered them to a corner. A sympathetic courthouse guard kept overeager reporters from coming too close. Keeping her voice low, she said, "How it happened so fast is I raised holy hell that they didn't let him surrender himself, and I got them to expedite. Apparently LAPD decided to turn this into a circus to let us know how happy they are *you're* involved." She turned to Sikorsky. "Let's deal with this now: you have to get rid of him."

Waldo said, "I'm happy to quit. I don't want to make this worse for anybody."

Sikorsky scoffed. *"Worse?* You're making it *better."* Clearly he wanted to end this conference and get on with his day. "What time is it? I think Charlie Sheen's waiting in my office."

Davis practically exploded. "How is this *better?"*

"Basic storytelling: the bigger assholes the cops are, the more sympathetic our protagonist is. And it plays to our greatest strength—people fucking love Alastair."

Waldo said, "You think? Still?"

Sikorsky said, "Believe me—I just bought a fucking *boat* on how much people love him." He clapped Waldo on the back. "Just keep being yourself. You're doing great."

SIXTEEN

It was the same car, it had to be, a blue Cadillac behind him on Oxnard and refusing to pass. He hung a right on Hazeltine to see what would happen, and when he looked over his shoulder half a block later, sure enough, it was right there. Left on Hatteras, same thing. Waldo pulled over by a hydrant and the Caddy stopped about twenty yards back without leaving his lane. Waldo stared at the driver, an ordinary-looking white man behind sunglasses, middle-aged or balding early. They waited each other out.

A Lexus SUV came up behind the Cadillac and was forced to stop. The Lexus driver tapped the horn but the balding guy just glanced at his rearview and looked back at Waldo. The SUV waited for a break in the opposing traffic, then pulled around the Caddy.

Waldo started pedaling again. He picked up speed, found a double driveway and glided onto the sidewalk. He braked hard, spun the bike and headed down the sidewalk in the opposite direction and, as the Cadillac went into a K-turn, tore down an alley and didn't look back.

Waldo was pretty close to his old neighborhood and knew the streets. Costello ended in a cul-de-sac, which backed onto the parking lot of a Mormon church; he got there just as the Caddy found him, walked his bike across the dirt divider where the Caddy couldn't follow and he was free. Crossing the church parking lot toward its front on Burbank, he glanced back and saw the Caddy backing up.

The guy would expect him to go left and parallel his original path on Oxnard, so Waldo jogged down to Chandler to go east that way instead, then overshot his target by passing under the freeway and going left back up to Burbank, where he took another left and came around from the far side with no sign of his tail.

Before he knew it he was in front of North Hollywood Division again, again racked with anxiety. But this time he knew he didn't have a choice.

He decided the play was to take it hard. He slammed open the glass doors with a force that stopped conversation dead in the precinct lobby. Three uniforms and a couple in street clothes, probably civilians, were standing in front of the reception desk, behind which sat a sergeant he didn't know, a black man with white hair whose name tag said STENNETT. Waldo thought two of the uniforms might look familiar but focusing to place them would slow him down.

He came right at the sergeant. "Charlie Waldo," he snapped. "You heard my name?" He didn't give the man a chance to answer. "Bet your ass you heard my name—I used to own this place. Fuck are you?" Sergeant Stennett opened his mouth but Waldo jumped him again. "I don't give a shit, that's who. Who I *want* is, first officer on the scene of the Pinch murder. Then I want info on: one, everyone on crime scene security; two, all transport, emergency and medical personnel who had contact with the victim; and three, all who had contact with the suspect."

Stennett caught the eye of one of the uniforms and tilted his head. The patrolman hustled through the doors that led to the squad room.

Waldo kept up the assault on the sergeant. "I just gave you a full morning's work, sweet cheeks—why you still sitting there?"

"I—I—"

"'I—I—'" he mocked. "If I still had my desk here, you'd be at K-9 with plastic gloves and a pooper scooper."

The sergeant gathered himself and said, "Lieutenant Conady's in charge of that investigation, but he's at lunch."

"Then who else you got?"

"Sir, I understand the position you had in the department, but I don't believe you have the authority—"

"I don't have the authority? Let me explain how this is going to go if the LAPD impedes the rights of the accused to gather exculpatory evidence—"

The squad room doors opened and an Asian-American police captain about Waldo's age came into the lobby. Waldo's relationship with Pam Tanaka was one of his most quietly complex during his North Hollywood years. She'd arrived at the precinct a year after Waldo, an atypical rookie in a bundle of conspicuous ways—not just intelligent but a USC grad with plans to get a law degree at night, not just attractive but eye-catching enough that Waldo once saw a modeling agent hand her his business card. She was effortlessly charming, great company over an after-work beer, and the way she looked at Waldo made him think she was interested until he realized she had the same effect on everyone. Naturally she was the object of all sorts of talk—desire, gossip, speculation—but the truth was Waldo never heard of her actually saying yes to any of his colleagues' overtures, and if her work and her law studies left her time for a romantic life, she kept it to herself. The two of them became easy pals without chemistry or sense of potential, and in time Waldo came to appreciate the additional challenges a woman with Pam Tanaka's gifts faced in that environment and to respect the ways in which she couldn't have handled those challenges better.

Except. The cops she rode with seemed to have mixed feelings about her, and the book was that in risky situations she tended to hesitate just long enough that her partner would invariably go through the door first; maybe no one actually asked to be reassigned another partner, but no one asked to be teamed with her, either. One partner got hit with a brutality accusation that proved false but that scrambled his life for a year; after he was cleared he grumbled that it would have happened faster if Tanaka hadn't played it safe with Internal Affairs instead of standing up strong for him. And one Friday night when she wasn't around, after more than the usual number of beers, a couple of female sergeants surprised Waldo with the ferocity of their resentment—they talked about cold shoulders in the ladies' room, subtle disrespect to her female superiors, lack of support for younger women coming into the division behind her, years of tiny slights that had piled up into full-grown beefs. Waldo first wrote it off as jealousy—neither of these women, much as he liked them, were blessed with anything like Pam Tanaka's looks or résumé or future—but he himself noticed, as the years went by and they rose through the ranks, that that effortless charm of hers indeed shined upward a lot more brightly than downward, and he came to distrust her. Still, there had never been an unpleasant moment between Charlie Waldo and Pam Tanaka, even at the end, and that made her one of very few.

"Waldo," she said.

"Hey, Pam." He nodded to her shoulder. "Star, huh."

"Division commander now. Maybe you heard."

He hadn't but wasn't surprised. "Nice."

"Problem?"

A few more uniforms and a couple of plainclothes had wandered out from the squad room—there were more than a dozen now—to see for themselves the legend in the lobby, back from the dead and raising hell.

"Just looking for some information. I'm working on the Alastair Pinch case."

"It's been on the news," she said. "We can't help you, though. I'm sure you understand the position I'm in."

"Cut me a break, huh, Pam? We both want the same thing."

"Do we?"

"We want to make sure this gets hung on the right guy."

"Already done. Your guy is the right guy."

"Then you've got nothing to hide."

"Sorry, Waldo. I'd love to help you but I can't. Good to see you, though." She said it warmly but it was a dismissal.

Waldo, though, had no intention of leaving. He looked past her to the pack of uniforms. "Who were the first officers on the scene? I'll start there."

Tanaka turned stern. *"Nobody gives him anything."*

The policemen looked at Waldo with open hostility, especially the ones he knew. He stared each of them in the eye, one at a time—Lemons, Ricketts, Oh, Cuevas—and the newcomers, too.

One young patrolman avoided Waldo's gaze and that was

enough. Waldo walked right to him, checked his name tag, and read it aloud. "Annis?" He pronounced it *anus*.

"Annis," the patrolman corrected, with a softer *A*.

"Goddamn," Waldo said, "high school must've sucked."

Annis nodded.

Pam Tanaka said, "Don't talk to him, Annis."

Waldo said to Annis, "You were at the Pinch house."

Annis didn't respond.

Waldo pressed. "You were the first ones? You and your partner?"

Tanaka said, "Annis . . ."

Waldo said, "Officer Annis, do you know who Fontella Davis is?"

Annis gave a small nod.

"Do you want her on TV every night, making this case about *you*?"

Annis shook his head.

Waldo asked, "Was the door dead bolted when you got there?"

Annis nodded.

Tanaka said, "That's enough, Annis."

Waldo asked Annis, "You sure? It's solid oak, no windows. You couldn't see him unlock it. You heard it that clearly?"

"The alarm was definitely on. We saw him disarm it."

"Annis!"

Waldo pressed. "Yes, but the real killer—if it wasn't Pinch, that is—the real killer could've set the alarm on the way out. If the door wasn't dead bolted. Right?"

Cuevas, one of the plainclothes Waldo knew, said, "Don't let him spin you, Annis."

Tanaka said, "Don't *answer* him, Annis."

Waldo asked Annis, "How about the murder weapon? The earthenware vase? Was it you, gathered up the pieces?"

Tanaka answered for him, "Yes, he got all the pieces of the murder weapon. Conady supervised. Now I'd like you to leave. I'm asking you as a friend."

Waldo said, "The earthenware vase."

Tanaka said, "Yes, the earthenware vase. We have the murder weapon. All of it."

Waldo said, "Good. Only the earthenware vase *wasn't* the murder weapon. Not if Alastair Pinch killed her. Earthenware that size, that had to weigh almost thirty pounds, and it came down over the victim's right eye. Have to be one strong lefty to take a killer swing with that thing. Not a drunken righty." Before she could respond, he said, "Yeah, Pam, Pinch is a righty. I've watched him pour." Waldo reached into his pocket and pulled out the *Architectural Digest*, rolled up. He opened it to the page with the photos of the room and showed it to Annis. "See that statue? That's an Olivier Award, for acting in England. Ever see it before?" Annis studied the picture but didn't respond. "No? Of course not. Because it's missing. *That* was the murder weapon. Three and a half pounds. The earthenware vase—the victim hit that on the way *down*."

Annis looked over at Tanaka.

Waldo said, "Don't look at *her*, Annis—this comes out the wrong time, believe me, she's going to let you get fucked on this. Remember—I used to work here." He didn't know how long this young cop had been at North Hollywood, but he figured the griping about Tanaka wouldn't have eased up since she got the big job. He was burning the relationship, or whatever may have been left of it, but he was used to that, and if this kid already didn't trust her, maybe he'd catch a break.

Tanaka said, "Waldo, I'll give you ten seconds to get out of here on your own; then—"

Annis blurted, "It sounded like Pinch fumbled with the dead bolt when he opened the door. He was still kinda drunk. We didn't know for sure it was bolted."

"*Really*," Waldo said, and looked at Pam Tanaka.

But before he could press the moment, Big Jim Cuppy burst through the squad room door. "Fuck are you doing here, Waldo?!"

One of the plainclothes muttered to Cuppy, "Annis is talking to him."

Cuppy exploded, "Shut the fuck up, Anus!" Cuppy glared at Pam Tanaka and said, "Everybody shuts up—*now*! Pinch's side wants anything, let 'em subpoena through the DA—but nobody says another word to this scum sack. He's a person of interest in two homicide investigations."

Waldo scoffed, said, "What bullshit is that?"

"For anyone who hasn't heard," Cuppy announced to the room, "the body of one Eladio Reynoso was found in Idyllwild, on Mr. Waldo's property. Presumably he was killed at the behest of his rival Don Q, with whom we have reason to believe Mr. Waldo has been associating."

Well, at least they'd ID'd the body and linked it to Q, and hopefully that meant Waldo wouldn't have any more problems with the locals in Riverside County. But what else were they hanging on him? "Associating, yeah, if you mean letting his gorilla work me like a heavy bag. What's the second homicide?"

Cuppy gave it a beat for effect and then said, "Lorena Nascimento."

Waldo felt his heart stop.

Cuppy continued: "She borrowed her husband's car. They

found it on fire off the freeway up by Magic Mountain, with the body inside. Here: worth a thousand words." He handed Waldo a photo: the burned-out Porsche with what was left of Lorena in the driver's seat, no skin, not even patches of red, just gray-black char in the shape of an openmouthed skull. Waldo gagged. Cuppy leaned in close and spoke quietly, enjoying it. "Somebody wanted to make sure she wasn't pretty anymore."

Waldo couldn't look away from the picture. What had he done? What had he *not* done? The little he'd eaten today was heading back up.

Cuppy said, "Look here, asshole—that item Lorena gave you? I can put your friend Don Q away for so long you'll both die of old age before he's a problem again. So why don't you give it to me, before the man goes all cherries jubilee on you, too."

Waldo ran out of the station house, the photo still in his hand. He doubled over, steadied himself with a forearm against the brick wall and vomited until he had nothing left inside him but regret.

SEVENTEEN

The dry heaves finally stopped. He noticed flecks on his shoes, found a leaf on the ground that looked fresh and wiped off what he could. He checked the rest of his clothes for puke; given his limited wardrobe and his daily wear-one, wash-the-other routine, he was grateful not to find any more. Still shaking, he unlocked his bike, but he couldn't pull it out of the rack: someone else's U-lock tethered it to a second bicycle beside it. He looked around for the biker who'd carelessly jammed him up, and when he saw no one nearby, Waldo lost it.

He cursed, every foul word he knew or could remember plus some he made up. He kicked the other bike, football-style, then stomped on it over and over until he'd bent its gear mechanism so badly that the chain dropped off. The bike ravaged, he focused his wrath on a metal trash can, hurling it against the side of the building and scattering garbage across the asphalt. Then he picked it up with both hands and smashed it against the brick wall again and again and again and again.

Spent, he propped himself with his backside against the wall
and his hands on his knees. He spit a few times to rid the foul
taste from his mouth, then wiped his face with his sleeve. He took
some deep breaths and began counting slowly, actually whispering the numbers aloud. By fourteen or fifteen he had calmed himself, and at twenty he stood, focused on the ground between his
feet, and exhaled.

When he looked up, there was the blue Cadillac.

It was parked on the far side of the small lot, facing away from
Waldo, and the man was getting out and heading in Waldo's
direction. He was indeed middle-aged and ordinary-looking and
wore a nondescript brown suit. "Excuse me," he said. "I had my
bike on that rack next to yours, and I must have left—"

"Bullshit!" Waldo stormed at him. "You've been following me
all day! Now, get that lock off my goddamn bike before I—"

The man held up his hands in front of him. "If you're thinking
about doing me bodily harm, you should know that I am an attorney specializing in personal injury, and I will seek damages."
The man walked past Waldo and squatted by the rack, inspecting the busted-up bike. He said, "Speaking of damage."

Waldo seethed. "Just get the lock off."

The man took his bike chain in hand but stopped himself
before opening the lock and looked up at Waldo. "You're a private eye?" Waldo waited for the man to open the lock. The man
waited for Waldo to answer.

"Yeah," Waldo said to move things along, "I'm a private eye.
Now, get—"

"Big mistake," the man interrupted. He dropped the chain
and stood. "You've just committed a felony, presenting yourself
as a private investigator in the state of California when in fact
you're unlicensed."

"I'm acting as an operative under a fully licensed investigator."

"Who's the investigator?"

"I don't have to answer your questions."

"You'll have to answer the California Bureau of Security and Investigative Services' questions, and I hope your boss can provide documentation to *them*. Otherwise you could be looking at a ten-thousand-dollar fine and/or one year in prison."

"Thanks for your concern, but I'll be back home long before that becomes an issue."

"To that house in the woods."

This guy knew too much about him and Waldo didn't like it. "Who the fuck are you?"

"Do you have running water up there?"

"I have a well."

"That must really cut down on waste."

"It does."

"Admirable. Did you happen to file a well completion report with the Department of Water Resources?"

Waldo hadn't even heard of a well completion report. He'd ordered the cabin and everything possible prefabricated, and the rest he had taught himself with online research and laborious trial and error.

The lawyer said, "You're not going to get a permit without a C-57 Well Drilling Contractor's License. And I sincerely hope you don't have a composting toilet."

"What's this about?"

"A client of mine is curious why you'd involve yourself with a murderer like Alastair Pinch."

"One of your personal injury clients."

"A legal client."

"Who would that be?"

"Let's just say a gentleman of resources who wonders why you'd get entangled with this, when you've had such a peaceful life in Idyllwild, undisturbed by the government or lawsuits from your neighbors."

"Listen, asshole, I've had a lot scarier than you trying to muscle me off this case—"

"You misunderstand, Mr. Waldo. I've made no threats whatsoever, and none are intended." He knelt again to fiddle with his U-lock and this time opened it, releasing both bicycles. He started back toward his Cadillac with the lock, leaving the busted bike in the rack.

Waldo said, "Aren't you going to take your bike?"

"Now that I looked closer, that bike might not have been mine after all." More shit: thanks to this prick, Waldo had just stomped somebody else's bike to pieces. As the lawyer got to his car he called back, "You know, Mr. Waldo, it's my hope— and my client's—that you enjoy your retirement to the fullest and that this pleasant, happenstantial conversation is the last dealing you and I ever have." He pointed to the bikes, said, "Sorry for the inconvenience," and got into his car. Waldo heard the electronic snap of the door locks, but the lawyer didn't start the ignition right away; it looked like he was making a phone call first.

From the bike rack, Waldo watched the back of the man's head and tried to make sense of the confrontation. This was the second time he had been warned to stay off the Pinch case. Either someone other than Alastair had killed his wife, or the Pinches had been involved in something else that some third party didn't want uncovered, something they thought the police less likely than Waldo to notice, or at least less likely than Waldo to reveal or exploit. The

people who'd tried to intimidate Waldo—the would-be gangbangers and now this nuisance-suit lawyer—were mismatched,
too. He wanted to know more about this guy and he wanted to
know whom he was talking to.

The lawyer was deep in conversation. Leaving his bike in the
rack, Waldo swung wide out of his view and, crouching, approached the rear of the Cadillac from the side. He knelt behind
it, keeping low enough so the lawyer couldn't spot him in the rearview. Then he waited.

A couple of minutes later the engine turned over and red brake
lights went on. Waldo braced himself, and as soon as the car
moved a few inches he reached up and slapped the top of the
trunk hard while letting the car tap him and knock him down.

The car stopped and the driver killed the engine. Waldo
stayed on the ground, curled and facing the passenger side. The
lawyer got out and rushed over, not asking if Waldo was all right,
but launching straight into a self-protective spiel, delivered to the
back of Waldo's head. "There is no liability on my part here. I
don't know what mischief you were up to at the rear of my car, but
I checked the mirrors carefully and you were deliberately below
the sight line."

But Waldo didn't answer. He was sobbing, his body racking.

"Mr. Waldo?" the lawyer said, thrown. "Mr. Waldo?"

"They killed her," Waldo got out between gasps.

"Are you all right?"

"It's m-my fault. If—if I had just helped her in the first
place . . ."

The lawyer, softening, came around to Waldo's other side.
"Let me help you up." He reached out to him, offering a hand.

Waldo didn't take it. "It's my fault . . ."

"Mr. Waldo, are you injured?"

"No."

Again the lawyer said, "Let me help you up," and this time Waldo let the lawyer pull him to his feet.

Tears streaming down his face, he reached into his pocket and took out the gruesome photo of Lorena's incinerated body. He showed it to the lawyer while he blubbered some more. "I'm sorry . . . this has been . . . three years . . . not even talking to anyone . . . and then . . . Lorena . . ." He wiped his nose with his sleeve. "I'm sorry," he said, "this is embarrassing."

"Yeah," the lawyer said, for lack of anything better.

"You've got one of those watches," Waldo said, noticing a Kudoke Skeleton, like Sikorsky's, the one Alastair coveted, and he felt the anger rising in his blood again. "Why do you need it?"

"What?" the lawyer said, again for lack of anything better.

"You have a phone. You know how many people you could feed with what that watch cost—" He stopped himself. There was just too much else wrong in the world, wrong in *his* world. He looked the lawyer in the eye. "I'm going back to my mountain. I'm done."

The lawyer looked surprised, then pleased. "It's the right decision. You don't need any more trouble."

"No. I don't. Thank you for being so kind." The tears coming again, Waldo threw his arms around him in an appreciative hug and sobbed some more into his suit, clinging until the lawyer managed to extricate himself and got back in the Cadillac as quickly as he could. The lawyer backed out of his space extra carefully and drove off with Waldo watching.

When the Cadillac cleared the driveway and pulled safely into the street, Waldo dropped the sobbing act and wiped his face again. "Fucking ambulance chaser," he muttered, looking down at the lawyer's iPhone, which he'd lifted during his weepy embrace.

Waldo went into settings, changed the autolock to "never," and stuffed it into his own pocket.

It wasn't until Waldo settled into a chair in the nearby public library to examine the phone that he started to fret over how it fit into the constellation of Things. In the confusion of the moment, he'd forgotten to discard something to offset it. He agonized over the infraction, finally granting himself absolution by establishing a new codicil: evidence, material gathered specifically for the case, was never really *his* and thus needn't count.

The crisis resolved, he got to work. A couple of taps identified the phone's owner—well, *former* owner—as Warren Gomes, Esq., and a couple of more taps confirmed that he indeed specialized in personal injury work as a sole practitioner with an office in West L.A. Waldo checked the phone history and learned that the guy's last call—the one placed right after strong-arming Waldo by the bike rack and right before tapping Waldo with his car—was to someone named Darius Jamshidi.

Waldo switched over to his own phone to research Jamshidi and quickly learned he was the founder and principal owner of something called the Darius Group, a global private equity firm specializing in acquiring and partnering with mature and growing businesses, with concentrations in technology and telecommunications. Waldo had no idea what any of that meant.

But he did know what it meant that Jamshidi resided in Beverly Park. First, it meant that Jamshidi lived in a walled community above the city among the richest of the rich, the very biggest movie stars and moguls and athletes in Southern

California; second, it meant that if Waldo wanted to confront Jamshidi at his home—more aggressive and likely more fruitful than doing it at his office, where he was sure to be insulated by layers of assistants and a small army of security men—he had a wicked canyon pedal ahead of him.

Waldo read a little more about the acquisitions Jamshidi's company had made over the past few years: a chain of shopping centers, a group of seventeen radio stations, a French manufacturer of terrestrial broadcast equipment, the library of a once-powerful independent television studio, and a biotech firm known for its revolutionary artificial knees. But the Darius Group's most legendary killing came from its purchase of a Belgian company called LGA Avianimmo, which had previously made a fortune in some advanced medical field called pharmacogenomics before losing a patent lawsuit and falling on hard times; after the acquisition the Darius Group secured a bankruptcy judgment in Bruges, shut down two-thirds of the company's operations, then resold the restructured firm to a Bulgarian holding company that Darius managed to buy in its entirety two years later. Somehow the result of these maneuvers—nothing but contracts and closures—was a four-billion-dollar profit for Jamshidi and his investors.

And Waldo found one more news item online that made the web of relationships all the more curious: the Darius Group was currently awaiting the Federal Communications Commission's blessing of its biggest acquisition yet, SignaCom Global, whose best-known asset was the television network that happened to be employing Waldo right now, whose production arm was on the verge of making hundreds of millions syndicating *Johnny's Bench.*

In other words, it looked like Darius Jamshidi was trying to become the biggest financial beneficiary of Alastair Pinch's popularity, while also trying to stop Waldo from keeping Alastair Pinch out of prison. Waldo squinted, as if behind the pixels on his phone he'd be able to find the logic. He might as well have been trying to teach himself pharmacogenomics.

EIGHTEEN

The pedal up Coldwater wasn't as steep or as long as 243 but excruciating enough. The light midday traffic at first seemed a blessing but ended up making the trip even more hazardous, Valley drivers living out the luxury car commercials in their heads, taking the wide-open hairpins fast and loose on their way to lunches in Beverly Hills. Waldo stayed right, hard against the cliffs, fear distracting him from the pain, holding his breath every time he heard a car approaching from behind.

The first thirty or forty passed him with nothing worse than an occasional peevish honk. But when a silver Dodge Charger practically brushed Waldo's left arm, then hurtled to the right and screeched to a halt in front of him, Waldo had no choice but to cut his front wheel and run himself straight into the hillside. He went over the handlebars, hit a rock and landed facedown, his bad elbow under his rib cage.

The next thing he felt was hands on his back and collar, lifting him and slamming his face into the hood of the Charger. "You're under arrest, asshole."

The voice was familiar, but he couldn't place it through the agony and adrenaline. "For what?" He felt more hands working his body, frisking him.

Someone leaned on the car in front of him. Pete Conady, that's who it was, and he was saying, "For shooting Warren Gomes in the head." It took another moment to recognize that as the name of the lawyer who'd just tried to squeeze him. "You argued with him outside the station house, and then you followed him, got in the back seat with a .38 and blew his brains through the passenger window."

"Yeah?" Waldo said, sentience returning. "Ever see me try to shoot with my left hand?"

"Fuck the lefty-righty, Waldo. Can't pull that shit twice in one day."

"Lieutenant?" one of the other cops said. It looked like there were three of them, two in uniform—one of them Annis—and one other plainclothes. The one speaking now held open Waldo's backpack for the lieutenant to look inside. Waldo knew he was showing him the Beretta 8045F.

Waldo said, "That's not a .38."

Conady said, "You got a permit?" Waldo didn't answer. "Didn't think so." Conady asked the patrolman, "Find the vic's wallet and watch in there?"

Waldo smirked. "What, you think I'm a robber, too?"

"I think you wanted to *look* like a robber. Probably took Gomes's valuables and dumped them somewhere in the canyon."

The cop checked the backpack pouches. "There's a phone in here. Plus the one in his pocket." Waldo had been too discombobulated to think about Gomes's phone, but now he knew he had a problem.

"Two phones," Conady said. "I hope to Christ one of them belongs to who I think it does."

They handcuffed him and pushed him into the back of the Charger, headed, no doubt, for the same Van Nuys jail and courthouse where Alastair had been taken that morning.

Conady took Waldo's booking information himself, both men using as few words as possible. Other officers photographed and fingerprinted him, and then there was the issue of whom to call. Whom did he even know anymore? Who would care? Jayne? Too weird. Alastair? Wrong any way you looked at it. Sikorsky? He might not return the call for days, or at best he'd bounce it to Fontella Davis. Waldo decided he'd be better off calling Davis directly, fucked up as *that* was.

He had to call information for her office number and then had to go through a receptionist and an assistant, and when he finally got her the conversation was short. "I've been arrested."

"For what?"

"They're trying to pin a murder on me. Or just playing at it."

"Shit follows you, doesn't it."

"I need you to get me out of here."

"Better idea—I tell Sikorsky to cut you loose; then you're not my concern."

"I think the victim knew something about Alastair. I'll explain when you get me out."

There was a silence. She said, "We'll see," and hung up.

He didn't know if she meant, *We'll see if your explanation is worth hearing,* or *We'll see if I get you out.*

He was turned over to a young cop named Ochoa, who silently

led him by elevator to the top floor. It wasn't what Waldo was expecting—he figured they'd put him in one of the larger holding cells downstairs for detainees awaiting arraignment—but it probably made sense not to throw a semifamous ex-LAPD in with the general population, no matter how much these guys hated him.

Upstairs they were joined by a guard who walked them into a block where the prisoners wore standard blue prison uniforms and found the arrival of a long-haired prisoner in civvies worth attention and extra catcalls. The guard opened a tiny one-bunk cell. Ochoa removed the handcuffs, then Waldo sat on the bunk and the guard slammed the bars shut.

He'd never been locked up before. He was used to long stretches of undirected time, but now he had no Kindle, nothing to distract himself, nothing to do but think about the implacable facts of the bars and of his helplessness and Lorena's violent death and then Waldo couldn't sit anymore, couldn't stay on the bunk, had to pace, but there was barely *room* to pace, and then there were the bars again and now it was impossible to be in here, in this cage, impossible for another minute, and who knew *how* long, really, whether Fontella Davis was even going to try to get him out, or whether he'd have to wait until an arraignment and ask for a public defender, and either way an arraignment could be as much as forty-eight hours if they really wanted to fuck with him. Which, of course, they did.

Maybe he could sleep, kill some minutes, if not hours. His body needed it anyway, if his mind would go along. He lay down on the bunk and tried to remember the last chess game he'd played, but it had been several days and nothing came. He'd never tried a game from scratch entirely in his head, playing both sides, but it was all he had, and why not. He closed his eyes and thought about where to start. If he played something pro-saic, he might slip into lethargy rather than exhaustion, so he needed something a little more Byzantine and challenging. He rarely played the English Opening, so he chose that, countered himself with an Adorjan Defence, and rode them both into a heavy afternoon slumber.

He awoke to wetness on his leg and the sound of a stream and he realized he was getting peed on. He swung his legs out of the flow and scrambled off the bunk. Cuppy stood outside the cell, pressed up against the bars, a stupid grin on his face as he kept pissing on the mattress. "Fuck!" Waldo said. "Really?"

"You have no idea how much I love seeing you here."

"You know it's bullshit. Get me out and I'll help you with Don Q."

"Oh, *now* you give a shit."

"Now he killed Lorena."

"Okay—tell me where I can find the item she gave you, and I'll work on Conady to shake you loose."

"Get me out first."

"You *do* think I'm stupid."

"I told you, she didn't give me anything."

Cuppy zipped himself up. "Then I'm good with you right where you are."

"Come on, I'll work with you. We'll get him on the murder."

"What do I need with a broke-down, out-of-practice cop with no badge? Have fun, Waldo. You're lonely, maybe I can get you some company. Ex-PD in here, you got plenty of neighbors would love a meet and greet." He walked away chuckling.

The first thing Fontella Davis said was "Whatever this is, we didn't need it." They'd been left alone in a holding room near the arraignment court and he had chains on his ankles and wrists and around his stomach. It was only an hour or two after Cuppy came to see him but the uncertainty and the wait made it feel like a day and a half. He never thought he'd be so glad to see someone he liked so little.

"Yeah, well, sorry to spoil your day."

"You smell terrible. Did you piss yourself?"

"Nah. Someone did it for me."

She started to ask but shook it off and moved on. "You said the victim knew something about Alastair."

"Yeah, I just don't know what yet. He followed me all morning, finally came up and threatened to slap me with all sorts of nuisance suits if I—"

She interrupted. "What, he was a lawyer?"

"Yeah, but personal injury. Not classy, like what you do." She glowered. Waldo said, "You know him? Warren Gomes."

"No."

He was about to ask if she knew Darius Jamshidi, but he decided to hold that name close for now. "He told me to get off the case, go back to Idyllwild. An hour later he got dead. Probably not a coincidence."

"What do you think it is?"

"Could be he had something to do with the Pinch murder, or with somebody who did. Or could be some cop killed him to frame me."

"Some cop—" she started to repeat, then rolled her eyes.

"Look, I'm only here because Sikorsky asked me to handle your arraignment and your bail. Soon as that's done, you need to find your own lawyer, unless you've got seventeen hundred an hour for my time." Waldo knew it wasn't a serious proposal, she just wanted to wave the number at him.

The door opened. "Okay," said a guard, planting himself in the room, "that's five minutes."

Davis told Waldo that she'd see him inside and headed for the door, turning back with an afterthought. "I assume you're going with 'not guilty.'"

"Uh, yeah."

She left. The guard led Waldo to the main holding area, where they left him with four other prisoners. A few minutes later all their shackles were removed and the group of five was brought into the arraignment court, where Davis already sat at a table with the other defense attorneys. She didn't cast her eyes in Waldo's direction, not when he was brought in, not while they listened to the first two defendants' cases. The judge, though, a woman in her fifties with kind eyes and no makeup, named Lisa Futterman Stein, kept stealing looks at both of them.

When it was Waldo's turn, a prosecutor named Walters stood and so did Davis. Judge Stein said that Waldo was being charged with first-degree murder and robbery, reading the charges slowly in a voice tinged with mystification at the unexpected turn this represented in the story of the law and their city. She told Waldo his rights, he said, "Not guilty," when asked, the prosecutor requested bail of two million dollars and the defense suggested half a million and the judge called it a million and that quickly it was over. Fontella Davis thanked the judge and walked out of the courtroom without ever glancing at Waldo.

———————

Next came a series of maddening waits—for the van that had to drive them the couple of hundred yards from the courthouse back to the jail, for another guard to tell him it was time for his release, for the clerk behind the cage in outprocessing to retrieve his bicycle and other belongings.

The first happy surprise of this wretched day was that the bike was in good shape, still aligned, even; apparently they hadn't been nearly as rough with it as they'd been with him. But there was an even bigger surprise in his backpack, where under his jacket and his sunglasses and helmet, along with his knife and keys and bike lock, along with his credit card and cash, he found his Beretta. He was dead certain they'd keep it, even though they already knew it wasn't the murder weapon, if only just to fuck with him.

Throwing his leg over the bike and starting south on Tyrone, he noticed a uniform on the far side of the street, staring until he caught Waldo's eye. Annis. That explained the gun. The patrolman put a finger to his cap, a subtle salute, then turned away and ducked into his squad car.

The sun was starting to set and Waldo still had to face the Coldwater climb all over again, this time with rush-hour traffic on his rear and one nine-thousandth of the LAPD at his back.

NINETEEN

H e couldn't let go of that good-bye, that last look at Lorena getting into her Porsche. What if he had kissed her, or let her kiss him? Would it have gone further? There weren't even two chairs inside for them both to sit, let alone room in the loft to luxuriate, the way they used to, in each other's bodies, in each other's caresses, in each other's breathing. He could have let her lead him into Idyllwild, could have followed on his bike and found a restaurant, one that served something he could eat or at least drink, then maybe one of those little inns. He could have lost himself again in the obscene thickness of her hair, could have let her undress him, the way she loved to, not looking up, always surprising him anew with her shyness at that moment, until he'd put a finger under her chin to raise her face to his, that beautiful face, that face that was char now, nothing but crumbling, flaking bone.

He knew pining wouldn't spur him through the pain as he climbed Coldwater for the second time that day, so he forced himself to focus on that image from the photo, remembering every detail, and the fury came, fury he could hold on to—fury at Don Q, at Cuppy, at these people who'd been sent to fuck with him, including the dead lawyer. Waldo could live on all that fury until he reached the top of the hill, and if he could channel it by the time he found this asshole billionaire who'd sicced the lawyer on him, it could even be an asset.

North Beverly Park was a private haven of sixty or so castles set on a couple hundred prime hilltop acres. If Beverly Hills was its own municipality, as lofty and imperious toward the Los Angeles that surrounded it as Vatican City was to Rome, Beverly Park, though not politically autonomous, sniffed at Beverly Hills itself in the same way. This would, in fact, be Waldo's first time within its borders; that is, if he could even get in. The gatehouse alone looked like a mansion, with three guards fixing him as he glided past on the bike. At least one of them would be armed.

Waldo pedaled away from the entrance along the canyon road, edged on the Beverly Park side by ivy-covered walls. He pulled to the shoulder when he reached an area far from any streetlamps and thick enough with foliage to blacken out even the moonlight. He found a thick branch growing from a tree on the other side of the wall and leaned his bike beneath it, hoping like hell it would be safe here unlocked. He stepped onto the seat, pushed up on his toes, and managed just enough purchase on the branch to take a couple of ivy-aided steps up the wall and swing one leg over the top. He shimmied down the other side and found himself in a grove at the edge of one of the estates. He cut across the lawn on a diagonal, looking to pick up the internal road far enough from the walls to avoid the security guards.

The properties were so large that he spent the better part of an hour looking for Jamshidi's address, trying to steer clear of a particular mansion that seemed to be hosting some kind of event until he realized it was the very one he was looking for. He'd rather have caught his target on a quiet night alone with his family; Jamshidi would have too many people around to run interference, possibly even an event security team. But at least Waldo could be sure the guy was home. Maybe he could turn the audience into a vulnerability.

He took cover behind a neighbor's thick oak to watch the action in the driveway. Dressy guests spilling from luxury cars stopped to marvel at the grandeur of the home's facade before regaining their L.A. cool, trying to look like they belonged here, like they were invited to soirees in palaces all the time. The cars themselves were swept off to an unseen lot by a squadron of red-vested valets. The very tableau, its heedless prodigality, rekindled the fury, swerving Waldo's thoughts back to Lorena and the grisly photograph. But tonight couldn't be about her; one job at a time.

He came out of the darkness and crossed the street. When one of the valets stepped into his path, Waldo muttered, "Don't even think about it."

The valet said, "I park the cars, man," and cleared out of the way.

Ascending the front steps and entering the colossal foyer, Waldo couldn't keep from marveling at the grandeur himself. There was marble everywhere and a five-foot circular mahogany table in the center with a perfectly centered crystal vase holding three dozen white tulips, and gilt-edged mirrors the size of picture windows on both walls. It reminded him of his junior-high trip to the White House. Waldo caught his reflection and realized the eyeful he presented, his wild mane now peppered with leaves and twigs from his clamber over the wall. He still smelled like urine, too. Fuck it, he thought. Use it.

A lively cocktail party was under way in a living room big enough for an NBA game. Long-limbed dazzlers in tall heels and short dresses passed out drinks and hors d'oeuvres to scores of guests in Zegna and Armani. There was a bar working at either end of the room; in between, a giant ice sculpture of a majestic eagle presided over a luxuriant dessert table.

The guests near the entrance were the first to notice him and stopped talking; within a minute their silence rippled through the hall as everyone turned and stared at the interloper. Loud enough to be sure everyone heard, he said, "Is this Darius Jamshidi's house?"

Nobody answered.

He'd pick an individual to work, make a show of it. He turned to the first woman on his left. But she was dark, Lorena's complexion, with a comparable build, now that he noticed, and he was back to that photograph, and the fury rose but not in a useful way. He spun to his right and locked on a dissimilar woman, auburn hair, porcelain skin, much better for the purpose, and asked her, "Do you know Darius Jamshidi?" The woman recoiled. "You the wife?" She gave her head a tiny shake. "Mistress?" Trembling, she stepped behind a nearby man, who didn't look like he wanted her.

Waldo crossed toward one of the bars, studying the partygoers one by one as he passed, each of them so comfortable, so complacent, so untroubled. His gaze landed on a man with tortoiseshell glasses and a silk pocket-handkerchief. *Up here on your hill, behind your walls* . . . He wasn't sure whether or not he'd said it out loud, but the man flinched as though he had.

At the bar, Waldo turned and asked the room, aloud for sure, "Which one of you is Jamshidi?" Nobody answered. This fucking day, and now these fucking people. He picked up a wine bottle from the bar and studied the label. "Château Gruaud Larose." He looked at the bartender. "Did I say that right? Château Gruaud Larose." He turned to a man in a cream silk jacket, holding a glass of red wine. "This what you're drinking?" The man averted his eyes. "California makes some of the best wines anywhere—and people still haul a bottle like this from clear over on the other side of the planet." He strolled toward the ice sculpture in the center of the room. "Put it on an extra ship, so what. Extra truck, who gives a shit." He tipped the bottle to his lips, took a deep swig and felt the effect, his body still unused to alcohol. He regarded the bottle again. "I mean, sure, this vino's tasty . . . but seriously, after two glasses, you might as well be drinking Ripple, right?"

With his free hand he plucked some kind of berry tart from the buffet. For damn sure none of these confections had ever been packaged. "All those extra ships and trucks?" He polished off the tart in two chomps and continued with his mouth full. "You know how many premature deaths we have from diesel pollution? Two thousand a year in California alone. *Two thousand.*" This was the best thing he'd tasted in longer than he could remember, and swallowing it reminded him how little he'd eaten today—no wonder the wine hit him hard—so he reached for another treat. "What do they call these? Macarons? Macaroons?"

"Macarons," said a man with close-cropped silver hair, impatient and condescending.

Waldo squinted into the man's wineglass. He said, "You like that *Château Gruaud Larose*?" this time warping the name with a snotty pseudo-French inflection. He stuffed the macaron into his mouth. "All these people dying in California from diesel pollution and still we bring wine all the way from France, Italy, Australia, because ours is too, what . . . *local*?" He swallowed the macaron. "*Shit*, that's good. Like macadamia or something. What's this pink one?" He wolfed down another and kept talking while he chewed and browsed the rest of the table. "You know where the pollution's the worst? The hubs. The port in Long Beach, the truck routes in West Oakland, the rail yards in Commerce. The death rates *there . . . fuck*." He turned to the silver-haired man, whose blue sport jacket somehow reminded Waldo of the navy. "But you don't live in Commerce or West Oakland, do you, Admiral?"

A statuesque blonde spoke up from across the buffet table. "Whoever you are, I'll have you know that the people in this room are very concerned about the environment. This happens to be a fund-raiser for global warming."

"Really." He took in the grand salon. "In this house."

"*This house* is quite green. All the furniture replaced in the last two years is bamboo."

Bamboo. He almost choked on his third macaron. These self-satisfied ass clowns, flying in private planes from one gargantuan house they don't need to another, mansions with room after supersize room, each of these stupid fucking mansions pouring millions and millions of pounds of CO_2 into the atmosphere, for nothing—*nothing*—but to show off to the other ass clowns coming over for a drink—but those mansions are okay, see, not just okay but *righteous*, even, because the furniture in those earth-choking rooms in those earth-choking mansions, furniture nobody but their Guatemalan housekeepers will even touch, is made of *bamboo*. Next she'd start gibbering about carbon fucking offsets.

Waldo shook his head and looked at the buffet again. "You folks may have your heads up your asses, but I've got to give it to you: you do have some fine grub." He leaned over the table and shook the leaves and twigs out of his hair and all over the desserts, ruining half the spread.

"Okay, mister, that's enough." Waldo turned and saw a brawny preppie type stepping forward to take him on, no doubt remembering glory days playing rugby at some candy-ass college.

Waldo said, "I'm sorry—am I hogging the macaroons?"

The young man made his move, an Ivy League cross that Waldo slipped easily, hooking a leg and tripping him into the table and bringing it down on top of the preppie, the frozen eagle landing across the bridge of his nose and leaving him stunned and preposterous under a heap of overpriced pastries. Waldo turned to the room and said again, in a weary voice, "Which one of you is Jamshidi?"

The crowd parted, making way for a matched set of immense security guards, everything about the pair designed for intimidation, from the bovine builds and shaved heads to the neck tattoos and gauges that stretched all four of their ears ostentatiously. One of them said, "That's enough, friend."

Waldo smiled at the blue-jacketed man from before and said, "Look, Admiral, I made a friend." The second baldie had circled so that one could charge Waldo from each side. Waldo said to that second one, "You my friend, too?" Then he squatted and smashed the bottle of Château Gruaud Larose on the marble floor, turning it into a jagged two-hundred-dollar weapon.

He looked from one behemoth to the other—left, right, left, right—and on the second turn to the right, the left baldie lunged. Waldo ducked his massive arm and came up with a grip on the back of the man's collar and the broken bottle at his throat, freezing the other attacker in his tracks. Waldo said into the nearest gauged ear, "Okay, Thing One, tell Thing Two to take those handcuffs from his belt and cuff one of his own wrists." When he didn't speak, Waldo nudged the broken glass harder against his neck. *"Tell him."*

Quickly the big man said, *"Do it."*

The second baldie obeyed, slapping a cuff onto his own thick left wrist. "Now," Waldo said to the man with the cuff directly, "I want you to turn around and put your hands straight out behind you. And step back toward us, slowly." Again the big man did as he was told. "Okay, Thing One, I want you to cuff Thing Two's hands together behind him. Come on, come on." When he'd snapped the second handcuff into place, Waldo said, "Now kneel." Neither moved and Waldo realized they didn't know which one he was talking to. He said, "Thing One, *you.* Thing Two, you keep standing." Waldo kept the bottle pressed to the man's throat as he knelt.

With his free hand, Waldo reached into his backpack and found his bicycle cable lock, then pushed one end through the kneeling man's ear gauge. *"What the fuck!"* the man said.

When the other baldie started to turn around to see what was happening, Waldo snapped, *"Don't move!"* He looped the cable around the fastened handcuffs and, tossing aside the bottle to free his other hand, quickly clicked shut the lock, pinning one man's ear to the other's wrists. Then he kicked the bottle out of the kneeling man's reach.

Waldo stood in front of the standing man, hooked a pinky through one of *his* gauges and said, "Now let's all find a comfortable sofa"—his eyes searched the room for the tall blond woman—"a comfortable *bamboo* sofa, and discuss how I might get to meet Mr. Darius Jamshidi." Tugging the ear of that baldie, who bent at the waist, Waldo started across the floor, the man on his knees whimpering as he struggled to keep up.

"I am Darius Jamshidi."

Waldo stopped short and looked for the voice. The baldies tripped over each other and toppled, one crying out in pain.

Waldo scanned the room. "Who said that?"

"I am Darius Jamshidi," the man repeated, and this time Waldo found him. He looked to be about four foot eleven, with piercing blue eyes. Persian-born, Waldo guessed from the man's name and gentle accent. The blond bamboo woman, apparently Mrs. Jamshidi, stood beside him, towering over him by an easy foot.

Jamshidi said, "The real police will be here momentarily. But I'll speak with you in private until they arrive."

Waldo knew he'd have to clear out of the house before then but left the baldies moaning on the floor and followed Jamshidi down seemingly endless hallways to a distant wing. They walked so far, in fact, that the din of the resumed party had faded to a hush even before Jamshidi closed the door to his stately study— leather and dark cherry, no bamboo in here. Jamshidi sat behind his desk and said, "How can I help you, Mr. . . . ?"

"You know my name. You sent Gomes to strong-arm me. I assume you sent those punks from the Palisades, too. Why do you want me off Pinch so badly?"

"I don't know anyone named Gomes."

"*Didn't* know," he corrected. Jamshidi's eyes narrowed. "Cops haven't come to see you yet? Your boy Gomes had a busy day. First he tried to put a scare in me, and right after that he called you, and right after that someone put a bullet through his ear."

The color drained from Jamshidi's face. Recovering, he rose and opened a set of French doors that led to a garden and said, "The wall past the next house backs onto Mulholland. Save us the embarrassment of more drama at my wife's event."

"Cops probably haven't tied you to Gomes yet. Lot more drama if I help them out. Tell me who he was—then I'll leave."

"Warren Gomes had a talent for special research, which helped my company make what it makes."

"Which is?"

"Money," he answered, as if it were a stupid question, as if there were nothing else a company might be interested in making.

"Say more."

Jamshidi spoke slowly and deliberately, like one would to a small child. "There's a group of shopping malls we acquired several years ago. They were an attractive target for us because their price was depressed due to chronic labor problems. Mr. Gomes's research enabled us to exercise certain . . . *leverage* and make those problems go away. We were then able to sell for a profit."

"So, okay, you're trying to buy the network. But who were you hoping to blackmail on this one?"

"I don't believe I said anything about blackmail."

"And what good would it do you to keep me away from Pinch? Why would you *want* the network's biggest star to go to jail? Is that going to drive the price down?"

Sirens wailed outside, at least three units, from the sound of it. LAPD was perennially undermanned and there were parts of town where a homicide call could take twenty minutes. Flatten a dessert table in Beverly Park, though, BH police were all over it.

Waldo, charged with murder only this afternoon, knew he had to disappear. He took a last, urgent shot. "But even if you drive the price down—if you've lost your star, the network you bought's still worth less, right?"

Jamshidi offered an enigmatic shrug and spread his hands with the flawless self-possession of a man who'd once managed to score four billion dollars without inventing or manufacturing a goddamn thing. "If everyone could understand business," he said now to Waldo, "everyone could live here."

TWENTY

Could an entire picnic set count as one Thing? Two plates, two forks, knives, spoons, plus glasses and a cutting board? If they'd belonged to him, he'd consider those alone to be eleven Things, and the basket built to hold them all a twelfth. And wait—were those candles? Candle*holders*? The whole concept seemed profligate, and that was before taking into account paper napkins—*paper*! Of course, the kit belonged to Jayne, and minimalism wasn't a part of *her* life, so was it fair to measure her by his standards? He should let go and enjoy every morsel of this spring afternoon—the cerulean sky, the trilliums in early bloom, the wine not only light and crisp but reassuringly local (Santa Barbara—hell, Waldo could've *biked* this bottle here). And, of course, there was Jayne herself, with her raven hair and heart-shaped face and azure eyes that never seemed to stray from his, Jayne as fresh as those trilliums in a corn-colored summer dress that played well on her slim silhouette. So different from Lorena's curves. Noting that brought home why he was uneasy, and he *was* uneasy, and not, if he were being honest, over the excesses of a picnic basket, or even the hours he was spending away from the job and the client who was relying on him. The unease—the *guilt*—was over being here at all, in *this park*, under *this tree*, where he'd lain with Lorena on a different sublime afternoon that had also felt like it could last forever. What was he thinking, picking the very spot, with thousands of acres to choose from in Griffith Park alone?

As if Jayne could feel his thoughts straying from her, she finished the wine in her glass, stood, kicked off her sandals and trotted away barefoot across the fresh-cut grass, confounding him all over again. But when she tossed a look over her shoulder before disappearing around a bend and behind some shrubs, this time at least he was able to recognize the flirtation. So he balanced his own glass on the picnic basket and followed her, the grass pleasantly prickly on the soles of his feet—when had he taken off *his* shoes? he couldn't remember—until the ground felt a little too soft on one step and softer still on the next and suddenly it wasn't ground under him at all but black muck, swallowing one foot all the way to the knee, and when he tried to put his weight on the other to pull himself out, that one got swallowed, too, and he was mired completely. What *was* this? He heard Jayne in the distance and looked up to see her by a eucalyptus grove, laughing like it was all a game she'd designed, another flirty and confusing trick to entice him, but when he looked down again and realized he was pinned by black tar, like the viscous asphalt that trapped the mammoths twenty thousand years ago, he knew it wasn't a joke, and then he heard the explosion and looked for Jayne again but the oil-rich eucalpytuses were consumed by fire and he screamed and then he could see Jayne in the flames only it wasn't Jayne but Lorena and he wanted to race over and save her from the fire but he couldn't extricate himself from the tar and Lorena said, "You should have called me, Waldo," and then she vanished, again.

When he awoke, it wasn't his feet pinned but his head, and not in tar but in the odd space between the bed and the overhanging night table, into which he must have somehow jammed himself during the night. He forced a swallow down his arid throat and tried to blink the dream away, then carefully extricated himself and sat up. The bedside clock said it was past ten and he cursed himself for having slept so late.

He considered again this ill-fitting table. He removed the clock and bouquet and set them carefully on the floor, and then the tablecloth, revealing a simple round slab of maple topped with glass. Alastair said his wife had been a tinkerer, always moving furniture around, but it was hard to imagine she'd have left this piece here very long. It wasn't the missing table from the *Architectural Digest* spread—that had been rectangular, with at least one drawer—but the odd placement of this one made Waldo wonder where in the house that one had landed.

He slipped on his clean set of clothes, grabbed the magazine and padded into the hallway, peeking into rooms in hope of finding the table that used to be in the living room and might have still been there the night of the murder. He'd scanned most of the house without success by the time he came to Alastair's closed bedroom door. He knocked, called Alastair's name, waited a few seconds, then opened the door carefully.

The room was empty, the bed made. Alastair's nightstand was also covered; Waldo shifted his digital alarm clock and assorted bedside knickknacks onto a bureau and removed the cloth, a solid royal blue. This table, rectangular with a light-colored wood top, maybe white oak, looked similar to the one that had been in the living room in the magazine photo, but for dark and irregular stains on top and a solid face instead of a drawer. Waldo was about to replace the cloth when he thought to reach around back, and there felt the drawer pull; this was it. He lifted the table from the wall and shifted it so he could open the drawer. It was empty, or seemed to be until he reached inside and ran his hand along its back wall and found a cheap-looking flip phone, probably a burner.

It seemed not to have been used much: the security code hadn't even been set and the call history was empty. There were some texts, though, all to and from one number. A whole bunch of incoming, mostly strings of unanswered question marks, and then this exchange:

Outgoing: *I miss you*

Incoming: *U wouldnt know it*

Incoming: *Miss U 2*

Outgoing: *Come over*

Incoming: *Really?*

Incoming: *Now?*

Outgoing: *Please?*

Incoming: *Where is she?*

Outgoing: *Gone all night*

There the messages stopped.

The exchange took place on the date Monica Pinch was killed.

When he arrived at the *Johnny's Bench* soundstage, they were about to shoot, so Waldo took an unobtrusive spot behind the director again while he waited for the chance to talk to Alastair. The scene took place in a kitchen, where the actress, a striking light-skinned black woman with straightened and tinted hair, scrambled eggs at a working stove. Alastair entered behind her, dressed in a woman's frilly pink bathrobe. "Good morning," the actress said, looking over her shoulder and tittering at the robe. "Hey, that works on you—I should get you one of your own."

"Do. And keep it in your closet for me. I might want to make a regular thing of this."

"*Johnny*," she said, warning. "If the DA finds out you've been involved with me all this time . . ."

He reached around her, took the spatula from her hand and tossed it aside, then spun her and kissed her. Her desirous response looked like a lot more than a stage kiss, perhaps answering Waldo's first question about the burner texts before he even got a chance to ask it. She was an eyeful, too, even by actress standards, and it was hard to imagine getting kisses like that from a woman like that and *not* wanting to bring your work home. Had she been to the Pinches' house the day of the murder? The night of, even? He'd have to talk to her, too.

The kiss ended and the lovers locked eyes for a long, profound moment. Waldo wondered how much of what he was witnessing was pure acting and how much was controlled exposure of a private reality, a silent sharing of actual history, actual secrets. Whatever, he couldn't wait to hear what Alastair/Johnny was going to say to her next.

What he said was ". . . Line?"

The actress didn't reply. Instead, the script supervisor, sitting beside the director again, called out, "'I'll recuse myself if I have to.'"

Alastair said, "Shit!" and turned away from the actress, who stepped out of the counterfeit kitchen herself, covering her exasperation.

"Cut," said the director, doing almost as good a job of hiding his own.

Alastair muttered to himself, "I'll recuse myself if I have to, I'll recuse myself if I have to." Then he turned to the actress and said, "Deepest apologies, Naomi—I must have been distracted by your perfume." The crew laughed.

Naomi herself, not laughing, exchanged a private smirk with a new young and athletic camera assistant, presumably the replacement for the one Alastair had battered on Waldo's first day. Waldo realized he'd been fooled again: in the cold light of cameras not rolling, the actress didn't care much for her leading man at all.

Unfortunately, that leading man had picked up on the wordless exchange. "Am I interrupting something?"

"What?" Naomi said. "No . . ."

Alastair looked at the camera assistant, then back to her. "Is *that* what you like? I have pimples on my arse older than that one." Nobody laughed, though it was arguably funnier than his perfume line. Alastair marched over to the kid, his rising temper risibly incongruous with his frilly bathrobe, but nobody laughed at that, either. "This is *my* set, love, and I'd ask you to show me some respect."

The kid said, "I respect you, sir."

Alastair took umbrage at even that. "'*Sir*'? How old do you think I *am*?"

Before the kid could find the right answer, Alastair head butted him. Stunned, he tried to answer with a blind, wild left but Alastair dodged it and came back with another proficient combination, and the kid staggered and wobbled and dropped without having landed a single blow. Waldo scanned the stage, a crew of about seventy, all inspecting phones or fingernails.

Alastair caught his breath and noticed something on the sleeve of the frilly bathrobe and called, "Wardrobe?" A tiny woman with a Mohawk scurried over and Alastair said, "I'm afraid we've gotten a spot of blood on this."

"Don't worry," she said, reassuring. "We always have a double." Alastair's team knew what to prepare for.

"I'll be in my trailer while she fetches it," Alastair called in the vague direction of the director on his way to the exit. Waldo decided not to follow him, figuring this wasn't the moment for a confrontation about the burner; he'd have better luck with Alastair later, after the flush from his pugilistic triumph had worn off.

To kill some time, Waldo took a turn around the lot. He was ravenous, not having eaten yet, so he stopped at the commissary. After an extended colloquy with a short-order chef over the provenance of the grilled vegetable medley, he settled for a banana, despite the thousands of miles it must have traveled and his misgivings about the repression of unionization efforts on plantations in Guatemala and Costa Rica.

Nearing the far end of the lot, Waldo saw two parked black-and-whites up ahead with almost a dozen patrolmen in conference nearby. He could have veered away and avoided the inevitable hostility when they recognized him, but the old curiosity kicked in and he itched to know what kind of incident had drawn this many uniforms out to a studio lot. He kept his head down, hoping to catch some of their conversation. As he passed, one cop was saying, "... So I go, *you* change her diaper, she's *your* fuckin' *mother*," and the others cracked up. Waldo slowed to hear more, preferably something more enlightening. A couple of the cops registered him and nodded friendly, unexpected hellos. That slowed him down, and now they all noticed him. But nobody seemed inhospitable; apparently, somehow, none of them recognized the infamous Detective Charlie Waldo. Maybe it was the beard, maybe the context.

"What's going on?" he said.

"Waitin'," one cop said. "Shootin' the shit."

"I mean, what are you here for?"

"Oh, pilot. *Delta Blues.*" He said to Waldo, "You in the soup kitchen scene? I hear they might not get to it today." Waldo glanced at the patrolman's shoulder patch and saw it had a New Orleans insignia.

"Thanks," Waldo said and kept walking. He didn't have any shit he wanted to shoot with a band of screen extras.

Passing the backlot, the maze of bogus streets and building facades used for the filming of city scenes, he saw in the distance an unexpected pairing: the camera assistant Alastair had just beaten up having a laugh and a cigarette with his counterpart from the first day, both with bandaged faces now, reenacting punches, sharing war stories. As Waldo neared, another familiar face from the *Johnny's Bench* set, a goateed assistant director with a headset resting on his neck, came up to the pair and handed today's victim an envelope. They shook hands, the AD left, and the young guys started cutting up again.

Waldo approached, putting on a laugh of his own. "That rocked," he said. "Where can I get a gig like that?"

They stopped laughing. Today's kid looked especially wary. "Don't know what you're talkin 'bout, dude."

"I was on the *Johnny's Bench* set. Come on—how much you get for letting that old guy kick your ass?"

The two camera assistants shared a careful glance. Then one started laughing and the other did too. Today's kid said to Waldo, "Get bent."

Waldo turned to his friend. "How are you still on the lot? Didn't I see you get fired the other day?"

"I'm on another show now."

"They move you guys around? And pay you extra to take a couple punches. Come on, how much?"

"A grand."

"*Larry,*" said the other one, nervous now.

Larry, full of himself, said, "Who gives a shit? *We're* not gonna get in trouble." He gave Waldo a *what are you gonna do about it* smirk; today's kid fingered the envelope and fidgeted.

Waldo figured he'd get more out of the cocky one. "How do they know Pinch'll come at you? You get paid even if he doesn't?"

"He does, he always does. Gotta be the alpha dog or somethin'." The kid couldn't resist adding, "It's a sweet deal, man. Dudes are linin' up for it."

For maybe the first time, Waldo felt a twinge of empathy for Alastair. What a world the man lived in: phony friends with phony laughter, phony police walking phony streets, phony adversaries throwing phony punches after phony kisses from phony lovers.

Knowing he'd never find a compost heap on the lot, Waldo tossed his banana peel into a garbage can and headed back to the soundstage. At least he thought it was a garbage can.

TWENTY-ONE

The rest of Alastair's morning, which Waldo tracked via the sighs and grumbling of crew members, was an exercise in dilatory inventiveness, the star finding one excuse after another not to emerge from his trailer: first the replacement bathrobe, which he swore didn't fit as well; then a headache, which he blamed on the wardrobe people who'd dragged him through so much tailoring; then a set of script revisions, which he claimed not to have received until the last minute and which he deemed inconsistent with backstory from an episode the prior season. At last the producers cried uncle and called the lunch break.

Through all this, Waldo kept his distance, taking advantage of the dead hours to peel off members of the crew for one-on-ones, wild shots at teasing out new threads. He started with the beleaguered director and his script supervisor sidekick, then found the embattled costume designer and also managed a few minutes apiece with three producers of different stripes, these last behind closed doors in their nearby offices. The various interviews were

uniformly cautious, nobody wanting to drop a stronger descriptor on Alastair than "intense" or "complicated." The words Waldo
kept hearing, unspoken, were "meal ticket."

After the producers, Waldo knocked on the screen door of the
actress's trailer, thinking that her relative irreplaceability might
make her less reticent. "Is he finally fucking ready?" she called,
confirming the instinct. He apologized for not being the production assistant she'd been hoping for and introduced himself. She
invited him in.

The trailer, or her half of it—the chunky actor who played
Judge Johnny's sardonic but fiercely loyal bailiff occupied the
other half, with a separate entrance—took a similar approach to
limited space as Waldo's own cabin, cleverly loading a surprising array of amenities into its walls, from microwave to gas
fireplace. The actress sat on the only chair and gestured toward
the built-in daybed. Her name was Naomi Tompkins-Jones and
she didn't need a prompt to start complaining. "I've got a director meeting at four in Culver City. They promised me I'd be out
by lunch."

"I just have a couple questions. I won't slow down your day, I
promise. Do you know Alastair well?"

"Nobody knows Alastair 'well.'"

"Ever meet his wife?"

"Sat next to her at the Golden Globes. *That* was a trip."

"How so?"

"English girl got a *mouth* on her. And she was not happy to be
there. You know that's the only awards where they serve alcohol
during the show, right? Plus they do TV right off, so then we're
all done and still got to sit there three hours, so everybody starts
getting shit-faced."

"Is that what Monica wasn't happy about? Having to sit there?"

"Everything—sitting there, this show, *L.A.* Kept calling it the City of Angles. Said, with every award she could feel more brain cells dying. Finally I go, 'Might not be the awards, girl— might be all them champagne cocktails.'"

"What'd she say to that?"

"She goes, 'You fucking my husband, too?'" Waldo waited her out on that one. Naomi lowered her chin and her voice and said, "Not even close, honey." She snorted.

Waldo offered a conspiratorial grin to let her know he believed her. He said, "What's it like, playing love scenes opposite a man accused of killing his wife?"

"What do *you* think? I'm on the board of the L.A. Coalition Against Domestic Violence. You know what that means? *All* this shit's messed up, is what it means."

A PA knocked and called from outside that they were ready to start up again. Waldo walked to the stage with the PA and the actress and watched her and Alastair get the breakfast scene right and then shoot another quick two-line scene in Judge Johnny's chambers—the unsatisfactory new pages having been revised twice more—and then Alastair was released for the day.

Waldo approached him while he was signing the end-of-day paperwork. The two men eyed each other; it was the first time they'd been together since the police took Alastair away, incredibly only thirty hours ago, and the energy between them had altered, profoundly and disagreeably. Alastair, unsmiling, looked much older. Waldo said, "Can we talk?"

Alastair said, "If we must." Softening an iota, he added, "I'll get changed and you can come with me to pick up Gaby."

They didn't speak during the walk to Alastair's trailer, or while he changed in the bedroom, or as they crossed the lot to his Hummer and he handed Waldo the keys. It wasn't like the silence of the first day, all unfamiliarity and uncertainty. This silence was soaked in mutual resentment: Alastair's over the sense that Waldo not only had failed to protect him but had likely made things worse—no doubt Fontella Davis had fed that impression since the arrest—and Waldo's over the burner phone and the likelihood that Alastair had been hiding at least one card from him.

Waldo steered off the lot. He decided not to start with the burner. "Warren Gomes, Darius Jamshidi—you know either of them?"

"No," Alastair said, not missing a beat, "but Robert Blake called last night. He asked if I cared to play pinochle with him on Thursdays. He's been without a partner since O.J. and Phil Spector went on their vacations."

Waldo had been through too much; there was nothing winning anymore about the mordant palaver. "Stop fucking around. Everyone else is sure you did it, and the only reason *I* have doubts is somebody keeps busting *my horns.* Me figuring out why may be the only thing standing between you and life without parole— so when I ask for your help, goddamnit, *help.*" He stopped for a light. He turned to Alastair and repeated the names: "Warren Gomes, Darius Jamshidi. Who are they?"

Alastair stared forward, shook his head.

Waldo watched him carefully. How much was this maddening bastard holding back, and how much did he truly not remember? Alastair still wouldn't look at him. Waldo waited for the light to turn before asking, "Is there anything you're not telling me?"

"Like what?"

"Like, did you invite anyone over to the house that night?"

"No."

"You're sure."

"Absolutely."

"How can you be sure, when you don't remember anything?"

"Because I never just 'invite anyone over to the house.' That's not part of my life."

He was lying. Yes, it was possible that the text exchange happened during Alastair's blackout, too. If there *was* one—for all Waldo really knew, that was bullshit, too. But even assuming the blackout was real, at the very least he had to remember owning a burner phone that he used to talk to another woman, and he had to know that it was missing and that he hadn't used it since the day of the murder.

"Were you faithful to your wife?"

"I don't see where that's relevant."

"Everything's relevant." It was clear that Alastair didn't intend to answer, or else felt that he already had, so Waldo moved on. "When did you shift the furniture around?"

"I told you, Monica was a constant tinkerer—"

"The night table in my room doesn't fucking fit, okay? It hangs way over the side of the bed. Nobody who gets pictures of her house in *Architectural Digest* would ever put that table there. I'm thinking it was moved from *your* bedroom and the one in your bedroom came from the living room. Probably on the night of the murder. Unless you've moved them since."

Alastair bit off his response. "I have not. Moved them. Since."

"Could you have rearranged furniture that night and dressed it with tablecloths and flowers—and not remembered the next day?"

"I've gotten married, fathered children and taken out mort-
gages and not remembered the next day."

They renewed their silence, Waldo wishing he could bellow
his frustration. The transposed furniture, Jamshidi—the reeds
were slim, but they were reeds, and any sane man invested in his
own exoneration would grasp at them with all he had. Why not
this man? It was as if he were hell-bent on his own undoing.
Could self-loathing possibly run this deep?

They'd reached Gaby's school. Alastair pointed wordlessly to a
procession of cars waiting their turns to collect elementary schoolers laden with colorful backpacks and art projects, and Waldo
steered the Hummer to the end of the line. Alastair scanned the
crowd for his daughter and said, "What shall you do, Detective,
when your vaunted skills lead you to the conclusion that I did, in
fact, murder my wife? Will you share your findings with the police? Will you stand for your client, or for Truth and Justice, like
the incorruptible Charlie Waldo of yore?"

Or, Waldo thought, there was that. Maybe Alastair wasn't
invested in exoneration because he knew on some level, even if it
was buried deep, that he killed his wife and saw punishment as
not only ineluctable but deserved. Which begged the question:
why had Waldo been so resistant to accepting the obvious answer as the true one, almost since the moment he'd met the man?
Again, was this the unavoidable nature of PI work, approaching
the investigation as advocate rather than disinterested analyst?
Or was it simply Alastair's movie star panache working its magic
from the start despite Waldo's best efforts to resist it?

Alastair's bone-weary sigh pulled him back. "I used to rather
like waking up somewhere I didn't know, with someone I didn't
know, and no idea what damage I might have caused the night

before. It kept life interesting. Gave me character." Waldo, edging the Hummer forward, spied Gaby just before she spotted them and came running full tilt. Alastair, opening his door, turned back to him and said, "Stick with Truth and Justice, Waldo. I've gotten away with far more than most men. If I killed my little girl's mother, this time I'll take what's coming to me, and we'll call the whole lot even."

Maybe he was just a chump for Alastair's acting—it wouldn't be the first time—but Waldo believed he meant it. And coupled with the little girl leaping into his arms, it was heartbreaking.

Alastair shed the heaviness and became the joyful daddy once again. "Princess Ozma!" he shouted, twirling her.

Waldo got out of the car too, hoping to catch a glimpse of Jayne among her kindergarteners. And there she was, a few cars ahead, chatting with a parent; she saw him immediately and flashed him a quick smile with her eyes while politely keeping focus on her conversation.

Waldo turned back to the car, and what he saw beyond it chilled him: a black Escalade sitting at the curb outside the campus entrance, Don Q in the passenger seat, staring in their direction, dead eyed, unblinking.

"Daddy," Gaby was saying, "I know all my lines for my play!"

"I can't wait to see your Rumpelstiltskin," said Alastair, oblivious to the danger. "One of the most coveted roles in all of theater!"

Gaby climbed into her car seat; Alastair leaned in to buckle her. Waldo rounded the car and put a hand on his shoulder. "Hey," he said, "you sober enough to drive?"

"If I must."

"You must. I'll see you at your house."

"What's wrong?"

Waldo opened the back of the Hummer and pulled out his bike. "Just keep your doors locked and don't stop for anything. *Anything*. Understand?" Alastair nodded.

Waldo shut the rear door and marched his bike toward the entrance, blood pounding in his ears. This motherfucker killed her, *killed* her, and set her on fire. He barely broke stride to drop the bike and backpack against a wall just inside the school gate. He picked up his stride and stormed at the Escalade. Don Q stepped out, and Nini, too, from the driver's side.

"Tell me about Lorena," Waldo said, inches from Don Q. "Tell it to my face."

"You tell me 'bout my Mem."

"I don't even know what a fucking Mem is!"

"I think you're prevaricatin', Waldo. That means lyin'." Was this fucker *smiling*? He *was*! "Bitch said she gave it to you. Last words she ever said, too, so I'm inclined to take it for true." Waldo could feel malice coursing through his body like a chemical. "You know, she was still alive when I poured the gas on her, and once that shit started, you couldn't get the bitch to shut up—"

Waldo lunged for Q's throat, driving him into the car door. He barely started squeezing off the bastard's larynx when he felt Nini's fist batter his kidney and the strength drain from his thumbs and everywhere else. Nini flung him against the Escalade and pounded his rib cage. The air went out of Waldo and he doubled over, first retching, then gasping frantically for oxygen like he'd been released into a different atmosphere.

There was no winning this. Lorena was dead and these guys were going to kill him, too, quickly or slowly, if he didn't find this Mem, whatever the fuck that was. "Okay," he wheezed, "tell me . . . exactly . . ."

But Don Q was massaging his throat and shaking his head, uninterested in negotiation at the moment. Nini stood Waldo up against the Escalade and put him to sleep a second time.

TWENTY-TWO

H e was facedown at the bottom of the ocean, or it could have been a deep well, because there was a pin of light somewhere ahead in the distance, though if he saw it he couldn't be face-down, could he, maybe he was on his back, he couldn't even be sure about that, maybe he *was* faceup now that he thought about it, and maybe it wasn't a well but the bottom of a tank at the aquarium, a tank that's *shaped* like a well, with tropical fish, be-cause it didn't look like sky when he cracked his eyes, there were colors, bright colors swimming past, but it hurt even to squint, so he closed them again, and how did he get to the aquarium, where would that be, Long Beach or was there a little one in Santa Monica, and who brought him here anyway . . . ?

Q.

Now he remembered. Q and the Eskimo, what were they going to do with him . . . ? He needed to pull it together, climb out of this tank, get away . . . but how was he even breathing at the bottom of a tank? It was excruciating, each inhale, but it was *possible.* So all right, he wasn't underwater. Also he was freezing at the bottom of his face, but no place else—what was that about? He decided to force his eyes open and start from there.

The colors. An assault. Not moving, not fish, but yellows and oranges and reds and greens. It was a drawing. Of what? A girl and a boy and a sink. Why? And there were words. It took some doing to decipher them, but at last he did, and they read:

GOOD HEALTH STARTS WITH CLEAN HANDS!

What the fuck.

He let his eyes drift to the overhead fluorescents while he explored his rib cage with his fingers: swollen but no protrusion, so good news, only bruised, but he'd been through that once before and knew it would be a month till he felt anything like good health again, and by the way, washing his hands wasn't going to help a damn bit. He put a hand to his frozen jaw and found an ice pack. He scanned the room without moving his head. It wasn't a hospital, more like a doctor's office, a pediatrician's, maybe, from the posters.

And now something touched his hair and he flinched at the assault, but it was a *kind* touch, and he contorted his neck to look.

Jayne, smiling at him. "Morning, sleepyhead."

"Is it . . ."

"No, it's about four thirty. Sorry, I shouldn't confuse you. You're in the school nurse's office." That pulled it together. "A couple of football players saw it happen and carried you in. The nurse had to go home, so I said I'd stay and take care of you."

"Thank you."

"Should I take you to a hospital?"

"No. But I could use another ice pack for my ribs."

"They got your ribs, too? Nice friends you have." Waldo grunted.

A little later he turned down a second offer of a ride to the hospital but agreed to let her drive him to Alastair's. She helped him off the nurse's table and out to a bench near the student pickup area, where he waited, still holding an ice pack to his side, until she swung her Civic around and helped him ease into the cramped passenger seat. Steadying himself on the roof of the car, Waldo happened to glance up and spot Dr. Hexter in a corner window of the top floor of the main building, watching them. Their eyes met but neither man offered any sort of greeting. Waldo got the sense that his chaos had outlasted the headmaster's patience, and that the man wasn't happy about whatever might be brewing between Waldo and Jayne, either.

It felt strange to be alone in a car with a woman, more so with her driving. They turned onto Laurel Canyon and found it stopped dead; the few miles to Alastair's could take half an hour or more. "Sorry to put you out," he said, stifling a wince.

She said, "Does it hurt to talk?" and he nodded. When on the next green they didn't even make it to the intersection, she said, "I might have a better idea. Do you trust me?"

Waldo said, "Why should I trust you?" and gave her a crooked grin that made his jaw ache.

But there was no smile in return; in fact she was almost solemn when she said, "Because you'll like it." Her unexpected seriousness dizzied him. It was the last either of them spoke for hours.

She lived in a standard midcentury two-story deeper in the Valley, the big looping cursive out front that read SHERMAN WAY

ROYALE promising more than it delivered, eight boxy units around a pool that had seen better days. Jayne's own apartment was sparse and shabby—Waldo guessed she'd rented it furnished—but clean. There was a Paul Detlefsen lithograph of a horse and buggy crossing a covered bridge with a boy in a straw hat fishing in the foreground, bucolic and nostalgic, a token of her kindergarten choirgirl side, or maybe it just came with the place.

He felt a hand on his shoulder and caught a glimpse of a long strip of dark fabric, which she brought to his eyes and tied into a blindfold. "Shhh," she whispered.

She took his hand and steered him into what, from the sound of their footfalls, he took to be another room, and then she maneuvered him to sit on a low, uncomfortable chair, which he eventually recognized as a closed toilet seat. She tied something else loosely around his neck. He heard the scraping of metal against metal—scissors?—then felt a soft tug at his lower left cheek and he realized she was trimming his beard. He started to object, but she quieted him with a soft finger on his lips. He was stunned by her boldness, even more surprised by how unhurriedly she worked, taking each pinch of hair between her fingers, twirling and caressing it before bracketing it with the blades and slowly closing them, the room so still that he could hear individual whiskers severing. Then she'd move on to the next patch, working her way bit by bit down his neck and back up to his jawline, then across his chin and over to the other side, idling as she gently pulled on the patch below his lip to glide a finger slowly across the lip itself, then tarrying for the same on the return trip as she clipped his mustache. When she'd finished the entire beard—or when he'd thought she'd finished—she began the whole process again, cropping closer this time, the backs of her fingers never losing contact with his skin now, skin that even his own fingers hadn't encountered in years.

He felt the coolness of a gel and then her fingers spreading it across the bristly remains, and after that the blade, in long, thoughtful strokes. She kept close to her work; he could hear her inhale and feel her exhale. And when the gel and the whiskers were all gone, she caressed his new naked face, every millimeter of it, less than a caress, really, the contact so slight that it was barely a touch at all, and his breathing became so quick and shallow that he forgot about his ribs.

Then she took off the blindfold and led him into the bedroom.

He hadn't realized she was awake, but as the first stirrings of dawn turned the room from black to iron gray, she propped herself on an elbow and said, "What are you thinking?"

He'd been thinking about all of it—the night, the strangeness of it, and the moment he realized it had stopped being strange. About how he never would have guessed she'd be so at ease in bed, so sexually fluent, and how grateful he was for the way her effortlessness so quickly melted his own initial awkwardness and rust. About how careful she'd been of his ribs, how she'd balanced her weight on his shoulders or his hands, how every time she shifted she'd check to make sure he was all right, and how she stopped checking once she'd lost herself completely, and how powerful *that* was to experience, how potent for him her ferocity had been. And he'd been thinking about how connected he felt to her now, more connected than he could recall feeling the first time with anyone, except maybe Lorena, of course, and he'd been wondering whether it was only because it had been so long or whether there was something stronger stirring here, something that would force a whole bunch of questions more consequential than whether this meant he was going to start shaving regularly.

Of course, he didn't say any of that. What he said was "I was thinking of a woman who looked like she was about seventy, with false teeth that didn't fit right, and a big, ugly wart on the side of her nose."

She laughed. "And why were you thinking that?"

"Because she was *my* kindergarten teacher."

Jayne laughed again, then rested a hand lightly over Waldo's heart. "Does that hurt?"

He shook his head. He could make out her face a bit, in this early light almost like a black-and-white photograph. It worked for her. But then again, everything did. Waldo said, "That was . . . intense."

"*Too* intense?" She put a hand over her face. "I'm embarrassed. I'm not usually like that."

"Who is who they are?"

"Stop!" But he could tell she liked the reprise.

On her bed stand he noticed a tall stack of DVDs. He reached over to pick up a disk and squinted to read the box in the half-light. It was a workout video. "Savannah Moon, huh?" He picked up another DVD and looked at it, then a third. "What do you have, twenty DVDs of her?"

"Something like that. And all five books."

"Twenty and five. That would be a quarter of my stuff," he said, marveling. "Why her?"

"Empowerment."

"*Really?*"

"Oh, definitely. Self-confidence begins with physical confidence."

"Well, you've got *that*."

"Stop!" she said again and slapped him on the shoulder, lightly, ever conscious of his injuries.

Waldo perused one of the discs. "I'm kind of fascinated by her, actually. She's sort of the essence of consumerism—she preys on people's insecurities, then gets rich pumping tons of nonbiodegradable crap into the ecosystem." He realized she was grinning at him. *"What?"*

"Was it really three years? Or was that a line?"

"It wasn't a line."

"Huh. Wouldn't know it."

"Truth," he said. "I thought I was retired."

"Maybe that's what did it for me—the idea of you going without for so long. Or maybe it's that you're so damaged."

"Damaged? Is that how you see me? Damaged?"

"Jesus, Waldo."

"Everybody keeps saying that."

"You live alone on a mountain. You've got all these insane rules . . ."

"I'm just trying to live more responsibly. Leave a smaller footprint." Seeing the way she looked at him, something else moved inside him, and he thought that this had to be deeper than a first-time-in-years postcoital flush, because something about this girl made him want to make himself . . . *known*. "The thing is," he said, "having some rules . . . some lines to color inside of . . . a plan for being a better person . . . and not *hurting* anything anymore, not another human being, not the planet . . . it's how life started making sense again. That's all."

Saying it out loud for the first time, he was certain that it *did* make sense, and that she'd see him as he saw himself, that she'd understand that he wasn't merely eccentric, let alone unhinged, that he was entirely rational.

She said, "Uh-huh. *Really* damaged."

Her words unnerved him, but just as quickly her smile steadied him. Sincere or ironic, she was telling him that she *got* it, and more important, that she was all right with it. This was what he'd never have living alone on a mountain, this was connection, and even with his jaw throbbing, his elbow aching, and the bruised ribs now making every full breath a white-hot rapier piercing his side, for the first time in what felt like forever, it didn't hurt to be alive.

TWENTY-THREE

They made love again and it was even better but he woke up the second time in a panic, remembering his bike, which he'd forgotten about in the trauma and the intoxication of the previous night. He vaguely recalled dumping it along with his backpack before confronting Don Q. Jayne was in the shower, so he suffered ten horror-filled minutes imagining some little schoolkid finding his Beretta before she got out and reassured him: the football players who brought him to the nurse's had retrieved his belongings too, and his backpack was in the trunk of her car downstairs and his bike in a rack at the school. She hadn't thought at the time to look through his bag for a lock, but the school entrance was secured at night and the bike would almost certainly be safe until they got there.

Jayne didn't keep much on hand that Waldo could eat for breakfast, but he let her give him an apple and a tomato after she vowed they'd been brought home in reusable bags. They drove to school together, Jayne singing to Katy Perry and Carly Rae

Jepsen on the radio. Waldo's thoughts drifted back to the case and the dead end he'd reached when Alastair couldn't—or wouldn't—shed light on the Gomes and Jamshidi connection. There were few threads left for him to pull on beyond the riddle of why people were intent on him not pulling on them. The only other utility he could see for himself was to keep picking at the initial police work, dredging up sand for Fontella Davis to toss in the jury's eyes—hardly what he'd signed on for. He wondered if it was time to step away from the case. But Jamshidi's interference had to mean something, and so did the Palisades Posse's, and he'd feel feckless abandoning Alastair with both of those left unexplained, especially when none of the actor's other supposed advocates believed in him.

He and Jayne had pleasurably distracted each other into a later start than she usually managed, so the campus was already crowded by the time they arrived. She pointed out the rack across the playground from the teachers' parking lot—it was too far for him to be able to identify his own bike among the several it held—and told him again that she was late. He said, "I'll call you soon."

She said, "I know you will," and headed for her classroom.

He was halfway across the yard when Gaby came running up to him. "Mr. Lion! What are you gonna do?"

"About what?"

"You lost half your mane!" She laughed at her joke and ran back to her friends. He stroked his clean-shaven face. It felt good.

It was a huge relief to see his bike, but when he tried to wheel it out from between two others, something interfered: a large yellow envelope someone had apparently stuck between the spokes. He yanked it out and looked it over. *MR. WALDO* was hand printed in thick marker, surrounded by sparkly stickers, like some kind of child's art project made with a teacher's help. He wondered if it was a gift from Gaby. That notion evaporated instantly, though, when he saw what was inside: a folded sheet of paper and a DVD, a pornographic parody of a historical drama called *The King's Peach.* The actress on the cover had her hair in tightly pasted 1930s curls and was naked but for heels and a large feathered hat, and she was straddling a man of whom little could be seen but an English bowler of the same period.

The naked actress was Jayne.

Unmistakably Jayne.

Waldo fumbled at the paper, on which was written, also in marker:

> Wonder how "Jayne" got hired with no teaching experience?
>
> Maybe you should "investigate" how well she knows the Headmaster!

He looked around: was anyone watching him read this? Not that he could spot. Studying the cover again, he went dizzy and heard a sudden, insistent ringing. It took the frantic scurry of kids to their classrooms to make him realize that the bell wasn't sounding in his head.

Who is who they are?

And who had sent him this, and why?

Waldo walked his bike across the freshly emptied schoolyard to her classroom at the far end of the campus. By the time he got there the door was closed. Through the window he saw that her kindergarteners were already in their seats and Jayne in front of the whiteboard, beginning the day. He caught her eye and she smiled, delighted at what she assumed to be bonus affection, an extra good-bye. She winked, then turned back to her students.

His phone buzzed and he took it from his pocket: an email. It looked to be a typical come-on from an unfamiliar address, unfinishedbusiness@gmail.com, with a blind subject line that read *Mammoth Opportunity!* Discomfited by Jayne and the DVD, he automatically dismissed it as junk or phishing, but he paused before deleting it, if only because of its novelty: he almost never received emails, even spam, since he'd unsubscribed from every-thing back at the beginning, corresponded with no one, and so rarely bought Things. He idly wondered how some marketer might have snagged his email of late and was about to wipe it to trash when he caught a second look at the address and subject lines, put them together and, dumbfounded, said aloud, "Son of a bitch," and opened the email.

There was no link or attachment, just a simple message:

you never know what you might find in your trunk

"Motherfucker!" he shouted, loud enough to draw dirty looks from two moms coming out of a second-grade classroom. He jumped on his bike, screaming, "Yes! Yes! Yes!" and, too exhila-rated to be hindered by his injuries, bolted the campus.

She was alive. He didn't know where she was, how it was possi-ble, let alone how to keep her that way, but she was alive. Her last words before driving from his cabin reverberated: *Unfinished business is a bitch.* Had she phrased it that way deliberately, know-ing it would stay with him like it did, so that it would make an impression and she could call it back later? She must have cached something in the elephant sculpture, a bit of legerdemain made possible by the way her appearance on the mountain had unnerved him. Every bit of the gambit was so quintessentially Lorena—the boldness, the craftiness, the wordplay. He was so giddy that he didn't even care that she was taunting him by call-ing it a mammoth again. And of course he was dying to know what she'd hidden there.

His curiosity made the two legs of the Greyhound trip back to Banning all the more interminable. Resting his ribs on the bus helped and he was able to bike the flats out there more easily than he'd handled North Hollywood. The worst of the ride was ahead, of course, but he was sure elation and curiosity would carry him, even with his wounds, and by the time he coasted into the low grade at the base of 243 he knew that this trip up the mountain would be manageable. All he'd need was more fre-quent rest than on the last trip, maybe a five-minute breather every twenty and he'd be fine.

That confidence lasted until his muscles' first cry for oxygen. As the huffs grew deeper, the stabbing in his side grew sharper, until the agony was so great that each breath brought tears. When he couldn't take it anymore he stopped.

He lay the bike on the shoulder and sat beside it until he re-gained control of his breathing and the throbbing subsided. He was hoping he'd bitten off at least three or four miles with this first push, though he truly had no idea; the agony had been so all consuming as to scramble any sense of time or distance. He took out his phone to estimate. If the app was right, he'd gone just under a mile. One lousy mile, twenty-three to go, and almost all of them steeper than the first. He was in trouble.

He took apart the Brompton and bagged it and stuck out his thumb. A Range Rover didn't slow. Neither did the string of motorcycles that passed a minute later, nor any of the next score of cars. He wondered how long he'd be out here. As a former cop, he sure wouldn't recommend picking up any hitchhiker screwy enough to be out on this death trap, let alone one who hadn't had a haircut in three years. But maybe he'd get lucky and some un-reconstructed Idyllwild hippie, lightly stoned, would take him for a kindred spirit.

Salvation came in the form of a Chevron tanker, of all things, its driver lonely for someone to talk at. The trucker's complaints about the weekly run up this road and his wife and the Lakers weren't quite compelling enough to distract Waldo from the an-imation playing in his head, the carbon dioxide and carbon mon-oxide and nitrogen oxide and unburned hydrocarbons and other particulate matter defiling the desert sky by the second. It was unforgivable, the damage these two men were doing together, especially that for which Waldo was alone to blame, the mar-ginal atmospheric destruction unleashed when the truck stopped for him and reaccelerated after picking him up. He kicked him-self for not anticipating the impossibility of biking in the first place and arranging a zero-footprint option ahead of time.

Still, thanks to the lift, he reached his property with a good half hour of daylight remaining. He rode along his dirt path, not-ing with relief that the corpse had been removed, dropped his bike outside the cabin and set out into the woods. In his excite-ment he pushed a little too hard, reigniting the pain.

Light played color tricks on the metal, and when Waldo

reached the clearing, the evening shadows had turned the sculpture as close to an elephant's natural hue as it would be all day. Waldo reached up into its raised trunk and stuck his fingers into the hollow, an indentation a few inches deep that he'd never even noticed before. There he found some leaves and muck, and something else too: a blue plastic USB flash drive.

I want my Mem.

He rested his back against the metal elephant's haunches and slowly sunk to the ground, respite for his legs, and controlled his pain with breaths just deep enough to be useful. He intended to rest there only a few minutes so he could make it to the cabin before the last of the daylight was gone but fell asleep with the memory stick in his fist. When he awoke hours later he had to navigate back in the scant moonlight that managed to permeate the high foliage.

In the cabin he set the computer on his table and turned it on, then plugged the flash drive into the USB port. It contained only one file, a Word document. Waldo tried to read it but got a pop-up instead:

Enter password to open file.

Waldo had no idea where to begin. He tried "Nanook."

The password is incorrect. Word cannot open the document.

He tried "Don Q." Same.

"Lorena." Nothing.

He knew maddeningly little about the trafficker, nothing to inspire a guess. He tried all the interesting words he could remember Q using: "Inuit," "pejorative," "Bowflex."

"Mem."

He tried all uppercase, he tried all lowercase. No luck.

He assumed the protected file contained incriminating details about Don Q's business, likely in code and meaningless to Waldo even if he *could* open it. Still, Don Q must have feared the possibility of it falling into the wrong hands—Cuppy's? He was desperate enough to kill for it, or at least to let the police *believe* he'd killed for it.

Believe he'd killed.

Waldo thrilled at the reminder: *she was alive.*

Fucking Lorena.

But how had she gotten her hands on this flash drive, and what had she been planning to do with it? Cuppy claimed she was working for Don Q; was that looking more plausible? And why would she run this kind of risk? Again—*what had she become in these three years?* A blackmailer—could it be? Or was she maybe holding the flash as some kind of insurance, protection because she'd already gotten on Don Q's bad side for something else?

Regardless, she had gone to ground now and it was on him to clear the way for her to come back. Maybe he could trade the flash drive for her safety. Of course, even reaching out to arrange a parley was risky; once Don Q knew he was holding the Mem, this whole thing could easily end with Waldo himself the next rotting message on somebody else's lawn. He'd have to dream up a hell of a play just to get the conversation started.

He knew that kind of inventiveness wasn't likely while he was in this condition. Before he could sleep, though, he wanted the Mem out of the cabin, in case he got any more visitors. He took his flashlight and trekked back to the elephant, replaced the thumb drive in the trunk, and on the way back stopped to pick a few vegetables from his garden for a late-night snack, much needed.

He needed a return to routine, too. Late as it was, he played his four games of chess, putting up admirable resistance in three of them before succumbing to the computer's inexorable, reassuring crush.

He climbed into his sleeping loft, the cocoon gladly received after the disconcerting exposure of Alastair's capacious rooms. Snug, exhausted by the day and drained by the chess, he was sure he'd drop quickly into a deep slumber.

But it didn't happen. There was one bit of nettling business wedged in the deeper recesses of his consciousness, hiding for most of the day behind the excitement and mystery and exertion and danger. Or maybe all that excitement had just given him permission not to let it out. Now, in the quiet of the night, there was no more avoiding it.

Surrendering, he climbed down from the loft and slipped *The King's Peach* into his computer's DVD drive.

The first surprise was the production values. No basement paneling or bad lighting here: *The King's Peach* was a full-on period piece made at some expense, a parody of the Oscar winner about the stuttering king of England, only in this version the speech therapist was a woman, equipped with a whole different set of exercises with which to teach His Majesty to relax his jaw muscles and strengthen his tongue, as well as a bevy of other goodies for incentive in his training. Jayne, playing the therapist, performed under the name Kandi Krush.

It was an odd sensation and then some, seeing things he'd seen only the night before, albeit now from third-person angles and sometimes augmented by the big feathered hat. Yet somehow it didn't feel like it had anything to do with *them*, because this didn't feel like *her*. This Kandi was someone else entirely, someone wholly other than the Jayne he'd been starting to fall in love with.

Until.

There was this one moment, several scenes in: the speech therapist was about to be taken from behind by the king's remarkably endowed chancellor of the exchequer (here the plot deviated from the original) and just before it happened Kandi looked over her shoulder at her lover with a fetching glimmer of vulnerability that brought Waldo up short. The camera had been placed near enough to the man's point of view that Waldo in that instant was seeing *exactly* the Jayne he knew, and either way—whether Jayne had been acting for Waldo the night before, or whether Kandi had been letting some kind of truth into her performance (shades of Alastair and Judge Johnny)—it tore him up, and he had to press the eject button and stop the scene.

He climbed back into his sleeping bag and tried to force his way out of consciousness. He reconstructed the opening of his last chess game but couldn't keep a grip on it. There was too much else competing: Jayne and Kandi and a murder charge still to face and Lorena and Don Q and Alastair and Hollywood and acting and stardom and the Mem . . .

. . . and suddenly lightning struck his undersense and he had the play. He scrambled down from the loft again and went back to the computer and pounded and clicked, clicked and pounded, until he found everything he was looking for. Then he dialed a cell number.

Someone answered the line with an unintelligible grunt.

Waldo said, "That you, Nanook?"

The Inuit grunted again.

"Tell your boss I got his goddamn Mem. I'll be in Hollywood tomorrow afternoon, two o'clock. Tell him to meet me at Alex Trebek and don't be late."

He hung up, nestled back into his cocoon and slept like a baby.

TWENTY-FOUR

In his gravity-fed shower, he released just enough water, hauled earlier that morning from his well, to lather his hair with the all-natural shampoo he'd ordered from Oregon, made with wind power from hand- and sustainably harvested bladder wrack seaweed. Even with the most eco-friendly product on the market, he still couldn't wash his hair without getting the willies, thinking of everything he'd spent decades massaging into his scalp without a care and then flushing into the ecosystem: sodium laureth sulfate, ammonium chloride, methylchloroisothiazolinone. Poison, poison, poison.

A smidgen of shampoo stung his eye and he was reaching for the handle and a sooner-than-planned rinse when the shower door flung open and a black-gloved hand flicked out and popped his nose. Through the water and burn he could dimly make out a figure clad in black from balaclava mask to footwear. He was a naked man confronting a ninja.

Instinctively he dropped his arms to shield his damaged rib

cage, allowing the ninja to grab him by his long, lathery hair and wrench him from the tiny stall and out into the cabin proper. The ninja gripped a wrist and wrenched it backward, pinning Waldo's face and naked front against a wall.

"Listen to me," said the ninja in an unexpected voice: a woman's. Of the too-many recent altercations, this was surely the most humiliating in every regard.

"Let me guess," said Waldo. "You want me to stay on my mountain."

The ninja hesitated before saying, surprise in her voice, ". . . Yeah."

"And especially stay away from the Pinch case."

That disconcerted her more. ". . . That's right."

"Who are you? Who sent you?"

Confidence returning, she said, "Doesn't matter. Just don't come back to L.A. unless you want more of this." Her voice was starting to ring familiar. But before he had time to place it she walloped him again, launching ripples of fresh agony from the small of his back and his ribs through his limbic system and cerebral cortex, which converted it into a preternatural animal ferocity that drove the pain from his mind long enough to fling himself from the wall and the lady ninja from his back. By the time she caught her balance, he had somehow gotten hold of the top of her balaclava and jerked it off. That same primitive instinct told him to flee to the woods, to exploit his knowledge of the terrain and find a safe hollow where he might nurse his wounds, so he whacked his predator with his MacBook and made for the door.

Just outside the cabin he lost his footing and toppled. He rolled in the dirt, taking a defensive fetal curl as his attacker followed him out, giving Waldo his first good look at her face and bewildering him to the core. He blinked the last of the shampoo out of his eye, making sure he had it right, and said, "You're Savannah Moon."

This flustered her again; in the heat of the scuffle, she evidently hadn't considered the implications of losing her mask. At last she came back with "I am not!" then scurried to her SUV and drove off. Waldo made a mental note of the license plate, not that he needed it.

He lay on the ground, filthy from rolling wet, his hair a goulash of shampoo and dirt, silently cursing each torturous breath. He stayed there for a while, still, eyes on nothing but the altocumulus drift miles above him, until the throes subsided enough to consider this third discordant puzzle piece.

The Palisades Posse.

Gomes and Jamshidi.

Now Savannah Moon.

What did they have in common? What could they all have against Alastair?

He'd have been tempted to stay out here all day, recovering under the cottony clouds, but he had a date in Hollywood with Don Q. He'd rest on the bus. But before that he was facing the mountain trip to Banning—down, at least—and before that, he'd have to haul a fresh bucket of water from the well and begin his shower all over again.

The kid was solipsistic as only a fifteen-year-old can be and he chafed Waldo's already frayed nerves from the moment he walked into the Banning station. His hair was long and unwashed, his pants so low you could see not only the seat of his impudent American flag boxer shorts but practically the hems. The kid's

Beats Pill speaker, blasted at a volume Waldo associated with Se-
attle Seahawks games, played a hip-hop song whose lyricist must
have felt pretty good about rhyming "smoking grass" with "eating
ass" because he celebrated by repeating the couplet two dozen
times. The kid bought a ticket to L.A., took a seat across from
Waldo in the waiting area and opened a bag of pistachios, the
shells of which he idly flung toward the middle of the floor. Waldo
decided to let the little shit board first so that he could find a seat
as far away as he could.

The bus was more crowded than on his previous trips, though,
and there weren't many doubles with both seats open. The Little
Shit, who'd turned off his music when it came time to board,
took an aisle seat about a third of the way from the front. Because
Waldo didn't want to annoy a passenger alone in a two-seater by
taking the remaining single, he settled for the lone open double,
just two rows behind. From there Waldo had a decent view of
the guy across the aisle from the Little Shit, too old and overweight to bring off the tank top he was wearing, but then his
bleached hair and white sunglasses on a neck cord sold him as a
jackass anyway. The Little Shit began the ride by opening a
smelly bag of fast-food chicken and chucking the wrapper onto
the floor near the Jackass's feet, leaving the Jackass a man in
perfect proportion, equally annoying and annoyed.

Waldo reminded himself that the peevishness two rows up
wasn't his problem and let it go. He attended to his breathing,
trying to keep his inhales consistent and just deep enough not to
trouble his ribs. Immobile in his bus seat and finally untroubled
by pain, he closed his eyes and began to doze.

Then the music came back on. Waldo assumed from the
volume that it was coming from the Little Shit's device, but he

couldn't be sure, as this wasn't bumptious hip-hop but rather a sweetly crooned R&B number, something about overflowing hearts and everlasting tenderness and souls touching. But it turned out the song only *began* with two minutes of hearts and tenderness; after that, another artist stepped in with a rap solo about how his bitch got a pussy like a bag of Skittles, whatever that meant. It sounded like the same guy from the eating-ass song, but either way the rapper didn't have a fan across the aisle, as Waldo could see the Jackass growing more and more agitated.

"*Don't be churchin' up no dirty south,*" blared the song. "*Just sid-down bitch and take care'a your mouth.*"

The Jackass was rocking in his seat like he was going to explode.

"*Brush every morning,*" continued the Skittles guy, "*brush every night, my muthafuckin' teeth is hella white! Teeth can be shiny, teeth can be gold, you fuck with my teeth bitch you ain't growin' old.*"

"Hey, dickhead!" screamed the Jackass when he couldn't take any more, leaning right into the Little Shit's face. "Ever heard of headphones?!"

"I got a right to listen to my music!" screamed the Little Shit over his music.

"Actually, you don't!" screamed the bus driver, joining the fracas from behind the wheel at seventy-five miles an hour. "Put on some headphones or turn it off!"

The kid snapped off the Pill.

It took Waldo a minute or two to place the lyrics. When he did, he stood and walked the few steps to the Little Shit, who looked up at him, braced for another altercation. But Waldo only said, "Who was that you were listening to?"

The kid looked at Waldo as if he'd been asked to explain particle physics, but then gave in to the straightforwardness of the question and answered, "Swag Dog."

"Swag Dog," Waldo repeated, and went back to his seat.

He took out his phone and Googled the name, which turned out to be spelled *Swag Doggg*. Wikipedia said his real name was Leonard Steven Roberson and that he was a rapper-singer-entrepreneur born in Staten Island. Waldo didn't recognize his photograph. He watched parts of two of Swag Doggg's music videos, which were pretty much as expected, then thumbed down through more videos until he got to the obscure interviews and other miscellany. What he was really hoping to find, of course, was a clip that showed off Swag's house, but he settled for something from the red carpet outside a music awards show, which teased Waldo with the descriptor "Swag Doggg explains spelling."

"We've seen it spelled D-A-W-G," said a blonde with a microphone, displaying a lot of cleavage for a journalist. *"We've seen it spelled* D-O-G-G. *But, Swaggy, you're the first artist to spell his name with three G's:* D-O-G-G-G. *What's that about?"*

"The third G *is for God,"* said Swag Doggg.

Swag Doggg's crew—three white kids—crowded into the frame around him and shouted at the camera. The first said, "God! Word!"

The second said, "God is dope!"

The third said, "Da Gizzay!"

Waldo paused the frame. He'd met these guys.

He kept scrolling through screens of YouTube videos until he found another one that intrigued him: Swag wrestling on the ground with a little boy about Gaby's age. It was adorable. And familiar. Waldo looked out the window for a moment, thinking.

His cell buzzed in his hand. He tapped his way to the mail screen with a silent prayer that it would be from Unfinished Business, and the prayer was answered. Her email read only:

Safe??

Waldo thought a long time before typing back, simply:

Working on it

He hit send, then Googled Savannah Moon and found exactly what he thought he might.

It was different being a PI, but maybe in some ways it was the same. Lot of noise when you start, nothing but noise, but then you'd begin to find the first faint beats of a signal hiding in there, and that instant, with all its thrill and promise, always gave him a tingle like nothing else. All these years away, he'd forgotten how he used to live for that moment.

He welcomed it back with a deep sigh of satisfaction and almost passed out from the whammy it put on his ribs.

TWENTY-FIVE

H e got there twenty minutes early, locked up his bike near the Roosevelt Hotel and walked the two blocks to scope the meet point. He was relieved to see that his internet research had gotten it right: Alex Trebek's star on the Walk of Fame was indeed right in front of the US Armed Forces recruiting center, the closest thing to a safe zone Waldo could conjure without involving the police.

He ambled west down Hollywood Boulevard, thinking about how to negotiate a face-to-face with Swag Doggg. Without the authority of a badge, simply locating him could be a challenge. He'd heard that stars do almost everything through their publicists, even arranging dates with each other, so maybe he should start by looking for Swag's. Publicists by definition shouldn't be hard to find.

He doubled back on the opposite side of the street, looking among the stores for a vantage on the foot traffic on both sides and from both directions. He wanted to spot Don Q and Nini before they saw him. He found a souvenir store that would work, with a big open entrance to the street and two racks of postcards to obscure him while he waited.

He was still ten minutes early, so he took a turn around the store and surveyed the cornucopia of shameless junk surrounding him, assaulting him. Having steered clear of the relatively modest kitsch shop at the coroner's, he hadn't been inside anything like it since his transformation. Picking up the first piece of crap he saw, a miniature fake Oscar with a tin plaque that read BEST NEPHEW, he felt the same brew of revulsion and fascination that compelled him to watch a man eat a dozen burgers. He surrendered to it now, studying every display, putting his hands on Thing after Thing that served no purpose but to *be* a Thing, garbage from birth— miniature cars and license plates and plastic animals, miniature currency with pictures of infamous murderers and bad presidents, miniature road signs for the 101 and 66 and Sunset and Wilshire. Hollywood, the store reminded, was hallowed ground, the very Mecca of the Religion of Pointless Waste, its Holy Trinity of Elvis, Marilyn and James Dean available for worship in your own home on matching commemorative plates.

A framed replica of Marlon Brando's Walk of Fame star re-minded him why he was there and he realized it was already one fifty-nine. He stood behind the postcards, looked both ways down the boulevard, and saw Nini and Don Q approaching from the east, half a block away. Across the street, a soldier in camouflage fatigues was coming out of the recruiting station. The grunt lit a cigarette and leaned on a rail. Perfect.

Waldo reached the meet point first and traded friendly nods with the soldier. He leaned on a rail opposite and dialed the gen-eral phone number of Swag Doggg's record label. As he listened to the ring, big Nini and little Don Q settled in on either side of him. The soldier checked them both, watchful, without the pleasant nod he'd given Waldo.

Don Q said, "Army–Navy–Air Force–Marines, I respect the play, Waldo. And Trebek—that's clever shit. 'I'll take Makin' It through the Day Alive for a hunnerd, Alex.'" He chortled, pleased with himself. "Truth is, though, you didn't need to sweat it. Gimme my Mem, you were walkin' away clean anyhow."

Waldo had been hoping to multitask, collecting some information from the record company while simultaneously taunting Don Q with his indifference. When all he got was a recorded message saying he could press his party's extension if he knew it, he settled for the latter and put on a show, ignoring Q and saying into the void, "Hi, my name's Colin Goldman and I'm writing a piece for *Esquire* on the new face of hip-hop."

"What the fuck," said Don Q.

Turning away from him, Waldo said, "I'd like to talk to Swag Doggg—could you put me in touch with his publicist?"

Don Q circled Waldo and looked up at him, eyes to chin. "You shittin' me? I'm takin' hours out of my busy calendar, and you gonna stand here on the phone and chitchat?"

Waldo ignored him again, turning and taking a couple of steps away. Still into the phone, he said, "I could cold call, but if you gave him a ring first as an icebreaker, that would be a big help—"

Nini reached out and snatched the phone from Waldo's hand. Waldo looked Nini in the eye and flicked a cool thumb in the direction of the soldier, who stared at Nini and exhaled smoke through his nostrils. Don Q tipped his head and Nini hit a button, ending the call, but handed the phone back to Waldo.

The soldier, eyes still on Nini, dropped his cigarette butt on the ground, stubbed it with his boot and went back inside. But he'd established himself as a presence and a witness and Waldo felt safe. Better still, he could see he was getting under Don Q's skin.

Don Q said, "Pretty bold to be disrespectin' me, especially in light of Lorena's final hours. You shoulda seen her eyes when I lit that match, bro—"

Waldo cut him off. "I talked to her." It was a stretch but not a lie. Don Q looked at him like it wasn't possible; no doubt he'd been told the same things about Lorena's fiery death that Waldo had, maybe even saw the same photograph. "Uh-huh, she's alive."

"Not what I heard."

"Yeah? Well, A, you weren't the one who killed her, and B, it wasn't Lorena that *got* killed. That was someone else in her husband's car."

Almost under his breath, Don Q said, "Shit."

Waldo said, "But I *do* have your flash drive. So how about you put a lid on the gas-o-line talk and tell me why Lorena was messing with you in the first place."

"I don't gotta answer your questions."

"You do if you want the Mem."

Don Q fell quiet and then said, "Nini, go buy yourself an ice cream cone."

Nini threw Waldo a glare but left, heading east on Hollywood toward the Chinese Theatre.

Don Q said, "When I find that bitch, she *is* dead. You know that."

Waldo didn't say anything.

"Lorena was workin' for me. Not what you think." Waldo

wondered what Q thought he thought. "Marital surveillance, for my sister. Watchin' my lazy-ass brother-in-law."

"Go on."

"First my sister don't like what Lorena drags up. Then she don't like *Lorena*. Then she wants me to renegotiate Lorena's fee."

Waldo shook his head.

"Don't look at me like that. My sister's trouble, man. She scares me. She scares *Nini*."

Two beatings, days of grieving over Lorena, plus somebody *did* get burned to death in Lorena's husband's car, whoever and whyever that was. Waldo said, "That's your problem with Lorena? A billing dispute?"

"Started that way. Coulda been resolved a lot easier, but your girl had to go and escalate. Came to see me at this chop shop in Pacoima I use for an office. I got my laptop out, bitch sees this Mem stick sittin' there and palms it. *Palms my Mem.* Calls me later, tells me it's collateral on the sum she claims I owe her."

"The sum you *do* owe her."

"Waldo. First rule of life in the private sector: you only owe what the owe-ee can collect."

Waldo said, "This is bullshit. You want the Mem, it's simple— let Lorena come back to L.A. Whack out the rest in small claims court."

"No deal. Fuck up my rep, I let her get away with that kinda disrespect."

"What do you suggest?"

"I don't gotta suggest nothin'. You need to hand that shit over. Time's on my side. Lorena pops up, I kill her. Mem pops up, I kill you. And before *that*, I find you alone, without the benefit of half the fuckin' Pentagon—"

Before he could finish the thought, Big Jim Cuppy was on them, saying, "Okay, assbags—against the wall. Both of you." He spun Waldo off the rail and began to pat him down. Don Q assumed the frisk position without assistance.

The same soldier burst out of the recruiting center, ready to bust it up. "Problem out here?"

"LAPD," Cuppy said. "All under control." The soldier looked Waldo's way, not sure he was buying it. Cuppy flashed his badge and said, "Back to your tank, GI Joe. I got this." The soldier took a step toward him but, presumably deciding that punching out an LAPD wasn't worth the paperwork, sniggered and went back inside.

Don Q said, "Cuppy, man—you should have more respect for the brave men and women who protect our way of life."

Cuppy found Waldo's Beretta tucked in the back of his jeans. "Looky, looky. You got a permit for this? 'Cause if not, I could send you to live in a *state* cabin for a couple years. You'd like it— they let you keep about *ten* things."

Don Q cackled. Waldo scowled at him. "Sorry, Waldo, but that shit is risible. That means it's *funny*."

Cuppy stuck the Beretta into his own belt and resumed patting Waldo down.

Waldo said, "If you're looking for this asshole's flash drive, you're out of luck. I didn't bring it."

Don Q flared. "*What?!* But you brought a *piece*?! You *are* one nervy muthafucker."

Cuppy turned Waldo back around. "Where is it?"

Waldo answered with only a shit-eating grin.

"Okay, then," Cuppy said, turning to Don Q. "We'll do it this way: you're under arrest for the murder of Lorena Nascimento."

He turned back to Waldo. "And you are an accomplice." He reached for his handcuffs.

Don Q cackled again and said to Waldo, "Want to read this boy the six o'clock news?"

Waldo said to Cuppy, "You can't arrest me for Lorena."

"No? Why not?"

"You didn't have an ID from the lab when you showed me that picture, did you."

"So?"

"So she's alive. I've heard from her."

"You're lying." Waldo imagined the mockery and abasement Cuppy would endure when it was discovered that he'd arrested two men for the homicide of a perfectly healthy woman. It must have bubbled into a smug and confident grin, because Cuppy read it and said, "*Fuck!*"

Waldo looked from Cuppy to Q and back. "Can I just say? Both of you suck at your jobs."

Q took his hands off the wall. "Cuppy wasn't gonna book us for Lorena anyway. He plays that bullshit with me alla time, reachin' for any new squeeze he can think of, see if it'll work. That's what *all* this shit's about, even the Mem: I'm the only businessman in town don't grease this cocksucker."

Seething, Cuppy said, "Little man, you ought to watch your mouth on days you don't have that douchebag Eskimo following you around."

Waldo nodded at something over Cuppy's shoulder.

Cuppy turned to see Nini standing right behind him, eating a pink ice cream cone, double scoop. He handed the cone to Waldo, crumpled Cuppy with an overhand right, then reclaimed the cone and took another lick.

Don Q apparently wasn't considering all this a bonding episode. He said to Waldo, "Next time I see you, you ain't carryin' a
little present for me, I'm breakin' a piece offa you instead. C'mon,
Nini."

Don Q stepped over Cuppy and he and Nini headed back down
Hollywood Boulevard.

Cuppy sat up, blinking like a man who hadn't been concussed
in a while. Waldo said, "'Eskimo' is pejorative," which befuddled
the woozy cop even more, as did the hand Waldo offered to help
him stand. Cuppy was big and useless and Waldo needed a second arm around his waist to lift him, giving his rib cage a fresh
twinge. Cuppy stood on the sidewalk, trying to shake out the
cobwebs. Waldo clapped him on the arm and pointed him in the
opposite direction from the others, and Cuppy tottered away.

Waldo took his Beretta, which he'd plucked from the rear of
Cuppy's belt, and discreetly shoved it back into his own. Cuppy's
badge he tossed in a sewer.

TWENTY-SIX

H is presence still unsettled the Stoddard campus, and when he entered the main office unescorted the receptionists looked skittish. He told them who he was and that he was working for Alastair, but they already knew and hearing it again didn't soothe them.

Hexter passed through from an inner office and asked if he needed something. Waldo said he'd like to see a roster of students, ideally by grade, with names of their parents as well. Hexter answered with his eyes that Waldo was about as welcome at the school as a lice outbreak. Waldo remembered the note in the mysterious DVD package urging him to delve into Jayne's relationship with the headmaster, and also his dark glower when Jayne was helping Waldo into her car. Thinking back on the first day, when Hexter hadn't even wanted Waldo to talk to Jayne, it was almost as if he'd known something would develop. Still, he now instructed one of the assistants to show Waldo a copy of the directory.

Waldo thanked him, accepted the wire-bound book, and started to leave. Hexter said curtly that it needed to stay in the office, so Waldo took a seat. Authority reasserted, the headmaster continued out.

Waldo thumbed through the directory, which opened with the twelfth graders and continued down to the kindergarteners. The elementary school classes were subdivided by room, two per grade. Alphabetically behind the other kindergarten teacher, a Lynne Solis, Jayne White's pages were the last in the book. Waldo's eye went first to "Gaby Pinch, parents Monica & Alastair Pinch," the ampersand giving their marriage a deceptively simple gloss. Other families' complications were on more open display via clumsy but eloquent punctuation, semicolons of divorce and sometimes a re-ampersand: Gaby's classmates included "Shannon Cameron, parents Kami Cameron; Cliff Cameron," and "Max Kemper, parents Leigh Kemper; Douglas & Isabel Kemper," and "Mariah Weaver, parents Amber Tate & Jacqueline Hough; Gregg Weaver & Pablo Etchevarria," the last of which surely betokened the most intriguing Thanksgiving.

More important, Gaby's classmates also included one "Travaris Roberson, parents Leonard & Elise," confirming Waldo's expectations. Little Swaggy Junior had learned "Brush Every Morning" from Ms. White, just like Gaby Pinch had.

Then there was "Yasmin Jamshidi, parents Soraya Jamshidi; Whitney & Darius Jamshidi."

But Waldo had trouble finding the third classmate. He scanned the list twice more and when that failed checked Ms. Solis's kindergarten roster. It wasn't until his fourth time through Jayne's list that his subconscious did a bit of hocus-pocus with "Jared Moskowitz, parents Sarah & Mitch Moskowitz" and he knew

he'd found his little man; he began smiling even before Wikipedia confirmed Savannah Moon's birth name.

He took pictures of the relevant pages on his phone, gave the
directory back to the assistant and went outside to the empty
playground. He leaned on a jungle gym and took inventory.
There are no accidents. Savannah Moon, Darius Jamshidi and
Swag Doggg were all fellow kindergarten parents of the Pinches,
and all three had gone to lengths to dissuade Waldo from the
case. Assuming they'd all met through their kids, what had these
rich people gotten into? Were they culpable for Monica's death?
Or were they just conjoined in their hatred of Alastair and desire to see him punished, guilty or not? And why had Alastair
claimed not to know Jamshidi? Or was it plausible that he in fact
didn't?

As long as Waldo was here, he'd start by checking in with
Jayne, who must know them all, probably even the semicolons
and re-ampersands. He crossed the playground to her classroom
and knocked on her window.

He'd intended to ask a simple, direct question—*What did the
Pinches have in common with the Robersons and the Jamshidis and
the Moskowitzes?*—but when he caught her eye and she smiled at
him, the constellation of parents flew from his head and all he
could think of was her vulnerable over-the-shoulder look at her
well-equipped costar, and when she opened the door what came
out of his mouth was "Who is who they are?"

With only that, she knew that he knew, or that he knew *something*, and her smile dropped; she looked at him like she was
waiting to be struck.

He said, "*The King's Peach?*"

"How'd you find out?"

"My guess? One of your coworkers doesn't like you very much." Jayne bit her lip and looked away. Waldo said, "Did you think you could keep it a secret?"

A little girl appeared in the doorway and pulled at her shirt. "Ms. White! Ms. White! I got glue in my shoe!"

Jayne said to Waldo, "Can we do this later?"

He realized he hadn't come near the subject that mattered and said, "I've got to ask you about some of the other parents—"

The girl held up the gluey shoe. "Look!"

She said to the girl, "I'll be right with you," and to Waldo, apologetic, "I have to . . ." He nodded understanding and surrender. She said, "Are you coming to the play tonight?" When he balked, she said, "You have to see Gaby. We can talk afterward." She closed the door and went back to her charges.

Waldo kicked himself for having lost focus. But still and always there was something about Jayne that wouldn't stop knocking him off his game.

He would come back tonight and try her again after Gaby's play. Anyway, she wasn't the one most likely to help him; that was Alastair, who, even if he honestly didn't know the relatively anonymous Jamshidi, had to be aware that his kid shared a classroom with these other children of the famous. And it was possible that, even through his perpetual haze of booze and self-absorption, he'd picked up on enough around him to offer some light on what this grab barrel of celebrities had to do with the murder of his wife.

An audacious young district attorney, better dressed and squarer jawed than any Waldo had encountered in his years in the criminal justice system, was calling out the secret affair between Judge Johnny and the defense attorney played by Naomi Tompkins-Jones. "Your Honor," he said to Johnny on the bench, "if an outside personal relationship *does* exist, I insist you recuse yourself from this case."

Judge Johnny narrowed his eyes at the cheeky prosecutor. Silence hung heavy in the courtroom, all present waiting to hear how the imposing jurist would respond to this challenge to his authority and integrity.

At length, Judge Johnny said, "'Two loves I have of comfort and despair, / Which like two spirits do suggest me still . . .'"

The DA's brow furrowed. The defense attorney deflated. The director started in on a cuticle.

"'The better angel is a man right fair, / The worser spirit a woman colour'd ill. / To win me soon to hell, my female evil / Tempteth my better angel from my side . . .'" Alastair played the lines alternately to the actors/lawyers before him.

The director leaned toward the script supervisor and whispered, "What the fuck is he doing now?"

The script supervisor whispered back, "I think it's a sonnet."

"'And would corrupt my saint to be a devil . . .'"

"Are you going to cut?"

"Yeah," the director whispered, "I'm going to stop him in the middle of this. That's exactly what I'm going to do."

"'Wooing his purity with her foul pride . . .'"

The script supervisor whispered, "We're not going to make our day."

The director, not really whispering anymore, said, "No shit."

So the cameras rolled and the other actors more or less held their positions and everybody waited until Alastair finished.

"'. . . Yet this shall I ne'er know, but live in doubt, / Till my bad angel fire my good one out.'" By way of final punctuation he simpered at Naomi, who raised a lip and walked off the set.

The director mustered counterfeit good nature, shouted "Bravo, Alastair!" and clapped his hands. He threw encouraging glances at the script supervisor and other crew members, drumming up a full-company round of applause. Alastair basked in the ovation.

"Now let's do one where we use the script," said the director, pleasantly, as if floating a spontaneous new thought. "Just for giggles."

"I think not," said Alastair, definitive.

Waldo studied the director, whose twitch had returned with a vengeance.

Alastair said, "I've been drinking vodka since this morning. *That*," he said, "is wholly inappropriate."

Waldo leaned in; he could feel the crew doing the same. Was this something new? Self-awareness?

Maybe not. Alastair said, "Vodka makes me confrontational."

The moment hung there, until the prop man had an idea. "Would you prefer brandy?"

"No!" shouted Alastair, slapping down the offer. He further explained, in a softer tone, "Brandy makes me cruel; lager makes me sleepy; tequila, sentimental." He pointed to Naomi, who was sitting in a director's chair near Waldo with her wardrobe heels off, rubbing her feet. "I just spent a night with this fair creature in glorious, multi-orgasmic splendor . . ."

"Whatever," said Naomi under her breath.

"This scene wants a romantic undertone." Alastair turned to the director. "Wouldn't you agree, love?"

The director, looking like a man with one foot on a land mine, said, "Absolutely."

"Therefore," said the actor, with a triumphant flourish, *"ouzo."*

After a moment, the prop man said, "What's ouzo?"

Putting on warmhearted patience, Alastair said, "It's an aperitif, flavored of anise. Have you any here?"

"I'll get some," said the prop man, knowing the gig, and scurried away.

"Well," said the star, "when he does, we shall play the scene properly. Till then, I shall be in my trailer." With that, he strutted toward the exit.

Waldo took one more look at the director, the poor bastard, then trotted after Alastair. He caught up with him just outside the door. *"Hey."*

Alastair said, "Detective. I thought I saw you lurking."

Waldo cut right to it. "Tell me about Swag Doggg and Savannah Moon."

"I don't know what any of those words mean." He corrected himself. "Not true: I know what they *all* mean, just not in that order."

"They both happen to be parents in your daughter's kindergarten class. Darius Jamshidi, too. They all wanted me to stay in my woods and away from your case. Monica was in the middle of something with them, and it may be that one or more wanted her dead. For damn sure they're happy to let you take the fall. *Now, what the hell is going on in that kindergarten class?"*

"Finger painting?" said Alastair, stepping onto the wooden steps to his trailer and opening his screen door. "Show-and-tell?"

First the lies about the burner and now this. Waldo grabbed him by the arm. *"Hey, asshole—I'm trying to save your life."* Alastair, stunned at the temerity, let the door swing closed. "Cut the self-indulgence and self-pity—you've got a terrific little girl who's lost a mother and doesn't need to lose her father too just because he doesn't have the stones for a real fight."

Alastair shook his arm loose. "Nobody talks to me that way. You know why?"

"Because they need the money."

"Because," he corrected, "they know they'll get a thrashing for the ages." He started rolling up his sleeves. Waldo shook his head and walked away. "Your turn now, love," the actor said after him.

"Come on, Alastair, I don't want to fight you," he said, turning back. "Seriously. Since this started, all I've *done* is fight—banger wannabes, Eskimos, *girls* . . ."

"And now," Alastair said, "one living legend." He took three deliberate steps and unfurled a roundhouse right, which Waldo slipped with ease.

Alastair tried the same but southpaw, again drew nothing but air.

Alastair charged like a mad bull; Waldo evaded like a cool matador. Alastair lunged again, arms out to the sides this time, sacrificing cover but making this rush impossible to dodge.

All Waldo wanted was to avoid a hit to the ribs, and the longer he let this go on, the more likely he was to get one. So he unloaded with a right cross to the jaw; Alastair did him the favor of multiplying its force by running straight into it. The actor spun a full one-eighty and landed knees first on the blacktop, then hands and face.

He lay still long enough for Waldo to worry, then flipped onto his back and shouted, "Well *done,* sir!" Propping himself on an elbow, he twinkled and said, "Now that we've got that out of our systems, let's the two of us have a drink. Help me up." Waldo did, flummoxed. "Do you like rugby, Waldo? You'd be right tasty company at the Scotland matches."

Steady on his feet again, Alastair cocked his fists, apparently ready for another round. Waldo grudgingly did likewise. But Alastair let loose a guffaw, threw an arm around Waldo and steered him back to the trailer. "Come on, now, Waldo," he said, "you remember having mates, don't you?" In truth, Waldo barely could; regardless, he was sure he'd never had a mate like Alastair Pinch.

Inside, Waldo took a seat at the table while Alastair poured two generous glasses of vodka over ice, downed one and refilled it before handing Waldo the other. "I'm drunk, Waldo."

"You don't say."

"I mean more than usual. Have been all day. I knew I was in no condition to play that courtroom scene worth a damn. That's why I behaved so unforgivably on the set. I'm not proud of it. I just want you to understand: it was all because I care so about the work." He raised his glass in a toast. "To 'self-indulgence and self-pity'—that's how you put it just now, wasn't it?" Alastair drank; Waldo didn't. The actor unfolded himself on the sofa, setting a pillow under his head. "Powerful observation, coming from the master."

"Meaning . . . ?"

"Meaning you and I are two sides of the same coin, aren't we." He yawned and stretched. He'd pass out soon.

Waldo wanted information before he lost him. "Savannah Moon," he prompted again. "Swag Doggg."

But Alastair was rolling down a different track entirely. "You know what you should have done when your young man Lipps was killed? You should've gone on an epic pub crawl—two weeks, at least. Just gotten it all out of your system . . . then gone right back to the job. Instead, you chose to make *his* tragedy *yours*. Self-indulgence and self-pity. Killing yourself, without killing yourself." He raised the glass again, a secondary toast. "But now here you are: back among the living, in a way you weren't a week ago."

The drunken observations shook him. "You see a difference?"

"All the difference in the world! The way you confronted me today—you didn't have that in you when you first shuffled onto my set with that rat's nest of a beard and those dead eyes. You've been brought back to life, mate." Alastair was slurring now, drifting toward slumber, but he kept muttering. "Brought back to life like so many of us . . . by singular carnal charms."

The truth of it abashed Waldo and he stood to leave. There was nothing more to gain from this interview anyway.

His footsteps obscured what Alastair said next, but it sounded like "Is Jayne keeping the baby?"

Waldo turned around. "What did you say?"

Eyes closed, Alastair mumbled, "I do think about her all the time . . . but I haven't felt I could telephone, given the circum-stances . . ." Waldo came closer to better hear Alastair's rambling as it grew softer. "I was such a cad . . . especially after she told me . . . but I was a married man, after all, and maybe it wasn't even mine . . . and then, after Monica . . ." Alastair heaved the heaviest sigh Waldo had ever heard. "I'm tired, Waldo," he said, and finally fell silent, turmoil unmistakable on his face even as he dropped off.

Waldo was sure he was out so he headed for the door. But before the last stray wisps of consciousness slipped away, Alastair murmured, "Fearing you're not as good as you're believed to be . . . that's common to all . . . but fearing you may actually be a monster . . . that's a whole different flavor of hell."

Waldo lingered to be sure that was really the last of it, then slipped out of the trailer, leaving Alastair to sleep, or maybe damning him to it.

TWENTY-SEVEN

All he wanted now was his solitude back, not to be seen, not to be known. He wanted his woods. The closest thing, literally, was Fryman Canyon Park, a recreation area very near to Alastair's house with a well-trafficked hiking trail that offered stunning city vistas but also tributaries into forests deep enough for isolation. He had almost five hours to kill anyway: if Alastair had nothing to offer on Swag Doggg or Savannah Moon, then Waldo's next moves were confrontations with Jayne or the other parents, any of whom he might be able to corner at the school tonight. Nor was there anything he could to do for Lorena until he heard from her again and could ask how she wanted to play it. Besides, the longer Don Q had to wait, the more inclined he might be to cut a deal.

Once he'd hiked far enough off the main trail that he could no longer hear voices or human footsteps, the thoughts started tumbling. This whole experiment, leaving his property and resuming contact with society, had gone horribly wrong. He was out of practice with humanness; he understood nothing; one morning he wondered if he was falling in love and just a day and a half later intimacy had crumbled into humiliation. The shame pushed him deeper still into the woods.

How had Alastair known? He said he hadn't been in touch with her, and his regret seemed genuine. Had he simply foreseen the inevitability of Waldo and Jayne from the first moment, when he'd left the two of them alone in Gaby's classroom? How could he? He didn't know Waldo. But he did know *her*, didn't he—and not the Jayne Waldo *thought* he knew, the kindergarten teacher choirgirl; he knew the *real* Jayne, and when Waldo didn't return to the house as promised and resurfaced two days later, Alastair had no doubt whom he'd been with, no doubt who'd taken his beard.

How many other lovers would Alastair have to have known about, to be so certain she'd seduce Waldo too? How many other men had seen that captivating look over her shoulder?

The real torment, truth be told, was that *Alastair* had seen it, had experienced her just as Waldo had. And Alastair knowing about Waldo—even before it happened—while he himself had no idea about Alastair made him feel like a dupe.

Not Alastair's dupe, though. Jayne's. How could she not tell him? The facets of the betrayal were too numerous to apprehend all at once. The most charitable explanation—the one that in his belly he desperately wanted to be true—was that her feelings for Waldo were real, that she'd lurched into an involvement with him and then found herself with no way to reveal her history with Alastair without fatally complicating their compelling new connection. But leaving his belly out of it, the explanation didn't hold. Real feelings hadn't developed yet that first night when they'd had a drink after her choir practice, a date she'd only drawn him into anyhow by dangling a spurious hint. No, she'd flirted with a purpose and must have seduced him with a purpose, too. But what was it?

He traipsed through the forest, turning it all round and round in his mind, trying to tease out reason from pain, sense from anger, understanding from jealousy. He wandered that way for hours, and though he couldn't quite decipher her motive in enchanting him, the rest of the puzzle pieces—even the ones that had seemed to be misfits—were starting to form a picture, albeit a picture that wasn't easy to look at.

He heard children's voices before he realized he'd reached an edge of Fryman Park and that the clearing ahead was someone's backyard, with three kids playing in a lavish tree fort, a large two-story Tudor beyond. The shadows had grown longer and Waldo decided he'd better find his way back to the main trail before he lost the light. These were not his woods.

The audience thrummed, scores of ampersands and semicolons anticipating the debut performances of their five-year-olds, cell phone videocams at the ready. He took a quick peek inside and noted Alastair sitting by himself on the far aisle, keeping a considerate distance. For all the actor's proclaimed indifference to the masses, the whispers and ostracism of the other parents had to torture him. It was a measure of his devotion to his daughter that he showed up anyway.

Waldo didn't linger in the auditorium. He followed shrieks and chatter to a nearby classroom, where Jayne, dressed for the event in a frilly lavender blouse and dress pants, fussed at the kindergarteners' costumes. A couple of class moms did the same. Jayne noticed him in the doorway and offered a nervous smile, invitation enough for him to wade carefully through the phalanx of overexcited five-year-olds.

"I'm glad you came," she said, fastening a little girl's bonnet with a bobby pin. "Now, don't touch that anymore before you go on—okay, Jessie?" The little girl ran off without thanking her.

Waldo said, "Why didn't you tell me about Alastair?"

Jayne studied him a moment before saying, "There's nothing to tell. He's a kindergarten dad." He wasn't sure what he'd been expecting, but the lie crushed him anew.

Her cell phone rang. She took it from the pocket of her slacks, looked at the number and went pale.

Waldo said, "Don't you want to answer it?"

With unsteady hands she killed the ring and put the phone back in her pocket. "It's not important."

"Don't worry—it's not Alastair," Waldo said, disorienting her more. "It's me." He pulled Alastair's burner from his own jeans. "I found this at his house, hidden away," he said quietly, leaning toward her. "Before his wife was killed he texted back and forth with someone, inviting her over." He nodded toward the phone in her pocket. "*Someone.*"

Jayne watched the roomful of kids while Waldo watched her. She inhaled, then checked the wall clock. "Let's go to my room." She told one of the moms where she'd be and Waldo followed her out and down the outdoor hallway to her classroom.

He closed the door behind them. "Did you also have a thing with Leonard Roberson? Swag Doggg?"

"Yes."

"And Jamshidi?"

"Yes."

"And what about Savannah Moon? Are you into women too?"

"I thought you watched the movie," she said. Shedding her secrets made her plucky.

It annoyed him. He said, "And you got pregnant."

Ambushed, her self-possession evaporated. After a beat, she confirmed it with a shaky nod.

"Are you still?"

She nodded again.

"Is it Alastair's?" She swallowed and looked like she might start crying. He asked her the same question again and she nodded a third time. "So that's it: I've been getting threatened and jumped all week, not because of Monica Pinch—because of *you*. It's just a bunch of rich people who didn't want their tawdry affairs with their kid's teacher found out."

"They're not tawdry." It was his turn to cock an eyebrow. "What do you want, Waldo? It's how I've made this work."

"How you've made *what* work?"

"*This*. Teaching fucking *kindergarten*." He sat on one of the undersize desks. She kept going, answering the unasked question of how she ended up there in the first place. "My life was messed up, okay? *Seriously* messed up. I needed stability—and someone wanted to help me and hooked me up with the job."

Waldo said, "I can guess who that was." Someone who had to watch, in pain, from his top-floor corner office as the girl he'd taken into his bed and under his wing carried on with Waldo, and Alastair, and God only knew how many others.

She said, "Don't even go there." There was a fierceness in her warning, a timbre he hadn't heard from her before; however she'd come to treat Hexter, she was going to protect him, repayment for whatever it was he'd once done to save her. "I mean it: do not bring him into this." Waldo held up his hands in acquiescence. "The thing is," she said, softening, "as fucked up as everything was back then? At least it was . . . *interesting.* Do you know what it's like to have your whole life be about a roomful of five-year-olds? It was like I'd suddenly gotten old. But then these incredibly successful people started flirting with me, and it was . . . a *lifeline.* I could have a *little* excitement, without the whole thing going off the rails again. And then when they started getting out of their minds jealous of each other? Over *me?* It was a rush."

She'd knocked him off his pins again, this time with the straightforwardness of her take on her own life, almost innocent, oblivious to the damage she radiated. He said, "It's all fun and games until somebody gets her skull bashed in."

"Look, after Monica, I backed off, with everybody."

"You didn't back off me."

"That was different."

"Of course it was. Sleeping with the detective investigating a death you were involved in? That had to be the biggest rush of all."

"Okay, yeah, at the beginning that's what it was about. But you know it turned into more, Waldo. I really felt something." She stepped toward him. "You did, too."

"Start from the beginning." His tone stopped her. "And no bullshit." He wasn't going to fall for it again. She'd been in the Pinch house the night Monica was killed and he had to know everything she knew. None of the rest mattered. And if Charlie Waldo had proven that he had any talent at all, it was for detaching, and staying detached.

"Okay," she said, stepping back, "the night it happened—"

"Not that beginning. The beginning where you told Alastair you were pregnant."

She considered her answer before speaking again. "It was an accident, but I knew who I'd been with and when, and I was sure it was his. Whatever I was going to do, he needed to know about it, and, yes, if I was going to do something, it would have been nice if he'd help me out with the money. This job doesn't pay a whole lot. But he didn't even engage—his whole response was to tell me how his wife wanted him to move back to England with her. Like he wasn't even hearing what I was saying to him. Or didn't give a shit. After that, total radio silence. On *his* end. I kept texting him, which made me feel stupid as hell. Finally, like three weeks later, I got this text saying he missed me. And that I should come over and that his wife would be gone all night."

It squared with what Waldo had seen on the burner. "What did you do?"

"I figured he finally wanted to talk about it. Or something, I don't know, maybe he did just want to see me again. And I wanted to see him. We had a thing, you know? I had his baby inside me. So I drove over. I had to get his address from the school directory, if you can believe that, which made me feel even stupider.

"Anyway, when I got there, before I could even ring the bell, *Monica* opened the door. I almost ran right back to my car. But she goes, 'Come in.' I didn't know what was going on—I didn't know if Alastair told her or something, or if she just came home unexpectedly and the move was for me to try to play it off like I was there for Gaby—the whole thing was so freaky, I wasn't even thinking straight.

"Then when I get inside, she's holding up Alastair's phone,

and almost, like, shaking. She tells me *she's* the one that texted me to come over. She goes, 'Alastair's upstairs, passed out.' And she says she found this second phone he has, and they had a fight—"

"A fight?"

"An *argument,* I guess. I guess he told her he got somebody pregnant, but he didn't say who. And then when he passed out, she decided to figure it out herself. So she sent me that 'I miss you' text—and I took the bait."

"What happened when she saw it was you?"

"She went bananas. Her daughter's teacher?"

"Bananas how?"

"The more she talked, the more . . . *unhinged* she got. She probably was drinking, too. It wasn't focused on me, it wasn't even *him* she was pissed at, it was *L.A.* She went on and on about what a mistake it was to come here, how the whole city was evil. But she was so intense about it—seriously, I was afraid she was going to get violent. So when I had a clear path to the door, I just ran out to my car, locked the door and drove the fuck away."

"That was it?"

"That was it. The next day it was on the news she was dead."

"What did you do when you heard?"

"I didn't know *what* to do. My first thought was to reach out to Alastair, but I didn't know how. I didn't want to get him in more trouble by calling *that* phone." She indicated Waldo's pocket. "And I didn't think I should call his regular cell. One time I did try their home phone from the school office—I figured that was safe—but I got the machine.

"After a couple days he started driving Gaby again, and I tried to talk to him, but he blew me off. *Total* asshole. I mean, yeah, I know he's got problems, but I'm still pregnant, right? You'd think he'd at least not *ignore* me at pickup.

"Whatever—I saw that was how it was going to be. So when the chips started falling on him, I figured, fuck it, and just let them fall." Jayne looked at the clock and said, "The play's going to start."

"Let me ask you one thing first. *Two* things." She bounced on her feet, restless. "Do you think he killed her?"

"What am I supposed to say to that?"

"Let me put it this way: do you think he *could* have?"

"*Could* have? Sure. Was that the second question?"

"No, one more: when you said that before, about all these people being out of their minds jealous . . . *how* jealous? Do you think anybody else might have gone over to Alastair's that night, because of you?"

"Because of me . . . ?" It was something she hadn't considered, but watching her weigh it and seeing the knowing smile sidle across her lips, he could tell it wasn't out of the question, that it might even have pleased her. He wondered which of the others she was picturing.

There was a rap at the door and it opened before Jayne could answer. It was one of the moms from the other classroom. "Jayne— we're ready to start."

"Right there," Jayne said, and the mom left. "I've got to go," she said to Waldo and started toward the door.

"I'm not done with you."

He'd meant it as a warning, but she somehow spun it into an invitation, saying, "I was hoping you weren't," then she left him alone, beguiled again despite himself.

TWENTY-EIGHT

No fool, Gaby's teacher, casting the progeny of Alastair Pinch in the title role. But even as the girl commanded the stage, Waldo's attention was elsewhere—in part on that teacher, wondering what she'd left out of her story, and in part on her other lovers and their spouses, scattered about the audience. There was Alastair, enraptured by his daughter's performance. There were the short and tall Jamshidis; there was Swag Doggg with a woman, presumably the still ampersanded Mrs. Doggg. There was Sarah/Savannah Moskowitz/Moon, whose husband annoyed the rest of the cell phone video crowd by planting himself unapologetically in front of the dozen who'd staked places earlier. There, standing alone against a wall, was Dr. Hexter, paterfamilias and über-impresario, haughty chin at prep school tilt.

Green eyes darted in every direction. Waldo had been granted full membership in their circle of sexual jealousy and knew that they were as aware of him as he of them. Indeed, more than wicked thoughts and glances might have been flying too, were it not for the conventions of polite society and fear of discovery; surely envy had juiced Savannah's blows when she had assaulted Waldo in his cabin. *Brought back to life like so many of us,* Alastair had said, *by singular carnal charms.* Jayne's charms were very much on Waldo's mind right now. They'd juice anybody's blows.

Sex, jealousy, violence—had Monica Pinch accidentally gotten caught in the middle of all that somehow? Once again he struggled to tease out the hints and data from the other distractions. Once again, Jayne was jamming his radar.

After the play ended to a standing ovation, there was a reception in the concrete courtyard outside the auditorium, store-bought baked goods for the kids, little plastic cups of wine for the parents. Waldo canvassed the crowd but didn't see Jayne. Gaby, still in costume, came running up. "Mr. Lion! Wasn't I good?"

"You were excellent."

"Next time I want a better part."

"You were the star."

"Yeah, but I had to play a boy. Next time I want to be a princess."

Actors, he thought. "Have you seen your teacher?"

"Ms. White?" Gaby turned to look around for her but immediately saw something more interesting. "Hey!" she yelled to a kid dressed as a jester on the nearby playground. "Where'd you get the brownie?!" and ran off after him to find out.

Waldo waited for Jayne, took in the scene. The second Mrs. Jamshidi gave him the stink eye. He'd have liked a minute or two with Swag Doggg, but the rapper had his son riding on his shoulders; any attempt would backfire. He settled for shoulder-bumping Savannah Moon as he brushed past and saying into her ear, "Nice to see you again, Sarah," just for effect.

After a while he wandered over to Alastair, by himself, affecting a deep study of the wall of plaques celebrating the school's original donors. When Waldo approached he said, "The innocents oughtn't have to shake hands with the leper."

"Why don't you go home?"

Alastair indicated the playground and Gaby, now atop a jungle gym, lesser cast members surrounding her on the lower levels. "The starlet deserves her night."

"You're a good dad."

Alastair snorted.

"Have you seen Jayne?"

"Unaccounted for, is she? Not the first time," he said, smirking. "Take attendance—that may be a clue; who's missing?" Waldo did a head count: the other parent-lovers and headmaster were all in view. Of course, that didn't preclude another conquest from beyond the known roster.

"Take your little girl home," he told Alastair. "You've done plenty for her this evening." He made sure to lock eyes until the actor nodded acquiescence and went to fetch his daughter.

Waldo waited until the crowd thinned before giving up. He tried the classroom where Jayne had prepped the kids, but it was shut down for the night, then tried her own classroom and found the same. He decided Jayne's no-show had been just another flirtation, designed to torque his curiosity and desire.

Well, it worked. He got his bike and headed for her apartment.

He knocked on her door. No answer. He tried the knob and was surprised that it opened.

The lights were on. The room looked more or less as it had when he'd been there before but something felt off. It took a moment for him to finger it: a hook on an empty wall, where that country lithograph had hung before. He went into her bedroom and straight for the closet. It was empty. His stomach dropped.

Skipping the reception and driving here while Waldo biked would have given her maybe a forty-five-minute jump on him, too little time to pack and load her car; she had to have started earlier. Bracing her in the afternoon had probably rattled her— not enough to miss the play she'd rehearsed so hard with her kids, but enough to blow out as soon as it was over.

Other than clothes and toiletries, she'd left most everything, even the Savannah Moon DVDs and books. The boy fishing by the covered bridge had meant more to her. Perplexed and disconsolate, ashamed and apprehensive, Waldo inventoried the room, wondering what else she'd been willing to leave behind. On her bed, atop the pillow, he saw a white letter-size envelope, with his name written in a girlish hand.

It contained one item: a pink disposable razor, a women's Schick Quattro.

He held on to it while he examined the rest of the apartment, but before he left he tossed it into the garbage can under the kitchen sink, a Thing he had no room for.

He didn't want to tell Alastair that Jayne had run off, but he didn't want *not* to tell him either, so back at the house that night he avoided his host, and pretended to sleep late the next morning. He only lit out for the Stoddard School after he was certain Alastair had already dropped Gaby off and was well on his way to the studio.

There he checked Jayne's classroom and saw the expected substitute trying to settle the kids, still worked up from their big night. He crossed to the main office, asked to see the headmaster and was told to wait. Twenty minutes later an assistant told him to take the stairs to the top floor and then a right. The woman at the desk in Hexter's outer office told him to go right in.

Hexter was seated at his desk. Waldo closed the door behind him and without pleasantries said, "Jayne White's disappeared."

"I don't know about *disappeared*. She did call in sick this morning."

"She cleared out of her apartment. I thought she might have said something to you first. Given your . . . personal history."

Hexter flinched, then went with a slippery nondenial. "Someone's been gossiping. Another teacher, I assume." Waldo kept silent, letting Hexter twist and seeing where he'd take it. "The rest of the elementary faculty wasn't happy I hired her. Trust me, though: a lot of what people say about Jayne's past is exaggerated."

Waldo had lain awake the night before, chewing on Jayne's flight and what had triggered it. She'd packed in the afternoon, before the play, before Waldo had challenged her on her relationships with Alastair and the others, before Waldo had called her on being at the Pinch house on the night of the murder. All he'd dinged her with at that point was the video, but it was enough to spook her. "If you don't know all of it," he said now to Hexter, "you should." He took the yellow envelope out of his backpack and held it out in front of him.

Hexter came around from behind his desk, reached into the envelope and took out Jayne's DVD. A cloud passed over his face. He shoved the video back into the envelope and thrust it at Waldo. "I assume our business is finished."

There was something discordant about the reaction. Waldo recognized some similarity to his own—he was sure that, like himself, Hexter hadn't seen *this* Jayne before—but Waldo had been *curious*, at least, crestfallen but at the same time darkly fascinated; this man displayed not a whit of that. True, Hexter was older, but not a prude, at least not too prudish to have had his own affair with—

The realization popped out of Waldo's mouth before he'd fully processed the thought. "You weren't sleeping with her. You didn't push that away like a lover." Hexter froze, caught between a lie that would tarnish him and a truth that would be worse. Hoping to coax him toward the second, Waldo said, "Tell me about your girl."

The headmaster went to the window, surveyed his campus awhile. At last he said, "I was divorced with a child before I was twenty. I didn't see her for years. Last summer her mother tracked me down and told me that Rosanna—'Jayne'—needed help."

"So you brought her here to teach kindergarten, even though she wasn't qualified."

"She'd been in Florida. No one here knew her, or even *about* her. Teachers at private schools don't need accreditation." He added, "Of course, I had to let someone go to open the spot for her. At the last minute, unfortunately."

"And the other teachers didn't like that. Especially when they realized she had no idea what she was doing."

"You don't need much knowledge to handle a kindergarten curriculum. Caring about the children is more important, frankly. Say what you will about her, she did care."

"And you let the teachers gossip."

Hexter turned back to him with a wan smile. "Rumors of an affair almost gave me a cachet. But hiring my daughter? That would be unsurvivable." He went back to his desk and sat. Again

Waldo waited him out. "She did call me last night, from the road. She said that you'd figured out about her past, and more, and that if she stayed here, our relationship was bound to be discovered. She ran off to protect me."

Maybe, Waldo thought. "Did she say what the 'more' was?" Hexter shook his head. Waldo returned the envelope with the DVD to his backpack.

Sipping from a coffee mug with both hands like a convalescent, Hexter looked older and smaller, the last of his haughtiness dried up and blown away. He'd made a small compromise to rescue his Rosanna from the degraded mess her life had become and now knew he might never see her again and could still be rewarded for it with the loss of his career. What men will do for their daughters. Alastair and Gaby fluttered across Waldo's mind.

Hexter looked up at Waldo, a supplicant now. "I know you don't owe me anything, Mr. Waldo, but can I rely on you to keep our secret? It's a favor I wouldn't know how to repay . . . but perhaps you'd consider doing it for Jayne."

For Jayne. He'd called her Jayne. The woman was no longer there to work her magic on Waldo, but her father hoped the name still would.

Why had she gone, really? If it was going to come down to the hope that Waldo would keep their secret anyway, couldn't she have just stayed? She had to know that running off in the night in the aftermath of a murder would look suspicious, maybe even incriminating.

Then again, whom would it look incriminating *to?* Nobody was paying any attention to her, save Waldo and the various flames who so badly wanted their affairs kept secret. Which meant Waldo was the only one who might conceivably hurt her.

For Jayne. It's what she was counting on.

Waldo walked out of the office, leaving the headmaster's request to hang there. He trotted down the stairs and left the building by the stairwell exit, then circled back to the entrance to unlock his bike.

He wondered where she'd run to. Where *do* you go to reinvent yourself, after you can't reinvent yourself in L.A.?

Anyway, Jayne was gone now, really gone.

And just like that, his radar was no longer jammed.

TWENTY-NINE

Waldo deciphered the signatures on the football: Bart Starr, John Elway, Terry Bradshaw . . .

"Every quarterback who's won two Super Bowls."

"Really." It wasn't enough to make him rethink the Things, but he had to admit that as purposeless keepsakes went, this one was pretty impressive. Actually, offices didn't get much more impressive than Sikorsky's in any way: floor-to-ceiling windows on two long sides, magnificent Oriental rugs, deep blue leather seats around a low walnut coffee table, handcrafted power desk of inlaid woods. Personal mementos were confined to a tall and elegant bookcase, except for this football, which merited its own pedestal.

Sikorsky said, "Commissioner gave it to me when we closed the last NFL contract. You get nice souvenirs in this job."

"I'll say. May I?" Sikorsky gestured permission and Waldo picked the ball up and studied it. Not many names, but the best names: Joe Montana, Troy Aikman . . .

"I have a table read in fifteen minutes."

"Sorry," Waldo said, and got to it. "I've hit a point where I thought I should come to you, since you're the one paying for my time. We hadn't really talked about an endgame for this."

"Do we need to? Are you finished with us?"

"Pretty close. I know Alastair didn't kill his wife."

"He didn't?" Sikorsky looked like he didn't trust the assertion. "Do you know who did?"

"I think so." Waldo spun the football in his hands. "There's a young woman named Jayne White—that isn't her *real* name, but it's what she's been going by. She's the Pinch girl's kindergarten teacher."

"*Kindergarten* teacher?" Sikorsky looked even more skeptical. "Why would *she* kill Monica?"

"Well, she was a lot more than that. She and Alastair were having an affair. You don't look surprised."

"They had a complicated marriage."

"So you knew them well."

Sikorsky shrugged. "You go to so many events together—wrap parties, award shows—you can't *help* but get to know each other. A little, at least." He took a deep breath and exhaled through pursed lips. "I'm so relieved it wasn't Alastair."

"I'm sure you are." Waldo lobbed him the football, a perfect underhand spiral.

Sikorsky smiled and tossed it back overhand, starting a catch, the two men flinging the precious ball back and forth across the length of the oversize office, almost in celebration. "Have you told Fontella yet?"

"Not yet," said Waldo. "Thing is, this Jayne White's disappeared. I'd love to find her before we take the next step. Did you know her, by any chance?"

Sikorsky bobbed his shoulders a couple of times to show he was reluctant to say it. "I knew *about* her."

"Did you know Alastair had gotten her pregnant? I've been wondering if that's a thing many people were aware of."

"Not many," Sikorsky said, tossing the ball. "Hardly anyone, I think."

"But *you* were aware."

"I guess I *did* know them pretty well."

"What was Monica Pinch's reaction, when she found out Jayne was pregnant?"

"Shit, what do you *think* her reaction was? She was beside herself."

"I bet. She probably pressed Alastair even harder to quit the show and move back to England. That was a big thing with her, wasn't it?"

"Was it? I guess I didn't know them *that* well."

"But you knew about the awards—the 'Shakespeare Awards' you talked about. They're called 'Oliviers,' by the way. You said they were in the bedroom closet."

"Figure of speech. They could have been in the attic for all I knew. I just knew that Alastair didn't like to keep them out."

"They actually *were* in the bedroom closet."

"So?"

"Alastair said he didn't know where they were."

"Alastair says a lot of things. Strikes a lot of poses. You must know that by now."

"True. But another thing I know is that Monica didn't find out Jayne White was pregnant until the night she died. So if she talked to you about it, it must have been that night."

"You said the murderer was Jayne White." He slung back the football with some mustard on it.

"Actually, I said I knew who the murderer *was*." Waldo fired it back just as hard; that's the way the catch continued. "I was also wondering about your watch."

"What about my watch?"

"Warren Gomes—this lawyer the cops said I murdered? Did you hear about that, by the way?"

"I did. I wasn't pleased."

"Me neither. Anyway, Gomes had the same kind of watch— what's it called? Kudoke?"

Annoyance mounting, Sikorsky said, "Kudoke Skeleton. They're getting popular."

"I researched them—they're individually made; no two are identical. The one he was wearing looked a lot like yours."

"He wasn't wearing mine," he said, all impatience and finality. He rolled up his sleeve and showed Waldo his watch. "Except when I sleep or shower, mine's been on my wrist every minute since my anniversary. Lot of trouble with the missus if it wasn't. They all look similar—you should know that, too, from your research." He threw Waldo the football like he wasn't expecting it back. "We need to wrap this up—my table read's on the other side of the lot."

Waldo said, "You asked Fontella what time it was."

"When?"

"At the courthouse, after Alastair's arraignment. You had to get to a meeting. I was surprised that a guy with a fancy watch like that would *ever* ask what time it was—I'd think you'd want any excuse to look at it. Then I saw you didn't have it on." He tossed Sikorsky the football again, back to underhand. Not expecting the throw, Sikorsky bobbled it but made the catch.

Sikorsky held on to Waldo's gaze too. He said, "Why don't

you tell me exactly what it is you're thinking?" and winged the ball as sharply as he could, face high; Waldo's reflexes were a match and he caught it cleanly.

So Waldo told him everything he was thinking.

He told him that he was thinking Sikorsky knew what Monica Pinch kept in her closet because he'd been spending time in her bedroom while Alastair was spending time with Jayne. And that the night Monica found out Alastair had gotten Jayne pregnant, Alastair passed out and she started climbing the walls and finally called Sikorsky. Though Sikorsky had told the police that the call that night had been from Alastair to gripe about candy bars, Waldo was thinking the call was in fact from Monica, in keeping with a practice of calling her lover, Sikorsky, from the family landline, which would always give them cover—as it did here—should anyone happen to look at their phone records.

Waldo said he couldn't know the content of the conversation they had on the phone, but his guess was that Monica told Sikorsky she was going to confess to Alastair about *their* affair, to get Alastair to quit the show and move back to England like she'd been wanting. But Sikorsky couldn't afford to lose Alastair, not with Jamshidi's takeover hanging over him. In fact, he couldn't even afford the scandal if it went public.

"I'm thinking," Waldo told Sikorsky now, "you drove over there and the argument kept going, and I'm thinking you picked up that Olivier Award and hit her in the head with it. Killed her."

He paused; there had been a bit of conjecture rolled into that and Waldo figured if he'd gotten a big piece wrong it would draw a reaction. But Sikorsky remained stock-still. Waldo took it as a general confirmation and kept going. "You wiped down everything you could remember touching, but the Olivier had been sitting on a wooden table, and that had bloodstains on it you *couldn't* clean. I'm thinking you were worried some of that might be *your* blood, so you moved the table to the master bedroom, moved the table that was there to the guest room, set the alarm on the way out the door, ditched the award in a Dumpster somewhere, and left poor Alastair to wake up and take the rap. You got a little lucky Alastair was still drunk enough to futz with the dead bolt when he was opening the door for the cops."

Sikorsky grinned and put on that killer charm again. "Very creative. I should give you a pilot deal. But you've got a big hole in your plot: why would I sabotage the biggest asset on my network?"

"You figured Alastair would get off; this is L.A.—the star *always* gets off. Even if he doesn't, you walk away clean. In the meantime, you told me yourself: the scandal made the show twice as valuable. And the more publicity, the bigger the windfall. So you brought in the lawyer who'd make the most noise." Waldo spun the ball in his hands. "And then, even better, the *investigator* who'd make the most noise. I'm sure Alastair was paying his lawyer himself, but *you're* the one who hired *me*. Because Fontella would've hired someone else. She was telling you all along I'd be a shitty choice—I'd never been a PI, the cops hated me, I was so out of practice I'd be useless. Turns out, those were exactly the reasons you *liked* me—because I'd be the *last* detective who'd ever figure out that you killed Monica Pinch. *And* Warren Gomes."

"Oh, I killed him, too? Remind me: why'd I do that?"

"Gomes was working for Jamshidi, digging up dirt on you he could use toward the takeover. But when Gomes found out you were sleeping with your biggest star's wife—well, that kind of information was too valuable to waste on Jamshidi. Especially after she wound up dead. So he blackmailed you, even made you cough up that beautiful watch, which you couldn't resist taking back after you shot him. One less thing to explain to the missus." He threw the football to Sikorsky.

Sikorsky said, "Lot of moving parts there. You must have been pretty sure of yourself to walk in here with a pitch like that," and fired back the ball.

"Actually, I only walked in ninety-eight percent sure." He winged the ball at Sikorsky.

"Is that so? What's the other two percent?"

"I wanted to make sure you were a lefty."

Sikorsky froze, the incriminating arm cocked behind his ear.

Waldo said, "Let's go see the cops."

"They know all this?"

Waldo shook his head. "They're about to hear it now. If I timed it right, they're already waiting downstairs."

Waldo had called Conady a couple of hours earlier to ask his erstwhile friend to meet him outside the Admin Building on Alastair Pinch's lot so he could turn over the real murderer of Monica Pinch and Warren Gomes. It turned into a testy conversation, Waldo not wanting to share his solution until he'd eliminated the final uncertainty of Sikorsky's handedness, the lieutenant demanding that Waldo tell him up front what he'd learned. Waldo held firm, counting on his own track record to keep Conady from dismissing the possibility of a dramatic reversal and risking months on the front page of the *Times* if it wasn't handled right.

So when Waldo walked out of the building with Sikorsky, he

was only mildly surprised to see that Conady had decided to one-up him by arriving late, sending as placeholders a couple of patrolmen who looked vaguely familiar from the week—probably from the day at the station house with Pam Tanaka—thus leaving Waldo and the murderer and the uniforms to wait awkwardly around the cruiser until Conady deigned to show. But Waldo wasn't too miffed over it; it was a passive-aggressive move he probably deserved for having played it so coy on the phone, and besides, nothing right now could dim his high spirits. He stepped away from the others to unlock his bike with a smile on his face.

He heard the ignition and turned to see Sikorsky pulling away from the building in the black-and-white. "Stop him!" The cops looked like they didn't give a damn. "Conady's going to have your ass!"

"Who's Conady?" said one of them.

Waldo realized where he'd seen them before; the New Orleans police insignias on their shoulders confirmed it. "Shit!" he said. The cruiser turned a corner and disappeared from sight.

Waldo jumped on his bike and took off after Sikorsky. He rounded the same corner just in time to see the cruiser take another turn, going about twenty, fast for a lot but not so fast as to draw attention. Every time Waldo got him back in sight, he'd take another corner. Waldo started to think Sikorsky was trying *not* to lose him, was trying to lead Waldo someplace specific.

Sikorsky turned into the backlot and Waldo followed him in, coasting through the brownstone facades and onto what looked like a deserted New York street—no production under way, no lot workers out for an afternoon stroll—a spooky scene, like from some movie about the dystopian aftermath of a biological disaster.

Waldo wheeled onto another street and saw the cruiser parked at its far end. He lowered his bike to the sidewalk and pulled the Beretta from the back of his pants. Sikorsky wasn't likely armed—he would have to have been carrying when Waldo first walked into his office—but then again he had shot Gomes, so Waldo couldn't be sure. He felt dangerously exposed as he walked down the silent street, the windows of the phony buildings looming on either side.

Sikorsky wasn't in the cruiser. Waldo looked to the facades; he could be behind any of those doors. Waldo crept to the nearest and threw it open. He stepped inside, gun at the ready, and found only debris and a metal stand left behind after some production. He went back out, leaving the door open behind him. He tried the next entrance and found more of the same nothing.

He looked up and down the block. Halfway down the other side of the street he saw a faux police station that said 21ST PRECINCT and decided to try that next, maybe because the thumping in his chest reminded him of his return to North Hollywood and that had worked out all right.

He yanked open the precinct door and started inside. A wood plank came down on his wrist, knocking the Beretta from his hand, and there was Sikorsky, kicking the gun past Waldo out into the street and winding up to clobber him again with the plank. Before Sikorsky could swing, though, Waldo threw himself headfirst into his midsection, the collision searing Waldo's ribs, like getting punched from inside. The two men crashed to the ground and grappled. Sikorsky, taking advantage of Waldo's impairment, flipped him onto his back. He dug one thumb into Waldo's throat while Waldo desperately grabbed the fingers of Sikorsky's other hand. Sikorsky pressed their locked hands closer to Waldo's neck; Waldo wedged a leg between their bodies.

Sikorsky let go of Waldo's hand so he could put him in a full choke, pushing his body weight onto his arms to finish him. Waldo channeled what strength he had left into his legs and kicked Sikorsky off, then rolled away.

Instead of pouncing again Sikorsky scrambled in the other direction, escaping through a passageway and into the space behind the next facade. The reversal confused Waldo. He pulled himself to his feet and followed, every gasping breath triggering waves of agony.

He had to step over a pile of scrap lumber to cross through. Sikorsky, hiding, shot out a leg to trip him, then grabbed an arm and pulled Waldo off-balance. Waldo's bad elbow hit a metal clamp and bore the brunt of the fall. For a few seconds he couldn't even think.

He rolled onto his back and tried to gather himself. Sikorsky came into view, standing above him gripping another one of those metal production stands, this one with what looked like a heavy metal lamp on one end, old and rusted. Sikorsky raised it high above Waldo's skull, poised for the kill.

Waldo said, "How'll you get away with *this*?"

"Self-defense. You came at me with a gun. LAPD already thinks you're crazy."

Waldo closed his eyes and waited for the deathblow.

When it came, it didn't hurt, but it was loud. In fact, it sounded like a gunshot.

Waldo opened his eyes.

Sikorsky was looking down at a red stain spreading across his shirt. He crumpled. The movie light fell with him, crunching the cement inches from Waldo's cranium.

Waldo, still flat on his back, had to arch to see who'd fired the bullet.

"Hey there, Waldo."

"Hiya, Q." Things were looking better, but not *that* much better. "Would it be ungrateful to ask what you're doing here?"

"Man, I been followin' you since Hollywood Boulevard. I even sat through that Rumpelstiltskin bullshit."

"How'd you get on the lot?"

"Snuck in with a studio tour." He walked over to Waldo. "Hope you don't mind, I used your gun." He wiped the Beretta on his guayabera, crouched and offered it to Waldo, who accepted it. "I was never here."

"I can work with that," said Waldo, nonplussed.

"You do understand why I saved your ass: somebody else kills you first, I can't get what I want."

Waldo rolled onto his side and pushed off the ground with his good arm. Don Q helped him up. "Got to say, Q: not too swift keeping your kind of business records on a flash drive lying around on a desk."

"*Business records?* That what Cuppy told you?"

"In so many words."

"Cuppy's a fool."

"Then what's on it?"

Q studied Waldo like he was trying to decide whether he was worthy. "Epic poem," he said finally. "Long-ass muthafucker, too. Only copy I got."

"Epic poem? What, that you wrote?"

"'Bout the life of a dealer," Don Q said, "tryin' to retain his integrity and independence in the era of corporate-style cartels, not to mention all that janky-ass legalization. Be one sick movie after some studio buys the rights."

"Why an epic poem?"

"Shit, man, I coulda written it as a screenplay straight up, but my lawyer says I got a stronger position on merchandisin' and such if I hold the copyright. He suggested a novel—but I'm drawn personally to the ancient classics, like *Beowulf* and *The Epic of* Fuckin' *Gilgamesh.*"

"What's *The Epic of* Fuckin' *Gilgamesh?*"

"You gotta get offa that mountain, Waldo, and *learn* your white ass somethin'. I'm an autodidact, see? That means I'm self-educated. Had to enrich my *own* life. Now, my little girl—I wanna make sure she gets a *real* education. That way she won't be stuck bein' no dealer or cop or whatever the fuck it is *you're* supposed to be." Waldo's head was spinning. "So," Q said. "My Mem."

Waldo pulled it together enough to say, "Can Lorena come back?"

"Shit, Waldo, you ain't listenin'. You gotta *do* for me—*then* Lorena can come back. You gotta get my little girl into that fancy private school—you know, where that English muthafucker send *his* kid. You got the juice for that?"

Waldo grinned.

THIRTY

On the back of a real ambulance sitting at a fake curb, Waldo let a real medic tend to his elbow. Real yellow tape sealed off a fake building down the fake block, inside of which the body of the real killer was being poked and measured and photographed by real cops, plus one of the fake ones, as nobody had thought to ask what a New Orleans PD was doing in the middle of a Burbank crime scene.

Don Q, of course, was long gone. Waldo had a date to meet him at the Banning bus station in two days to return the flash drive. Now Waldo worked his iPhone with one thumb and emailed Lorena:

Safe

Conady *had* taken his sweet time getting to the studio and ended up reaching Sikorsky's body around the same time as the Burbank police, who'd been summoned after Waldo flagged down a security woman cruising the lot in a golf cart. Waldo laid out for

Conady every detail of the solution to the murders of Monica Pinch and Warren Gomes, telling him about the Pinches' affairs and the kindergarten teacher's pregnancy and the intrigue around the school, implying that the teacher may have been getting it on with the headmaster as well. Waldo detailed the mistake he'd made leaving Sikorsky unsupervised and how Sikorsky got away from him and lured him onto the backlot. He left Don Q out of the account, of course, and walked through the choreography of his fight with Sikorsky, explaining that he'd saved his own life by shooting him in self-defense.

Conady told Waldo that even if the rest of it held up, he was going to be in trouble for having a second unlicensed firearm.

Waldo said, "Actually, it's the *same* unlicensed firearm, a second time."

It might have been true but it sounded smart-alecky and it didn't play well with Conady. "Pretty convenient that your story about Sikorsky killing Monica Pinch doesn't have any hard evidence behind it."

"Really? I was thinking it's not convenient at all."

"You might have a problem, Waldo."

"Nah. You'll catch up to it." He gave Conady Alastair's burner and told Conady what to look for on Gomes's phone, then walked him through the people he should interview—Jamshidi, Hexter, Jayne's unhappy coworkers, the New Orleans faux police—and the bits of the story they could corroborate. He knew Conady was a dedicated enough cop to follow all the leads and would, even without Waldo suggesting it, find confirmation that Sikorsky was left-handed. When enough of Waldo's details checked out, they'd hang the Pinch murder on Sikorsky and in turn accept Waldo's account of the executive's death, too.

Still, he wondered how much hell Conady would put him through first, and whether he'd face charges for the unlicensed weapon. He wondered whether Alberto Suarez or Patrolman Annis might end up catching some flak. He also wondered whether the network would ever make that donation to the Sierra Club, which at this point, if he was counting correctly, ought to be sixteen thousand dollars. He wondered whether Gaby Pinch and Don Q's little girl would become friends.

He wondered where Jayne was now.

They made him sit there for hours, telling the story over and over to a parade of detectives out of L.A. and Burbank. Conady himself made him go through the whole thing twice more. Waldo laid it all out for Fontella over the phone, too, but hadn't been able to reach Alastair, who was on set. When Waldo was finally allowed to leave, he headed across the lot to see him in person.

The soundstage was nearly empty; the AD who'd paid off Alastair's tomato cans said the crew was on lunch break, back in fifteen. Waldo went out to Alastair's trailer and knocked on the screen door.

The Alastair he found inside looked lightened by decades. "My hero!" he said when he saw Waldo. "My savior! Sit, sit."

Waldo said, "You've talked to Fontella?"

"Indeed. She's expecting the charges to be dropped presently. And she's positively giddy about the prospects for a lawsuit for wrongful arrest."

"Go for it."

Alastair shook his head. "No need. But why not let the lady dream?"

"One thing I still don't get. You knew that Jayne was involved with those others?"

"I suspected. Maybe I knew. She'd drop hints. I think she rather liked having us wonder about each other."

"Why didn't you tell me? Especially when I asked you about them?"

"One tries to be a gentleman about these things, to the extent one can. No need to drag other marriages down into my muck. My fidelity was irrelevant. After all, I had no reason to suspect *Jayne* killed Monica." He beamed at Waldo. "Is it too much of a cliché to say I don't know how to thank you?"

"I might have an idea."

"Do tell!"

"How about after your season finishes, we go off together and get into whatever trouble we get into?" Waldo put up his fists. "A right tasty vodka drunk. Somewhere they're playing rugby." The extravagance was out of character but it wasn't a violation. He'd given it careful thought: experiences weren't Things.

"Sounds brilliant," said Alastair, delighting Waldo. But then he continued: "Unfortunately, starting today, this is my liquor of choice." He opened his refrigerator and took out a Vitamin Water. He tossed it to Waldo and found a second one for himself. Waldo was stupefied. Alastair opened his bottle. "Never tried before. I used to say, 'I don't have a drinking problem, but if I did, I hope I'd have the courage to drink myself to death.'"

For what felt like the hundredth time, Waldo found himself trying to figure out where the character ended and the actor began.

"I cocked it all up, Waldo. My Monica is dead; Jayne's run off carrying a son or daughter I'll never know. All I have left is Gaby, and the least I owe her is the best I have."

"That could take more courage than drinking yourself to death."

"Don't I know it." Alastair raised his water in a toast. "Courage, Waldo."

Waldo toasted back without opening the plastic bottle. "Courage, mate."

"You gave me back my life. And my daughter hers. You did for us what you couldn't do years ago for that poor young man. Could be your little jaunt down the mountain balanced the books."

Lydell Lipps had never been less present for Waldo than he'd been these last few days. Now the reference brought it all back in a rush.

They were quiet together. Waldo thought about what Alastair said and decided he was wrong. There were books that could never be balanced. But maybe this would make them a little easier to live with.

Waldo pedaled off the lot for the last time, waving at the two security dickheads as he coasted past and out the main gate. The one with the mullet pretended to scratch his eyebrow with his middle finger, flipping an artful bird.

There were no pedestrians so Waldo opted for sidewalk rather than street. He still had the climb up 243 to figure out, but right now he felt renewed and unburdened, and the smooth, flat glide into Burbank was almost rapture.

A well-timed car door put a sudden and nasty end to that, sending Waldo tumbling across the pavement and his bike skittering into the gutter. He rolled and saw Big Jim Cuppy climbing out of the passenger seat of his Corvette. "Supposed to ride in the street, asshole." Waldo groaned. Cuppy perched on his trunk and watched him. "I hear you and Q kissed and made up. I bet you even gave him that flash drive."

Waldo pushed up onto a knee, then to his feet. His pants were torn and his leg was bleeding. He limped to his bike and checked it: the front wheel was bent—he tried to spin it but the rim kept brushing the brake pad—and one of the spokes was broken, too. Cuppy grinned at his handiwork.

Waldo sighed deeply through his nose. "Cuppy," he said. "I don't need you busting up my bike and pissing in my pond. Tell you what: if I do you one great, big, corrupt solid, will you call it a truce and stay off my ass?"

Cuppy frowned, confounded. "What are you selling?"

"You know TV actors are all cokeheads and tweakers, right?"

"I never heard that."

"Hell yeah. To work the hours they work?"

"So, what," Cuppy said, catching on, "you got a supplier on the lot I can jack?"

Waldo nodded. "The gate guards."

Cuppy said, "Really. *That* gate?" Because of the wall and driveway, they couldn't actually see the security kiosk from here, but Cuppy kept looking in that direction anyway, starting to dream.

Waldo said, "Don't let on at first that you're a cop."

"No?"

"Here's the deal: they comb their hair, they're letting you know they're holding. Let it play out."

"Nice. Okay, pigfucker, this works, you and I are square." Cuppy heaved himself off the trunk and made for the driver's side door.

"No-no-no—dressed like *you*, in *this* car? That *screams* 'I'm gonna shake you down.'" Cuppy looked at him, lost. "*Walk.*"

"Yeah?"

"Trust me. People come to a drive-on gate without a car? Fucks the guards up from the jump."

Waldo could see the confidence flowing into Cuppy, who hitched his belt, said, "Shit, Waldo—you may not be worthless after all," and sauntered off toward the gate. Waldo watched him go.

When Cuppy turned into the driveway and disappeared from sight, Waldo flipped open his Swiss Army knife and carved a two-foot gash in Cuppy's ragtop. This street had a steep California flood-control curb, leaving the car at the perfect height for what came next: Waldo unzipped his fly, leaned over the torn cloth and, steadying himself on the frame with his good arm, took a nice long leak into the cabin of the Corvette, closing his eyes to savor the moment in full.

When he opened them, not quite done with his piss, he saw a Mercedes across the street finishing off an impressive parallel park into a tight space. The door opened and there was Lorena. "Go ahead," she called as she jaywalked toward him. "Finish."

"I don't think I have a choice."

"It's okay," she said. "I've already seen it."

"How long you been watching?"

"Couple minutes. Thanks for squaring things with Q."

"Welcome back," he said, zipping himself up.

"You were the only one I trusted could fix it for me. Hope it didn't cause you too much trouble."

"Oh, no trouble at all," he said, amusement dancing in his eyes and inviting hers to dance too.

"I've got something else we could work together, if you're up for it."

That made him laugh out loud, reminding him of his ribs and

how they got that way. "Yeah, I don't think my body can take more of your business."

"Don't be such a princess," she said. "You loved every minute of it." She gave him a full-frame survey, down then up, settling on his jawline. "Bet you even found some damsel in distress worth shaving for."

"Is that jealousy I hear, Mrs. Vander Janssen?"

"Yeah," she sighed. "Guess I could've told you about that."

"How about you tell me how you made yourself dead. That one's had me more curious."

"Coroner in San Berdoo owed me a favor, let me have a Jane Doe they were about to cremate." Fucking Lorena. "I burned her in my husband's car instead of my own because—well, because he's a cheating prick."

"*Good-looking* prick."

"If you like 'em that way." She smiled at him. This felt easier now, easier than when she came up the mountain. "Sure you don't want to work this new case with me?"

"Sleazy divorce?"

"Hey, sleazy's in the eye of the beholder." He wanted to say no but suddenly couldn't remember the word. "How about I give you a lift to Idyllwild while I tell you about it?"

"Better idea," said Waldo, recapturing his resolve and picking up his wreck. "How about I find a bike shop, then figure out how to—" He stopped himself. "Ah, fuck it." He tossed the whole pricey Brompton onto Cuppy's compromised ragtop, which tore and collapsed under the weight.

He tipped his head toward her Mercedes and they crossed the street together. They got in and Lorena pulled away from the curb.

"So what does this clunker get? Like four miles to the gallon?"

"It's not a clunker," she said, irritated, as she got the car up to speed with the traffic on Alameda. "It's a brand-new Mercedes SLK. It set me back sixty-two-eight and it's my fucking baby and I'm not going to apologize."

"Sixty-two-eight?"

"Sixty-two-eight. Now, what'll it take for you to shut up about it?"

He turned to her with the answer, smiling like a man who was down to Ninety-Nine Things and somehow still had all he needed. "Let me drive."

She shook her head. "Jesus, Waldo."

ACKNOWLEDGMENTS

There would be no Waldo without Andrew Lazar, whose insight and heart breathe in every chapter. My thanks also to his partners in Tango West, Christina Lurie and Steve Shainberg, who've been there from the beginning. And to Aaron Kaplan, who was there for a little while before the beginning.

Larry Doyle was the big brother any first timer would want.

Glenn Gers is as fine a writer as I know, and an even finer writer's friend. Nothing I say here could do justice to what our decades have meant to me and to my work.

Susan Dickes, Laurie Gould, Neel Keller, Tony Quinn and Russ Woody also made the book better. Seeing those five names together in a sentence reminds me what a fortunate man I am.

Though he probably doesn't realize it, Jay Mandel's initial enthusiasm for the half-finished manuscript was a watershed, validating a midcareer experiment that I know had some people scratching their heads; then he turned out to be the rare agent who actually did exactly what he said he'd do. I'm thankful also to have had Jared Levine, David McIlvain, Danny Greenberg and Corinne Farley in my corner during the project's unusually complicated genesis.

Deepest gratitude to everyone at Dutton, particularly Jess Renheim, who brought this book into the world, graced it with her insightful notes and guided me through the experience. I'm too new at this to know what a novelist should reasonably expect from an editor, but I have a strong suspicion that I'm getting spoiled.

Though I've never met her, I want to mention Annie Leonard and her dazzling video *The Story of Stuff,* which got under my skin at just the right (or wrong) moment in my life. And while I'm at it, Kenneth Millar and Eudory Welty and Ray Wylie Hubbard for the same.

A shout to everybody at Peet's.

My children's contributions went beyond the usual love and support. Amanda planted the seed by showing me *The Story of Stuff* way back when. Milo, an artist with a powerful sense of the value of simply making and sharing, affirmed and illumined when I needed it. Gary asked to look at chapters very early on and had some sharp and useful observations—doing, in his inimitable way, just enough of the homework.

My mother didn't have much to do with this book directly but had everything to do with it indirectly, so I'll take this opportunity to say: Thanks, Mom.

Terri Gould, she of infinite kindness and patience and all-around wonderfulness, has been my first and best reader for most of my life. No writer ever had it better. No husband, either.

ABOUT THE AUTHOR

Howard Michael Gould is a writer, producer and director in television and film. *Last Looks* is his first novel.